Second Duke's
the Charm

BY KATE BATEMAN

RUTHLESS RIVALS

A Reckless Match
A Daring Pursuit
A Wicked Game

BOW STREET BACHELORS

This Earl of Mine
To Catch an Earl
The Princess and the Rogue

Second Duke's the Charm

KATE BATEMAN

St. Martin's Paperbacks

This is a work of fiction. All of the characters, organizations, and events portrayed in this novel are either products of the author's imagination or are used fictitiously.

First published in the United States by St. Martin's Paperbacks, an imprint of St. Martin's Publishing Group.

SECOND DUKE'S THE CHARM

For information, address St. Martin's Publishing Group, 120 Broadway, New York, NY 10271.

www.stmartins.com

ISBN: 978-1-250-90736-3

Our books may be purchased in bulk for promotional, educational, or business use. Please contact your local bookseller or the Macmillan Corporate and Premium Sales Department at 1-800-221-7945, ext. 5442, or by email at MacmillanSpecialMarkets@macmillan.com.

Printed in the United States of America

St. Martin's Paperbacks edition / January 2024

10 9 8 7 6 5 4 3 2 1

A cynic is someone who
knows the price of everything
and the value of nothing.

—OSCAR WILDE

Prologue

Spring 1814.

Tess Townsend was accustomed to men falling at her feet metaphorically, but this was the first time one had ever done it literally.

And on her wedding night, no less.

The decrepit Duke of Wansford—her husband of less than a day—lay prone on the rug, but unlike many new bridegrooms, he was not drunk.

He was dead.

When he'd entered Tess's bedchamber ten minutes ago, the lascivious look he'd cast her had turned her stomach. She'd just opened her mouth to tell him to go away, when he'd clutched at his chest with an expression of faint surprise. He'd staggered sideways, knocked over a table, and dropped to the ground like a stone.

Despite her dislike of the man, Tess had instinctively rushed forward to help, but instead of lurching to his feet, or taking the opportunity to grope her, he'd simply lain there, eyes closed, limbs slack.

With a growing sense of alarm, Tess had shaken him,

then slapped his cheek. Belatedly realizing she couldn't recall his Christian name from the ceremony, she'd hissed, "Wake up, you!" and pressed her fingers to his neck in search of a pulse.

To no avail. He was definitely dead.

A wave of incredulous relief rose in her chest, swiftly followed by guilt. She'd prayed for a miracle to save her from this dreadful marriage, but she'd never envisaged anything as drastic as *this*.

Indeed, when nothing had happened that morning to interrupt her vows, she'd taken matters into her own hands, and placed a loaded pistol under her pillow.

Her father might have forced her to the altar, but Tess had no intention of allowing the lecherous old duke his "husbandly rights." She'd half hoped that if she threatened to shoot him, he'd demand an annulment on the grounds of her insanity. Better to be considered mad for the rest of her life than submit to his repellent touch.

Whether such a plan would have been successful was now a moot point: the man wasn't in any state to demand anything, ever again.

An insistent pounding on the bedroom door made Tess start—until she remembered the desperate plea she'd issued to her two best friends. Ellie Law and Daisy Hamilton had sworn to do everything in their power to save her from the unwelcome attentions of her new husband. The three of them had met at Miss Honoria Burnett's Ladies Academy as children, and as far as Tess was concerned, they were far more her family than the father who'd treated her so shabbily.

"Your Grace, you must come!" Ellie's urgent voice was muffled by the heavy wooden door. She'd affected an accent, to sound like one of the servants. "The dower house is ablaze!"

Tess stumbled to the door and swung it wide. With a frantic look up and down the corridor, she seized both girls by the arm, and hauled them inside.

"Quick! Before someone comes!" She slid the bolt home behind them.

"Are we too early?" Confused, Daisy glanced at the door connecting the duchess's room to the master's suite. "Is the duke still in his rooms?"

"No. He's *there*." Tess pointed at the body on the floor, which was half-obscured by a wing armchair.

Ellie stepped sideways to get a better view, then sucked in a breath. "Oh, Bloody Hell. Tess, what did you *do*?"

"I didn't do anything, I swear! He came in, leered at me, and collapsed. He's not breathing."

Daisy, always the most practical of the three of them, knelt and put her ear to the duke's scrawny chest. After a tense moment she sat back on her heels with a sigh that was more irritation than dismay.

"She's right, he's dead." She sent Tess a wry glance. "Considering how fetching you look in that robe, my love, I'd say it's no surprise."

Tess bit her lip. A lifetime of comments had made her aware that most people considered her beautiful. With her dark eyes, pale skin, and lustrous hair, she'd lost count of the number of times she'd been compared to a Renaissance masterpiece or an ancient Greek deity. She supposed she must take after her mother, who'd died when she was a baby, because she bore only a passing resemblance to the dissolute scoundrel who was her father.

Guilt tightened her chest even more. The duke was—*had been*—awful, but the thought that she might have caused the demise of another human being, even inadvertently, was unsettling.

"You think I killed him?"

Ellie snorted. "Of course not. His own lechery killed him. A man of seventy-two has no business wedding a girl of nineteen. His shriveled heart probably gave out from all the excitement. It serves him right."

Daisy grimaced. "He didn't touch you, did he?"

"Thankfully not." Tess shuddered at the thought of the man's papery skin and rancid breath. She'd truly had a miraculous escape.

Daisy rose to her feet and dusted off her skirts, as Tess sank weakly onto the edge of the bed.

"Oh God, do you think people are going to think I killed him?" She shot a glance over her shoulder. "Daisy, your pistol's under my pillow. I was going to threaten him with it if he tried to force himself on me."

Daisy gave an approving nod. "Excellent plan." She rounded the bed, slipped her hand beneath the linen, and withdrew the pistol. With the ease of long practice, she unloaded the weapon and slid it into her skirts. "There."

The mattress sagged as she sat down next to Tess, and Ellie crossed to sit on her opposite side. All three of them gazed down at the corpse.

The duke's lined face was pale and waxy, and the powdered wig he'd worn to hide his thinning hair lay on the expensive rug like a small, furry creature that had fallen from a great height.

"We need to think this through," Ellie said levelly. "It's quite possible that you'll be suspected of killing him. After all, it was no secret that your father forced you to say your vows."

Tess grimaced. Her father had, for all intents and purposes, sold her to the duke.

Her family had been wealthy once, but a series of bad

investments, a disastrous loan to Mad King George that had never been repaid, and her father's drinking and gaming had squandered what they'd had.

Tess's childish hope of marrying for love had earned her a scornful laugh from her father; her pretty face was his ticket to a fortune. When the twice-widowed Duke of Wansford's roving eye had fallen on her during her first London season, her father had jumped at the chance to offer her up as an unwilling bride.

None of her other suitors could match the dual entice-ment of a title *and* a fortune, so Tess's objections had been soundly ignored. Her attempts to escape had been foiled, and she'd spent the week leading up to her wed-ding locked in her room, or under her father's inescapable gaze.

"It's obvious you didn't shoot him," Daisy said, break-ing into Tess's bitter recollections. "Or strangle him. There aren't any visible injuries. But you could have poisoned him."

Tess groaned. "As soon as the servants realize he's dead, the whole house will be in an uproar. If they find you two here, they might even think we planned it to-gether."

"The first thing anyone will do is call the doctor," Daisy said reasonably. "If he suspects there's been foul play, then the magistrate will be called and he'll start an official investigation."

"But he's not going to suspect anything," Ellie said. "Because you've done nothing wrong. The duke clearly died of natural causes."

Daisy pointed at the body. "I can't think with him just lying there. We need to put him back in his own room so everyone will think he died in his own bed."

Tess nodded. "Agreed."

The three of them stood.

Ellie tilted her head. "How, do you suppose? I've never had to deal with a corpse before."

"It can't be that different from moving a drunkard," Tess said. "Heaven knows, I've done *that* enough times, when Father's been three sheets to the wind. El, you grab him under his arms. Daisy, you and I can take his feet."

"Good Lord, he's heavy," Daisy groaned as the three of them hefted the duke's lifeless body. His head rolled forward so his chin rested on his chest.

"Who'd have thought someone so spindly could weigh so much?" Ellie panted. "He's like a sack of potatoes."

"When have you ever carried a sack of potatoes?" Daisy scoffed.

"Well, never. But this is exactly as heavy as I'd *expect* one to be."

With faltering steps, they staggered through the doorway and into the sitting room that separated the duke's room from the duchess's quarters. When they finally reached the duke's bedchamber, they deposited him on the bedcovers with universal sighs of relief.

Tess wrinkled her nose. "We need to take his robe off."

The duke had appeared in her room in a voluminous pea-green striped banyan, his skinny legs protruding from the hem like two pale sticks of rhubarb.

"I have a horrible feeling he's not wearing anything underneath. Look, that's his nightgown." Daisy indicated a square of linen folded neatly on the pillow and Tess quelled an instinctive shudder.

"It has to be done."

With a fortifying breath, she edged the duke's arm out

of the sleeve. The front of the robe slid open, exposing his entire—naked—body, and granting the three of them the unwelcome sight of his flaccid member lying limply between his legs amid a tangle of sparse gray hair.

"Eughhhh!" Daisy leapt back with a gagging sound. "My eyes! I'm never going to be able to unsee this as long as I live!"

"Far be it from me to speak ill of the dead," Ellie said, "but can I just say how unfair it is that *this* is the first man I've ever seen naked? Couldn't we have found a handsome prizefighter in an alley? Or nursed a wounded soldier back to health?"

Daisy snorted. "You read too many novels, Ellie Law." She angled her chin toward the duke's groin. "Real life is clearly a badly stuffed sausage."

Ellie grinned. "I should put that on a sampler."

Together they wrestled the duke into his nightgown and maneuvered him until he lay in the bed, the covers pulled up to his chin, his hands resting peacefully on his chest.

Tess stood back with a satisfied nod. "That'll do."

Ellie placed the duke's wig carefully on the stand in the corner, while Tess folded his banyan and laid it over a chair.

Back in Tess's room, Daisy righted the table that the duke had knocked over, then turned toward the bed, but the sound of footsteps approaching along the corridor had all three of them glancing around in panic.

Daisy, wide eyed, darted around the bed, pulling Ellie down beside her to hide.

Tess froze as a tentative knock came on the door.

"Yes?" Her voice held an alarming quiver.

"Your Grace? It's Hannah. Mrs. Jennings sent me to see if you'd like a bath?"

The servant's tone was soft, with a trace of pity. Tess had seen the commiserating looks the girl had given her when she'd brushed out her hair in preparation for the duke's conjugal visit earlier.

At the time, Tess had felt as if she was being readied for the guillotine. Or like Andromeda, about to be chained to the rocks as a sacrifice for some hideous sea monster. Only, unlike Andromeda, there would be no heroic Perseus coming to rescue her; Tess was going to have to save herself. Hence the pistol.

She cleared her throat and aimed for a normal tone.

"Er, no, thank you, Hannah. I'm too tired this evening. His Grace has . . . just retired to his own rooms." She gave an internal wince at the suggestive inference of those words. "I'll have a bath in the morning." Her heart pounded as she waited for the servant's response.

"Very good, Your Grace. Is there anything else I can get for you?"

"No, thank you. I'll see you tomorrow."

Tess expelled a huff of relief as the girl's footsteps retreated, and she turned to see Ellie and Daisy emerging from their hiding place.

"When one of the servants finds him in the morning, you can act surprised and dismayed," Ellie whispered. "You can say, quite truthfully, that the last time you saw him *alive* was when he came in here tonight. You certainly don't have to mention that the last time you actually *saw* him, he was dead."

Daisy sent her an admiring grin. "You have a fiendish brain, Ellie Law."

Ellie bobbed a mocking curtsey. "Thank you."

"Wait," Daisy said, turning back to Tess. "If you and the duke never *did the deed*, is the marriage even legal? What if his relatives find out, and try to get it annulled?"

Tess sank onto a chair with a groan. "I'll be sent back to my father—who'll probably try to marry me off to some *other* horrible, rich old man, now he's got the idea."

Ellie shook her head. "That's not going to happen. Non-consummation is *not* a legal reason for an annulment. As long as the marriage itself was valid, with the right names and witnesses and so on, then you're the Duchess of Wansford. Whether you're still a virgin or not."

Tess's anxiety ebbed a fraction. Ellie definitely knew what she was talking about when it came to legal matters. Her father was Sir Edward Law, Baron Ellenborough, one of England's top barristers. He'd been Attorney General for England and Wales, and was now Lord Chief Justice. Ellie had inherited her father's love of the law and his brilliant, incisive mind. Only the fact that she'd been born a female had stopped her from becoming a barrister herself.

"So where does this leave me?" Tess frowned.

Daisy flopped gracefully onto the bed. "As the envy of every woman in England, that's where. A widowed duchess, with all the benefits of the position and none of the aggravation of a husband."

"But my father—"

"—can't force you to do anything, ever again," Ellie finished with a smile. "In the eyes of the law, you're independent now. Your father has no right to control what you do. And with no husband to bully you, either, you're *free*, Tess."

A heady rush of excitement filled Tess's chest, but it was immediately quashed by her next thought. "But I don't have any money of my own. Father didn't even provide me with a dowry. The duke paid *him* two thousand pounds."

"There should have been provision for you in the marriage settlement," Ellie said. "A widow's jointure. Did you read it?"

Tess nodded. "Oh, I'd forgotten about that. Yes, I think I get lifetime use of the dower house."

"It's not actually on fire, by the way," Daisy grinned. "We just said that to get you out of here."

"I gathered that."

"You should get financial support, as well," Ellie pressed. "Like rent from some of the duke's properties. The standard percentage is usually a third of the estate, but even if you only get a fraction of the duchy's income, you'll still be better off than with your father."

Tess nodded as hope blossomed anew. "There was definitely something about rent in there, but I don't remember the particulars. I was too disgusted with my father to pay much attention."

Ellie gave a satisfied smile. "It's going to be all right. The duchy earns more than enough to support you. You *deserve* this, Tess. You said your vows. It's the duke's misfortune that he didn't live long enough to enjoy it."

Daisy wrinkled her nose—a sure sign that she was thinking.

"Even if the marriage doesn't have to have been consummated, it wouldn't be a bad idea to let everyone assume the duke bedded you." She held up her hand to stave off Tess's instinctive protest. "It will buy you some extra time before you have to deal with the next duke, because the executors will have to wait a few months to make sure you're not carrying an heir. When it becomes clear you're not, they'll go and find whoever's in line to inherit."

"That's not a terrible idea," Ellie agreed.

"In *fact*," Daisy continued, warming to her theme, "you could always try to get pregnant, quick, and tell everyone it's the duke's. That would really cement your position."

Tess gasped, half amused, half appalled by her friend's flippant suggestion. "I'm not against having children someday, but I'm not *that* desperate! And besides, how would I even go about it? Pounce on the first drunkard I see outside the Dog and Duck and beg him to make love to me?"

"You wouldn't have to beg anyone." Daisy sent her a playful grin. "They'd be lining up and thanking their lucky stars. But men in their cups aren't known for giving the best performance, so to speak. You'd be better hiring a professional."

Tess frowned. "A professional *man*? What do you mean?"

"A male whore," Daisy said, matter-of-factly. "I've heard people talking about them at my father's parties."

Officially, Daisy's father was the dissolute Duke of Dalkeith, but it was an open secret in the *ton* that her real sire was an Italian count with whom her mother had conducted a torrid, and very public, affair.

"I know they exist, too," Ellie nodded sagely. "Male prostitutes, that is. My father called one as a witness in a case he prosecuted last year. I read about it in his notes."

Tess threw up her hands. "I'm not hiring a man to lie with me. That's ridiculous. Not to mention *expensive*. At least, I expect it would be."

Daisy shrugged. "It was just a thought." She pulled back the bedcovers and gestured to Tess. "Come on, get in. We'll stay with you tonight. We'll leave before dawn so we're not seen."

"Won't you be missed at Hollyfield?"

Daisy's father owned the neighboring estate, on the far side of the village.

Daisy snorted. "Unlikely. Father's hosting a hunting party, which means everyone will be foxed. He thinks Ellie and I are both safely tucked up in bed. We won't be expected down before breakfast, at the earliest."

"How did you get here?"

"We left our horses in that empty cottage by the spinney. Then we sneaked in through the tradesman's entrance while the staff were having dinner. They were all gossiping about you, of course."

Tess made a face. "They probably think I'm a scheming harpy who only married the duke for his money."

"They do indeed. Because there's no *other* reason anyone would have married him. It's not like he was young, handsome, or even charming."

"Perhaps that's why Fate's giving you this second chance," Ellie mused.

A glowing excitement swirled in Tess's chest as the reality of her situation finally began to sink in. For the first time in her life, she didn't have to answer to anyone.

English law usually decreed that a woman passed directly from her father's control to that of a husband. They were little better than chattel, powerless to exert any authority over their own lives or finances.

But Fate had granted her an astonishing reprieve. Widowhood, combined with a modest income, would mean blissful independence. A chance to *do* something with her life. Something interesting. Something worthwhile.

"Think of all the things you can do now you're a duchess," Ellie murmured, almost as if reading her thoughts.

"You could start a charity," Daisy suggested. "Isn't that

what rich widows do? Open a hospital for orphaned puppies, wounded veterans, and fallen women."

"All in the same building?" Tess teased. "Wouldn't the soldiers trip over the puppies?"

"And wouldn't the harlots fall *onto* the veterans?" Ellie chuckled.

"It wouldn't be the worst thing." Daisy shrugged. "In fact, it's a brilliant idea, now I think about it. Flirting with women and playing with dogs are both excellent reasons for the veterans to recover. I bet our rehabilitation rates would be incredible."

Tess shook her head. "You are absurd."

"But brilliant." Daisy grinned. "Admit it."

"Yes, that, too."

Tess pleated the sheets as determination unfurled inside her. "I've spent nineteen years being told what to do, with no control over my own fate, and I *never* want to feel that way again. From now on, I'm going to do what makes me happy, not what pleases someone else."

"Bravo!" Daisy clapped.

"But," Tess continued, "think of all the women who *can't* choose. We know scores of girls who've been bullied or manipulated by the men in their lives. What if I use my new position to help those who haven't been so lucky?"

Daisy raised her brows. "It's a nice idea, but you'd have to be discreet."

"*We'd* have to be discreet," Tess amended. "I couldn't do anything without the two of you."

Ellie's eyes sparkled with excitement at the prospect of a new challenge. "We do make an excellent team. And you know how much I like justice."

"And you know how much I like annoying men." Daisy chuckled.

Tess smiled at her two best friends, grateful beyond words to have them in her life. "So this plan has something for everyone. Are you with me?"

Neither Ellie nor Daisy hesitated for a moment.

"Absolutely."

Chapter One

Two years later.
Spring, 1816. Thornton Shipping & Trading. Bristol.

"The Duke of Wansford? Me?"

Justin Thornton sent a scornful glare at the black-clad apparition hovering in the doorway of his study. "Don't be ridiculous."

The solicitor clutched his leather satchel to his chest. "I realize that this is unexpected, given your distant connection to the deceased, but there's no doubt. None at all."

Justin pinched the bridge of his nose. He could feel a headache coming on. He'd only been back in England for a month, and he had a hundred things to do today. Why was he wasting precious time listening to the ravings of this clearly deranged individual? How had the man even managed to get past Simms?

He glared at the intruder. "Mister . . . ?" he tailed off with an expectant lilt.

"Turnbull," the lawyer provided instantly. "Josiah Turnbull. Of Turnbull, Blomfield, and Brown. We are the executors of the late duke's estate."

"Mister Turnbull. Explain to me how, exactly, you have arrived at this erroneous conclusion."

The younger man pushed his spectacles higher on his nose and gestured toward Justin's desk. "If I may?"

Justin gave a permissive wave of his hand, and the man stepped forward. He pulled a sheaf of yellowing papers from the satchel and spread them on the leather top. Justin glanced down at what appeared to be a family tree, with lines and names neatly recorded and an official-looking wax seal on a ribbon at the bottom.

The clerk pointed. "Here, you see, is the eighth duke, one Archibald Thornton. He was married three times, but since none of those unions resulted in any offspring, his brother, Cecil, was his heir. Unfortunately for my colleagues and I, Cecil moved to Italy before the war, and it took us several months to locate him. When we finally did, we discovered he'd drowned in a canal in Venice, not six weeks after the death of his own brother."

"Unfortunate for Cecil," Justin muttered.

"Since he also died without issue"—the clerk pointed again, his finger following an inked line sideways and upward—"we had to go back a generation, to the seventh duke. *He* had two brothers. The elder died six years ago, and although he left twelve children, only one son was actually legitimate. That child, one Clarence Thornton, celebrated so enthusiastically on hearing the news that he fell from his horse, drunk, and broke his neck."

Justin rolled his eyes. He had no patience for such idiotic behavior. He hadn't made it to his current position in life by drinking and gaming his days away. He'd worked bloody hard to gain his fortune.

"The seventh duke's *other* brother died of a head injury in his twenties, so we were forced to go back *yet another* generation, to the duke's grandfather, Sir Sidney Thornton."

Justin drummed his fingers on the desk, wishing he'd installed a bell to summon Simms for moments such as this.

The solicitor, aware of his impatience, rushed to finish. "Sir Sidney had a younger brother, Bertram, who himself had two sons. The eldest, George, was killed in a duel a month ago. Which brings us to *his* brother, William." He paused meaningfully. "Your father."

Justin frowned. "My father died in Canada three years ago, on a fur-trading expedition."

The younger man nodded. "Which brings us to *you,* one Justin Trevelyan Thornton. Heir presumptive to the duchy of Wansford, and all its associated incomes and estates. The principal seat, Wansford Hall, is a fine example of the Jacobean architectural style, I believe."

Justin shook his head. "I don't care if it's a fairy-tale castle made entirely out of gingerbread. I don't want it. Give it to someone else. Whoever's next in line."

Turnbull sent him a pained, regretful look. "That's not how it works, I'm afraid. You can't refuse a dukedom. Even if you choose not to claim the title by applying to the Lord Chancellor's office for a writ of summons, the title can never be granted to anyone else until you yourself are dead."

Justin groaned. "This sounds very much like a Trojan horse: something that *looks* like a gift, but in truth will be nothing but aggravation. There's always a price to be paid. Come on, out with it. Is the duchy in debt? I bet it is. Mortgaged to the hilt. Crumbling into the ground. Sinking into a swamp."

"I don't believe so, no. I'm not privy to the accounts,

of course, but the duke's widow has been running the estate with the aid of the estate manager since the old duke died, and I've heard nothing but high praise."

Justin squinted at the dates inked above the eighth duke's name and did some swift mental calculation. The man had been over seventy at his death. His widow was doubtless similarly decrepit, but at least it sounded as if she had competent advisors. That was something, at least.

"There *will* be costs involved, though," he said. "Am I right?"

Turnbull pursed his lips. "Well, as to that, yes. There are homage fees: one on acceptance of your claim to the title, and another the first time a peer makes his appearance at the House of Lords."

"Of course," Justin said acidly. "How much must I pay for the privilege?"

"I believe for a duke, it's around three hundred and fifty pounds."

"Bloody Hell. So I'm expected to rejoice in suddenly becoming responsible for an estate I've never seen, a title I don't want, and an army of dependents I don't need?"

The solicitor swallowed. "Er. Yes, sir?"

"I *also* suppose that I'll be expected to choose some well-bred, empty-headed chit to provide the duchy with an heir?"

"Well, yes," Turnbull conceded. His lips twitched with a hint of amusement. "But there are *worse* things a man could be required to do."

"I disagree," Justin countered sternly. "It sounds like a fate worse than death. An inescapable one."

The clerk schooled his expression, and made a deferential bow. "You have my condolences. But I'm sure you'll be equal to the task. After all, you already run one of England's most successful trading companies, do you not?"

Justin snorted. "I do indeed. I gather you think I should be more grateful?"

The solicitor shrugged. "With respect, a dukedom is the highest rank a man can achieve in this country, short of being born a royal prince. You will have power. Respect. Wealth."

"I already have power, respect, and wealth. And I've *earned* them, not had them handed to me on a silver platter." Justin glared at him, but there was no escaping the inevitable. He let out an impatient huff. "Fine. I'll give it a year, no longer. I'll go to London, set the duchy's affairs in order, find a wife, and be back here by Easter."

The solicitor rolled his papers and neatly stashed them away. "You'll be coming to London soon, then?"

"I suppose I must. Did the eighth duke keep a town house?"

"He did, sir. In Portman Square. But I believe it's currently being occupied by the late duke's widow. As the new duke, you do, of course, have the right to occupy the premises, but it might be politic to give the lady a few weeks' grace to remove to the dower house at Wansford, or to some alternative lodging of her choice."

Justin frowned. He had a well-deserved reputation for ruthlessness in his business dealings. No doubt half of London would expect him to evict the old crone as soon as he arrived in the capital, but he had no desire for a fight in this case.

"Agreed. I have my own house on Curzon Street. I'll stay there until matters are resolved."

"Very good, Your Grace."

Justin winced at the honorific title.

Turnbull placed the leather satchel on the edge of the

desk. "I'll leave these documents for your perusal. And should you need any further assistance, I am entirely at your disposal."

Justin waved him away. "Thank you. I'll be in London by the start of next week. Simms will see you out."

When the clerk finally left, Justin sat back in his chair and gave an audible growl.

What in God's name had he done to deserve *this*?

His acquaintances—friends and enemies alike—said he had the devil's own luck, but it had been his own tenacity that had turned Thornton & Co. from the modest, single-ship enterprise he'd inherited from his father into the astonishing success it was today. His fleet conveyed everything from luxury goods from the Continent, to timber and furs from Canada and North America.

Being named heir to a dukedom was a surprise, certainly, but Justin had no doubt of his own abilities. The duchy would be lucky to have him. He would be infinitely better at running it than any of the previous incumbents, had they stayed alive long enough to accept the position. Those idiots would have gambled the place away, or fleeced the tenants to line their own pockets.

Justin rubbed his cheek, testing the dark stubble that shadowed his jaw. He hadn't bothered to shave that morning. He'd expected no visitors, had no woman to impress. Anne-Marie, his most recent paramour, had finally tired of what she called his "cruel inattention"—namely, his desire to get back to work instead of lounging around in bed after pleasuring her—and had flounced back to her French homeland two weeks ago.

She'd undoubtedly used him for a free voyage back from Canada—Montreal being less lucrative in terms of potential suitors than she'd hoped—but he'd been perfectly amenable to sharing his cabin for the tedious

Atlantic crossing. He'd been neither shocked nor saddened to see her go. Her parting words, however, rang in his ears, and to his surprise, they still stung.

"You are a beast." Anne-Marie's magnificent eyes had flashed with indignation and her equally magnificent bosom had quivered beneath her lace fichu. "And you know what? I pity you!"

Justin had unwisely allowed his snort of amusement to escape. "*Pity* me? Why? I'm one of the wealthiest men in England. I can buy whatever my heart desires."

"You *'ave* no heart. Only desires."

His raised brows had incensed her even more. Anne-Marie plopped her bonnet on her head and tied the ribbons with furious, shaking fingers. Her accent always became more pronounced when she was emotional.

"You 'ave passion, but no *love*." Her eyes filled with a scornful, withering expression that caught Justin like a punch to the chest. She stabbed her gloved finger at him. "*You*, Justin Thornton, are a man who knows the cost of everything, and the value of nothing. Nothing *important*, at least."

With that excellent parting shot, she'd slammed out of the house and out of his life.

It was just as well that she'd left, Justin reminded himself. He made it a rule to limit his liaisons to a maximum of three months, which not only avoided boredom, but also prevented either side from developing deeper feelings that might complicate an otherwise agreeable relationship.

His parents had married for love, and the dreadful toll that grief had wreaked on his father following his mother's death was something he planned to avoid at all costs.

He'd blamed his recent stretch of celibacy for why he was so on edge, but if he was honest, he'd been plagued by a smoldering sense of dissatisfaction for long before Anne-Marie had left. Until her parting diatribe, however, he'd never considered that the thing he might be missing could be . . . something that couldn't be bought.

Something like love.

He instantly dismissed the notion as absurd. He was a grown man of thirty, not a child in leading strings. He had no shortage of friends, colleagues, acquaintances whose company he enjoyed. When he had a physical desire, he sated his passions with whichever woman happened to catch his interest, as long as they were amenable. His affairs were mutually satisfying arrangements, in which love played no part.

Abstinence was clearly addling his brain. The brief, clinical pleasure he received from his own hand was no substitute for being with a woman. But women were, on the whole, a pain in the arse. Even semiprofessionals like Anne-Marie. They always *claimed* to be happy with a casual arrangement, but they always secretly wanted more.

More commitment.

More emotion.

More than he was willing to give.

Justin exhaled loudly. *God, what a morning.*

The weight of the unexpected dukedom felt like a lead cloak around his shoulders and he rolled them to relieve the tension.

He'd be inundated with women in London, even more so than usual, once word of his inheritance got out. Matchmaking mammas would be thrusting their quivering, doe-eyed daughters at him as prospective brides, while society wives and widows would be privately offering him carte blanche.

Engaging a new mistress would be good, but to do so while he was also publicly selecting a wife would require a great deal of discretion. It would be a situation fraught with potential for disaster, and he preferred to minimize risk wherever possible.

His gaze fell upon the uppermost envelope on his stack of correspondence. He'd been about to refuse Careby's invitation; his old school friend's house parties were infamous for their raucousness, and Justin generally avoided them, finding the dedicated pursuit of drunkenness and pleasure rather puerile.

But now an intriguing possibility struck him.

Careby's house was *en route* to London. It would be bursting at the seams with disreputable people, both male and female, all looking for a good time.

It was, therefore, the perfect place to find a willing partner for the night. A one-off solution for his physical needs before he arrived in the capital and found himself under the critical gaze of the *ton*.

It would also be a rare opportunity to find a partner who wanted nothing more from him than his body. Here in Bristol, he was instantly recognizable. Women lusted after his bank balance as much as his face. In London, with a dukedom to boot, he'd be lucky to go anywhere incognito, and the women he'd attract would be jockeying for the title of duchess and the elevation in rank he could provide.

At Careby's, there would be zero chance of inadvertently ruining some innocent and being trapped into a hasty marriage. The women would all be harlots: either professional prostitutes paid to provide entertainment, or bored society wives and widows looking for some racy entertainment a safe distance away from the wagging tongues of London.

Justin pulled a fresh sheet of paper toward him and scrawled a hasty acceptance, then rang the bell for Simms.

His trusted manservant appeared within a suspiciously

short space of time, indicating that he'd probably been hovering within earshot just beyond the door.

Justin shook his head. Simms's ability to lurk had been extremely useful to him over the years. The man seemed to know everything about everyone.

"Post this please, Simms. And tell Walker I'll be traveling to London tomorrow, with an overnight stop at Hinchcombe Park, Tom Careby's seat in Bedfordshire."

Simms, ever unruffled, bowed. "As you wish, Your Grace."

Justin scowled at use of his new title. "Your reputation for omnipotence—or perhaps I should more accurately call it eavesdropping—remains intact, Simms."

His fine sarcastic tone had no visible effect on the servant, who merely bowed again with a pleased smile. "You have my sincere felicitations on your good fortune, Your Grace."

"That's enough 'Your Grace-ing.' 'Sir' will do just as well." Justin handed him the note. "And you needn't look so smug. You'll be coming to London with me. Your eyes and ears might come in useful."

Simms bowed again. "Very good . . . Your Grace."

Chapter Two

Hinchcombe Park.

"This is a terrible idea." Tess made a desperate grab for the leather strap above her head as the carriage bounced along the rutted driveway. "The worst."

"It was *your* idea," Daisy reminded her. "And it's not the worst. Remember the time Ellie disguised herself as a fishwife to catch that man who'd abducted his cousin? That was the worst."

Ellie gave a theatrical shudder. "I still have nightmares about the smell."

"Well, it's definitely second-worst," Tess muttered. She tugged at the scandalously low-cut bodice of her gown, but her breasts still jiggled above the lace like two of Mrs. Ward's blancmanges. "I look like a harlot."

"We *all* look like harlots," Daisy said happily. "That's the point. How else are we going to get into this disgraceful event? And how else are *you* going to persuade some handsome-yet-morally-lax stranger to seduce you?"

Tess groaned. "I said I wanted someone to *kiss* me, not

seduce me. I can't risk doing anything that might leave me in an 'embarrassing situation.'"

Daisy grinned. "There are plenty of wonderful things you can do that won't result in a child, I promise."

Ever since Daisy had described in glowing detail her own first amorous encounter with Tom Harding, the cheeky stable hand who'd worked at Hollyfield, Tess had been burningly curious to discover physical pleasure for herself. But she was caught in a terrible dilemma.

As a widow, everyone assumed she'd had a physical relationship with the duke. If she took a lover from among the rakes of the *ton*, the secret of her virginity might be revealed. The resulting gossip would put her in a difficult position regarding the other wives and widows of London. They'd treated her as one of their own, included her in discussions no virgin should ever have heard.

Tess would be labeled an impostor. A brazen, shameful hussy who'd bent society's rigid rules and pretended to be worldlier than she really was.

Becoming a social pariah would *not* be beneficial for the work she did at King & Co.

She, Daisy, and Ellie had started the investigative agency a few months after the old duke's death. Since women with vocations were generally treated with disdain and suspicion in the *ton*, Tess had suggested that they operate under a male pseudonym. "Charles King, Esquire" was entirely fictitious. The three of them were King & Co.'s sole employees, not that many of their clients were aware of the fact. Whenever anyone asked to see the notoriously elusive Mr. King, they were told he was "out following a lead."

King & Co.'s headquarters—a handsome brick building in Lincoln's Inn Fields—had been one of the first purchases Tess had made with her widow's portion, and the satisfaction she'd felt on signing the deeds, that heady rush of independence, had gone a long way to lessening her guilt about the lies she'd told to get there.

Their first "case" had been to help Cecelia Talbot, an old school friend. Cece had lost her necklace while kissing a "gentleman" at a party, and the cad had been trying to blackmail her into marriage by threatening to send it to her father as proof of their "affair."

Tess had lured the blackmailer into a maze at Vauxhall. Instead of the kiss he'd been expecting, he'd been greeted by Daisy's loaded pistols, and a lengthy speech from Ellie reminding him that blackmail had been considered a capital felony instead of a misdemeanor since the case of *R. v. Jones* in 1776. As such, it was technically punishable by transportation to Australia—if not the death penalty outright—and that Ellie was quite prepared to ask her father to pursue a prosecution on Cecelia's behalf.

This information had been enough to scare the miscreant into returning the necklace the following day, and to take an extended tour of the Greek Islands "for his health."

After that, business had flourished. They'd gained cases through whispered word-of-mouth recommendations and a few newspaper advertisements, and now King & Co. was known for dealing with "sensitive matters" for London's fashionable elite with the utmost discretion and remarkable success.

Professional satisfaction, however, was not the same as *physical* satisfaction. It had been almost two years since her disastrous marriage, and Tess still had what Daisy called "an inexperience problem."

Her situation was uniquely challenging. If Tess took a lover, she risked falling pregnant, and the gossip she'd heard suggested that methods of prevention were notoriously unreliable. Any child of hers would be obviously illegitimate, and it would be cruel to subject an innocent to the inevitable stigma and disadvantages of such a position.

She couldn't choose another husband, either. Marriage would mean losing the income she received from the duchy and handing control of her person and her finances to a man who might forbid her to continue her investigative work.

That would never do. There was a mortgage to pay on the property at Lincoln's Inn Fields, and Ellie and Daisy relied on their salaries for their own limited independence.

The only way Tess could ever marry again would be to find a man as rich as the old duke, whom she could trust implicitly. A man who would love her enough to allow her to make her own decisions.

Since solvent, attractive, trustworthy gentlemen were notoriously thin on the ground, she'd resigned herself to a lifetime of widowhood.

But not to a life of complete celibacy.

The solution, the three of them had decided, was for Tess to become someone other than the Duchess of Wansford for a night. As an incognita, a masked woman with no name and no morals, she could find a handsome stranger and do a little "passionate experimenting" without fear of discovery.

According to Daisy, Hinchcombe Park was the place to do it. Tom Careby's masquerades were notorious for their licentiousness.

Still, Tess was having second thoughts. "I should never have suggested this."

"Of course you should," Daisy insisted. "You're the

most beautiful girl in England and you've never even been properly kissed. Or *im*properly kissed, for that matter. It's a travesty."

"Do you mean she's never been kissed with proficiency?" Ellie mused. "Or that she's never been kissed in an indecent manner?"

"Either," said Daisy. "Both." She shook her head with a frown. "London's full of rakes and scoundrels. I can't believe so few of them have propositioned you."

"Maybe there's something about me that suggests I wouldn't be open to advances? Am I too aloof? Too unapproachable?"

"Not at all," Ellie said soothingly. "You're utterly irresistible. And you looked radiant in half mourning. You're the only person I've ever met who looked good in lavender. Lilac makes me look seasick."

"You *have* developed a bizarre interest in modern agricultural practices, though," Daisy teased. "Not everyone's as excited by truffles as you are."

"You don't think they can tell I'm still a virgin, do you?"

Daisy snorted. "Of course not. Despite my father's claim to being able to spot one at fifty paces, men are not born with an innate maidenhood detector. Purity can't be divined, like water. If it *could*, every man would keep a dowsing twig in his pocket to see if it quivered whenever he got close to a girl."

Tess chuckled at the mental image that produced.

Ellie gripped the windowsill as the coach lurched through another rut. "It's more likely they haven't asked because the matrons have scared them off, or because they're afraid of being rejected. Most men would rather not try, than admit they'd failed."

Tess let out a long sigh. When she'd first been forced

to marry the duke, she'd worried that the *ton* would brand her a shameless fortune hunter—or worse, a murderess—but that hadn't been the case.

While she'd eschewed social events for the first six months of full mourning, Daisy and Ellie had started a campaign to smooth her reentry into society by reminding everyone that she'd been forced into an unwilling union by her domineering father.

Her father's own death, a mere eight weeks after the duke's, had prevented him from denying this unpalatable truth.

The irony of him not living long enough to enjoy the benefits of having a duchess for a daughter had not been lost on Tess. She'd felt guilty at how little she'd mourned him, but he'd been an unloving, selfish parent and she was unaccountably relieved to be beyond reach of his manipulations.

Since a large number of society's heiresses had been also forced into loveless unions themselves, she'd encountered an unexpected degree of sympathy when she'd finally returned to London.

Instead of being shunned, society's wives and widows had taken her under their wing. Ladies commiserated with her for having to bed an older man, and she'd tried not to wince as they'd described their own unsatisfactory bedroom encounters in excruciating detail.

As an attractive young widow, she'd inadvertently become the ultimate matrimonial prize, and those well-intentioned women had closed ranks to deter all but the most honorable suitors.

Unfortunately, none of them had ever considered that Tess might *welcome* a few scandalous advances.

"We should put our masks on," Tess said. "We can't have anyone guessing who we are."

Daisy and Ellie both nodded, and the three of them fumbled with their disguises.

Ellie's gown was pale blue. The excessive frills made her look like a sweet, if rather impractical, shepherdess. Daisy, having decided that none of her own outfits were "harlotty enough," had borrowed a deep indigo dress from a friend who worked as a chorus girl at Drury Lane Theatre. Her bosom was quite as exposed as Tess's.

But Tess's dress was still the boldest: a sinful, scandalous red.

She'd never worn anything this color in her life, but after a year of drab lavenders and dull browns the deep crimson made her feel daring and thoroughly wicked. She was simultaneously terrified of attracting attention, and emboldened by the fact that she would be completely anonymous.

Flaming torches illuminated the front of the house as the carriage joined the row of vehicles waiting to disgorge their passengers on the front steps. Laughter, music, and conversation floated through the open windows.

Tess's stomach lurched in panic, but Daisy caught her eye with a knowing smile.

"You can do this. You're a scarlet woman. *Literally*. You've spent far too long poring over rent books and grain yields. It's time to have some fun."

Tess nodded. Daisy was right. It was time to stop hiding in the shadows, and take something for herself.

Tonight, she would get herself kissed.

Chapter Three

Tess noticed him the moment she entered the cardroom. He sat at a table, half in profile, a pile of mother-of-pearl gaming chips heaped on the green baize in front of him, a glass of amber liquid by his wrist.

It was his stillness that drew her, the intensity of his concentration. He was an oasis of calm amid the crush of guests who eddied and flowed around him like the rushing waters of a stream.

His opponent shuffled his cards and drummed his fingertips impatiently on the table, but *his* movements were sure as he laid down one card and requested another from the dealer with a flick of his hand.

Intrigued, Tess started forward, using the crowd as cover. The candles overhead highlighted his dark hair, a straight nose, and the shadow of an evening beard on his unfashionably tanned cheek.

He was the only one in the room not wearing a mask.

The implied arrogance of that gesture, as if he disdained to play by the same rules as the rest of humanity, fascinated her. She'd always wished for the courage to dismiss society's expectations so brazenly.

Who was this man?

She edged closer, drawn by the aura of effortless command that surrounded him.

She'd never seen him before in the *ton*. Was he a soldier, newly returned from the war? He certainly had the physique. His shoulders were muscled beneath his dark jacket, his body lean and athletic.

He had money, too, judging by the exquisite cut of his coat. A foreigner, perhaps? A professional gamester? Definitely not some impoverished country squire. Still, in a gathering like this, he could just as well be a good-looking footman who'd stolen his master's clothes for the night.

Tess hovered near his elbow, desperate to see his whole face.

She almost hoped he'd open his mouth and say something imbecilic, or bray like a donkey when he laughed, and the allure would be shattered.

He did neither of those things. When his opponent made a comment, the deep sound of his laughter vibrated through her and produced a quivery feeling in the pit of her stomach. Tess took an amazed breath, shocked by her body's reaction.

After the next hand, his opponent gave a disgusted snort and tossed his cards faceup on the table.

"Damn it, Thorn, you've bested me again!"

The good-natured complaint was accompanied by a groan as the loser pushed his tokens forward and his chair back.

"Should've known better than to try my hand against you. You've the devil's own luck."

As if sensing Tess's presence at his side, the stranger raised his head.

A shock of something elemental, almost like recognition, flashed through her as their eyes met. If someone had asked her to describe a "dangerous man," it would be him. Flint-gray eyes, high cheekbones. Lips that looked like they could command—or kiss—with consummate ease.

They'd never met in person, she was sure, but she knew him: he was every wicked fantasy she'd ever dreamed, come to life.

Handsome seemed too weak a word. Shrewd intelligence blazed in his eyes, and Tess had the strangest sensation that he was looking right through her, through dress and skin, to the very heart of her. She felt exposed, all her secrets laid bare.

She gave herself a mental shake. She was being fanciful. He wasn't reading her soul. He was probably just imagining her naked.

As she was doing to him.

His gaze traveled the length of her body in a searing head-to-toe appraisal that took in her crimson gown and bloodred mask in one calculating sweep. His dark brows rose.

In interest? Disdain?

She couldn't tell.

Tess returned the bold appraisal with one of her own, even as heat flushed her body at her daring. A thrill shivered along her spine. So *this* was the lust the poets raved about. This dizzy, drunken feeling of excitement.

At last.

She felt breathless, and also extremely relieved. In recent months she'd started to worry that there was something wrong with her, that she was somehow numb. The lukewarm interest she'd felt on a few previous occasions paled into insignificance when compared to the scorching reaction she was having to this man.

Surely this was a sign from the universe?

The stranger's lips curved up at her prolonged inspection of him, as if he appreciated her boldness. He stood in a fluid movement and Tess took an involuntary step back; he was taller than she'd expected. More intimidating.

He must have thought she was about to leave, because he reached out and captured her wrist, encircling it gently with his fingers.

"Don't go, sweet. You've brought me luck."

Tess's belly twisted in glorious confusion. His voice was as delicious as his face; deep, with a hint of cynical amusement.

She managed a scornful laugh. "Pfft. Your friend just said you're always lucky. My presence had nothing to do with it."

He smiled at her refusal to accept the easy compliment and adjusted his grip to raise her hand to his lips. He kissed the back of her glove, like a gallant, and the heat of his lips burned through the satin.

"I don't believe we've been introduced."

"I don't believe we have. I'm—" Tess quickly tried to decide which alias to use.

"Masked," he finished smoothly, noting her hesitation. "And therefore disinclined to reveal your name. Or your face." He bowed over their joined hands, and the gleam in his eye was an invitation to spar with him. "Forget I asked. I'd rather have no name than a lie. I'll call you Scarlet."

Tess smiled, amused by his perspicacity, and matched his playful tone.

"Scarlet will do nicely. And yes, I like the anonymity of a masquerade. Unlike *you*, it seems. Do you think yourself so handsome that you don't want to deny the ladies the pleasure of looking at your face?"

His brows rose. "Not at all. Although I appreciate the

compliment. Are *you* so beautiful that you're wearing a mask to prevent every man in the room from falling at your feet?"

"Maybe." Tess shrugged. It wasn't far from the truth. Her looks were usually at the root of her problems. Tonight, she would take them out of the equation entirely.

His fingers tightened on hers as he turned them both toward the ballroom. Tess glanced back at the card table. "Don't you want to collect your winnings?"

"Simms will see to it. We should dance."

He ushered her through the throng, never releasing her hand, and when they reached the dance floor, he swirled her effortlessly into his arms.

Tess glanced at their joined hands. Her gloves were red, to match her dress. His fingers were long and elegant, his skin lightly tanned, as if he'd spent time outside.

They swung into the first dip of a waltz, bodies moving in perfect rhythm, and she tried to slow her pounding heart. The strong muscles of his shoulder rippled beneath her palm.

She glanced up in what she hoped was a coquettish manner. "So really, why no mask? Aren't you afraid of being recognized?"

"Not particularly. I have nothing to hide, and no patience for subterfuge. I prefer to be straightforward in my dealings, both business and personal. People can either take me as I am, or leave me."

It was Tess's turn to raise her brows. How nice it must be not to care about anyone else's opinion. Unfortunately, she didn't have that luxury. At least, not in the *ton*. "You think I'm hiding something?"

The look he flashed down at her was cynical, ironic.

"Apart from my face and my name," she added wryly.

He leaned in, so his lips brushed her temple, and the

woodsy scent of his cologne teased her nose. Dear Lord, he smelled amazing.

"I think you're hiding a hundred things, Scarlet," he murmured. "Not least a very lovely body beneath that scandalous dress."

Tess sucked in a breath, both shocked and delighted by his direct approach.

He fancied her! Without even seeing her face or knowing who she was!

"I could be as ugly as a horse beneath this mask," she managed.

He pulled back, just a fraction, and his cool gaze dropped to her lips. "Perhaps. But you have the most kissable mouth I've ever seen."

Tess missed a step.

He righted her with ease. "Are you married?"

She shook her head.

"Engaged?"

"No."

"Another man's mistress?"

"No. Are you?"

His lips curved. "Neither married, nor engaged. Nor any man's mistress, for that matter." His eyes bored into hers. "Did you only come here to dance tonight, Scarlet? Or are you after something more?"

Tess bit her lip. Now was her chance. "What if I said I'd come here for an adventure? Could you offer me that?"

He tilted his head, considering. "For an hour or so, yes. I think we could enjoy one another."

His candidness was refreshing. He wasn't trying to woo her with pretty words or sweetly whispered lies. Tess could feel herself crumbling.

Scandalous it might be, but there was something incredibly liberating about not being judged by her face.

"Beauty" was just an accidental combination of pleasing features that owed everything to luck and current fashion. Her looks would fade, and so few people ever bothered to look beyond them, for her intelligence, her kindness, her wit.

This man thought she was a woman with no morals. Apart from her lips, visible beneath her mask, he didn't know or care what she looked like. He just wanted her body to pleasure his own.

And for the first time in her life, Tess wanted exactly the same thing.

The waltz ended and they swirled to a stop, her skirts clinging to his legs as if reluctant to let him go. Her chest rose and fell as she tried to catch her breath.

She wanted this man to kiss her, more than she'd ever wanted anything in her life. If he wanted to do more than kiss . . . well, she had one of Daisy's knives in her pocket. She would use it if she had to.

She pressed her palm to the front of his shirt and threw caution to the wind.

"I'd like to do more than dance."

Chapter Four

Was she really doing this?

Tess shook her head in disbelief as she followed the handsome stranger through the crowded rooms. The force of her attraction was both wonderful and terrifying.

His opponent had called him Thorn, but was that his surname, or a nickname? Either way, it seemed oddly appropriate. There was a sharpness about him; a dangerous kind of beauty, like the perfectly honed edge of a blade.

Perhaps it was better not knowing his name.

He still held her hand. He glanced over his shoulder with a smile that made her belly flutter.

The crowds thinned out as they ventured deeper into the house. Couples pressed together in darkened alcoves. Tess glanced around for Ellie and Daisy, but there was no sign of either of them.

The first room they entered was occupied. Tess heard a male bellow of outrage as the door slammed shut again, and she sent a silent apology to whomever they'd inadvertently interrupted.

The second room was empty, lit with a solitary lamp.

She glimpsed tall rows of books that lined the walls before she was whirled around and pressed flat against the door. The stranger's chest met hers, his body caging her, and she felt a flutter of delicious panic.

This was madness.

Imperative madness.

She could barely see him in the gloom, just his outline, but she felt him lean closer. His breath teased her jaw.

"So, what does this adventure of yours look like?"

Her fears slid away. She wanted this. *Needed* this. She just had to be brave.

"It starts with a kiss."

He studied her mouth with an intensity that should have been unnerving, but instead made her body tingle in anticipation.

"A kiss? I can manage that."

He bent his head and Tess closed her eyes, determined to savor every movement. She'd never been kissed on the mouth before.

His lips grazed hers, warm, softer than she'd expected. She'd thought he'd devour her, abandon all restraint, but there was no urgency in his kiss, no aggression. Instead, he kissed her with a delicious, unhurried languor, as if she were something to be savored. As if they had all the time in the world.

Heat spread up her throat and into her cheeks.

His hands came up to cradle her face and she stiffened, thinking he meant to remove her mask, but he only brushed his thumbs across the edges of her mouth in a way that made her shiver out a breath.

He kissed her again.

"Delicious," he murmured. "Your mouth is delicious."

He angled his head, and she felt his tongue glide along the closed seam of her lips. Tess experienced a moment of confusion, but when she opened her mouth to ask him what he was doing, his tongue slid inside to mingle with her own.

She almost swooned at the delightful new sensation. Cautiously, she swirled her own tongue against his, kissing him back with artless enthusiasm, and when he gave a low groan of encouragement her body tingled in wicked response.

He tasted of the brandy he'd been drinking, smoky and dark, and heat pooled low in her belly. His big hands slid into her hair, cupping her skull as he deepened the kiss, pulling her into the darkness like an undertow current that was impossible to resist.

One kiss became many, an endless game of advance and retreat—drugging, addictive, deliciously overwhelming. Tess sagged against the door, weak at the knees.

Oh, this was *glorious*!

Emboldened, she slid her hands around his neck and threaded her fingers into his hair, wishing she'd removed her gloves to feel the texture of his skin. His chest pinioned her against the door as his mouth stole the breath from her lungs.

This man certainly knew what he was doing.

Little by little his kisses became more urgent, fusing them together, drawing her into a dizzying swirl of black and red. He pressed against her, heavy and hard, so overwhelmingly male that it thrilled her to her bones.

Tearing his lips from hers, he placed a scorching row of kisses down the side of her neck and across her collarbone, and Tess tilted her head back against the door to give him better access. The light, scratchy stubble on his cheeks raised goose bumps on her skin.

His low groan mirrored her own longing perfectly.

"God, Scarlet, tell me you want more than kissing."

The roughness in his voice, his fervency, was her undoing. Tess struggled to catch her breath, to muster any semblance of sanity, but her entire body was clamoring for his touch, for more of the delicious heat he was kindling so effortlessly.

How was it possible for two strangers to be so attuned? For her body to react in such a way? It had never happened before, and it made absolutely no sense, but she didn't care. If this was madness, then she was happily destined for Bedlam.

"More," she whispered. "Please."

He didn't wait for further encouragement. His mouth slid to the top of her breasts, shamefully exposed by the outrageous dress, and she gasped as he gave her skin a playful bite, then soothed it with his tongue.

And then his hand slid inside the low bodice and her mouth fell open as he cupped her breast.

Dear Lord, what a sensation! His fingers gently squeezed her while his hot mouth feathered kisses lower and lower. And then her nipple was *in his mouth*, and the swirling of his tongue and the faint suction of his lips made her belly quiver.

Oh, this was wicked!

"Touch me." His rough demand pulled her from her dazed languor. "Put your hands on me. Please."

Tess blinked. Touch him where? His face? His chest?

He caught her hand and drew it down between them, pressing her fingers to the front of his breeches, and she let out a shocked breath as she felt the rock-solid length of him beneath the cloth.

Touch him there? Oh, God, she hadn't the faintest idea what to do.

But she wanted to.

Thankfully, he didn't seem to notice her hesitation. As

she tugged off her gloves, he unbuttoned his falls with unhurried dexterity. And then she felt him: hot, velvety flesh against her palm. Her fingers closed around him automatically, and he uttered a growl of pleasure against her neck.

"Yes, Scarlet. Exactly like that."

Fascinated, aroused, Tess encircled him; her fingers only just touched.

With an impassioned curse he placed his hand over hers, molding her to his length, and her eyes widened in amazement as he began to move their joined hands up and down in a fiendish rhythm. His big body moved, hips rocking into her touch, as he released his grip to let her continue on her own.

Tess could scarcely believe what she was doing. She couldn't see anything in the jumble of clothes between them, but she could *feel*: soft skin sliding over ridged muscle and a slippery wetness on her fingers. It was astonishing.

His hoarse moan was breathed against her lips. "That's so good."

A heady feeling of elation filled her. She felt like she'd just solved one of the great mysteries of the universe. *Her touch was giving him pleasure! He liked this!*

"Slow now. Slowly. That's my girl."

With a muffled groan he caught her hand again, guiding her, and with three more strokes his body convulsed against hers. His face pressed into her neck and his free hand gripped her hair almost painfully as he shuddered, jerking in her hands.

For one brief, delicious moment he leaned against her, utterly spent and oddly vulnerable. His breathing was harsh, as if he'd run a race, and she felt a surge of satisfaction that she'd produced such a result in such a man.

And then he hissed out a long, satisfied sigh.

"Bloody Hell, Scarlet. That was—" He swallowed, as if trying to find the right words. "Not what I'd planned, actually. But good. So good." He pressed a kiss to her bare shoulder. "I apologize." His gravelly voice held a rueful laugh as he tucked himself back into his breeches. "I never meant to do that alone. You got the better of me."

Tess held back a laugh of delight. "No need to be sorry."

She'd wanted to experience passion, hadn't she? And this definitely fitted the bill. She'd learned more in the past ten minutes—about men, about *herself*—than in her previous twenty-one years combined.

He shook his head, as if chiding himself. "Ah, but I promised you adventure, and so far, I'm the only one who's done anything exciting."

"The kissing was exciting."

He was so tall, so broad. The way he loomed over her should have been menacing, but for some reason the obvious disparity between them only made her feel deliciously feminine. She felt hot and on edge, her body jittery with a strange humming current.

"I owe you more than kissing, Scarlet. I owe you satisfaction."

His chuckle twisted her stomach into knots, but his choice of words made her lips quirk.

"That sounds like a duel." She lowered her register to mimic his masculine tones. "*Sir, I demand satisfaction.*"

His teeth flashed white in the shadows as he smiled at her quick wit. "Oh, you'll get it, my lady. You'll be so satisfied you'll be dreaming about it for weeks."

Tess laughed, even as her body tingled at his absolute conviction. "You seem very sure of your abilities."

His fingers brushed her jaw in a devastating caress. "I've never had any complaints."

Dear Lord, she was tempted to see exactly what he could do, but things had gone far enough. She was about to tell him so, but he kissed her again, and the sensible part of her brain went a little fuzzy.

Maybe just a few more kisses—

He cupped her bottom through her skirts and pulled her into his body. The feel of him against her full-length was delicious, and she tilted her hips, pressing closer still.

He was hard again, despite what they'd just done. He stroked his hand along her thigh, wordlessly coaxing her to lift her leg up around his hip, and the new position settled him perfectly into the lee of her body.

Tess wriggled against him, lost to sensation, desperate to ease the throbbing ache that pulsed between her legs.

Without breaking their kiss, he slid his hand under her skirts and up her calf, then higher, to the silky ribbon of her garter. Tess gasped against his mouth as his hand gripped the bare skin of her thigh. No man had ever touched her there, but it felt so good, so naughty.

She wasn't wearing drawers, so there was nothing to stop his hand from moving higher still. He made a deep rumble of satisfaction as his fingers slid up the outside of her thigh and cupped her bare bottom.

"So soft." He gave her bottom lip a playful nip with his teeth.

Tess felt as if she had a fever. His big hand squeezed her bottom and everything inside her quivered. And then his hand slid lower, his fingers following the crease of her cheeks, and Tess strained up toward him, desperate to feel his touch between her legs. There had to be some way to stop this wicked, yearning ache—

The door at her back suddenly thrust her forward as someone attempted to gain entry to the room. Thrown off-balance, she clutched her companion's shoulders as her leg dropped back to the floor and his hand fell from her skirts.

Her forehead bumped his chin as the unwelcome intruder gave the door another forcible shove, presumably thinking it was stuck on an unseen obstacle.

"This room is taken!"

Her companion's growl blasted by her ear, and the furious jiggling of the doorknob ceased abruptly. A moment of silence reigned.

"Apologies! Didn't mean to intrude." The male voice on the other side of the door was both regretful and bawdily amused. "Have at it, my good man."

Footsteps receded along the corridor and reality intruded like a splash of cold water to the face. Tess flushed to the roots of her hair—not that her companion could see, between her mask and the darkness. She slid her hands from his shoulders to the rock-hard planes of his chest and gave him a gentle shove.

Regret mingled with relief as he obligingly stepped back, and with a start she realized the coolness on her chest was because her right breast was still exposed to the night air. She tugged up her bodice with unsteady hands.

Her heart was still pounding with unfulfilled desire, and she wasn't sure whether to bless or curse the strangers for their interruption. Five more minutes, and she'd probably have let this man take her up against the wall, or down on the floor like a dockside whore.

A wicked, desperate part of her still wanted him to, but sanity prevailed. She had others to think of, beside herself.

She cleared her throat. "I think that's enough adventuring for tonight."

She sensed his confusion, even in the dark. "You want to stop? Now? But why?" He reached out and stroked her chin. "Were you not enjoying it?"

The hint of uncertainty in his tone made her heart contract. How could he even doubt it?

"Oh, I was enjoying it very much."

Almost too much.

"Then let me return the favor." His fingers slid to her hips and squeezed lightly. "Please."

Tess forced herself to shake her head. "I have to go."

Home, she added silently. *To bed. Alone. To marvel at everything we just did.*

He took a step back. "I apologize. I seem to have misread the situation." His tone was suddenly curt. "I didn't realize you were a professional."

There was a rustle as he reached into his jacket. "How much do I owe you?"

Heat flushed her cheeks as she realized what he meant. Most women looking for an illicit liaison would have been begging him to continue; it wasn't unreasonable for him to assume she was a whore, eager to find her next mark.

"Nothing," she said quickly, pushing his hand away. "Really. I don't want any payment."

He gave a soft, cynical grunt of disbelief. "As a businessman, being offered something for nothing always makes me suspicious. Nothing's ever truly free."

Blast. She should have demanded ten pounds and let him think the worst. She forced a teasing lightness into her tone.

"Perhaps I've stolen your pocket watch?"

He didn't even bother to pat his pockets. "You haven't."

"Perhaps I've stolen your heart."

His stiffness eased a little. "I don't have one. Or so I've been told." He traced the tip of his finger over the outer corner of her lip, smoothing the little freckle she had there. "But in case they're wrong, then guard it well."

His playful riposte made her smile. She'd never had such an enjoyable flirtation. The knowledge that they wouldn't meet again left a hollow ache in her chest. Now that she'd found him, this man who made her senses come alive, she never wanted to let him go.

Impossible.

Tess debated whether to go up on tiptoe for a final kiss, then decided against it. She'd probably lose what remained of her wits if they started kissing again.

"Are you sure we've never met before?" he asked. "There's something familiar about you."

Tess's heart gave a jolt of alarm. "Oh yes, very sure."

She'd certainly have remembered him if she'd seen him in the *ton*. His face was unforgettable.

"Good night then. And goodbye." He took another step back, giving her space to leave. "Perhaps we'll meet again?"

"I doubt it. And even if we did, you wouldn't recognize me."

"Ah, but you might recognize me. If you do, I hope you'll introduce yourself, so we can have another adventure."

"Perhaps I will."

She'd never dare.

He gave her chin a playful pinch, as if chiding her for the lie. "Goodbye, Scarlet. You were exactly what I needed tonight."

Tess pushed off the door and turned the handle. "Likewise."

With one last glance over her shoulder, she slipped out into the corridor.

What a night!

&

Justin let out a long, slow breath. What an extraordinary encounter. And what an extraordinary *woman*.

His blood was still pounding in his veins, his brain swirling as the intoxicating remnants of her perfume lingered in the air.

He reached for the doorknob, then forced his hand back to his side. He shouldn't follow her. To discover her name, to see her face, would ruin the magic. The illusion.

Perhaps, as she said, she was ugly beneath her mask. Possessed of a bulbous nose, or crossed eyes, or covered in pox scars.

He shook his head. She wasn't. He knew it in his soul.

Her lips had been perfection: pillowy and soft, and the shy hesitation in her responses, the pretense that she wasn't as well versed at kissing as he knew she must be, had excited him nonetheless.

If she wasn't a courtesan, then what *was* she? The skin of her jaw beneath her mask had been as smooth as velvet, her hands equally soft; she was no dairymaid or washerwoman, with rough, calloused palms from manual labor.

She'd made no attempt to disguise her accent. Had she forgotten? Or was she so certain that her mask was an adequate disguise? Either way, her precise speech and rounded vowels didn't place her as a member of the working classes. He'd bet a hundred pounds she was a member of the aristocracy, or at least landed gentry.

He'd come here tonight with the lowest of expectations, but had ended up having the most erotic experience he'd had in years.

His cock throbbed again in memory, at the way her breast had fitted so beautifully in his hand, his mouth. The scent of her, some elusive combination of floral fragrance and warm female skin, had made him dizzy with desire.

His body recognized her, even if his mind did not. As if they'd been lovers before, in some long-distant past.

Justin let out a snort at his own uncharacteristic whimsy. He didn't even know her name, for God's sake. She'd claimed to be no man's wife, but people lied. She was probably kissing another man, right now, in another room.

A flash of possessive jealousy, completely irrational and unwarranted, stabbed at him. He had no claim on her. They would probably never meet again, as she said.

But he hated the feeling that they had unfinished business. If she'd been a bored wife or unattached widow, why not allow him to pleasure her in return? Had his hand-induced climax disappointed her? Had she thought he'd be unable to perform? That certainly wasn't the case; he'd recovered with almost miraculous speed. His cock was as hard as an iron rod again in his breeches.

And even if she hadn't wanted his cock, he could have pleasured her with his hands, or his mouth, and returned the favor. He would have loved to make her fall apart.

Justin sighed again. She'd left him with more questions than answers. This night was probably best left as a delightful memory, but he suspected he'd still be studying the lips of every woman in London, just in case his mystery woman was there.

Chapter Five

King & Co., Lincoln's Inn Fields.

"They've found him."

Tess glanced up in surprise, her pen poised above a copy of *The Times*, as Ellie bustled into her office.

"Who? The footman who stole Lady Bressingham's silver?"

"Not one of *our* cases. The new Wansford heir."

Tess gave a dismissive snort. "How many does this make? Five? Six? I've lost count."

"Seven, I think," Daisy said, her mop of curls appearing in the open doorway. She sidled into the room and sank in the leather club chair to the right of Tess's desk. "What are the odds that this one will live long enough to claim the title?"

"Slim," Tess said. "I'm beginning to think the title's cursed. The accidents that have befallen the other claimants have been truly unprecedented."

Ellie shook her head. "I'd put money on this one sticking."

"Why? What's different about this one?"

"He's young. Just turned thirty."

"Youth isn't any guarantee. The one who fell off his horse was twenty-two."

"True. But this one isn't stupid, either. He's made a fortune shipping fur and lumber from Canada."

Daisy raised her brows. "Sounds promising."

Ellie sent her a wicked, teasing look. "Not only that, but he's also tall, dark, and devastatingly handsome."

Tess frowned as her brain unhelpfully provided an image of her mysterious stranger. Memories of their interlude had haunted her ever since Careby's party ten days ago. Against all logic, she'd found herself searching for him at every event she'd attended since, her heart skipping a beat whenever she glimpsed a tall, dark male across a room.

Heat rushed to her cheeks and she fanned herself surreptitiously with *The Times*. She had to stop thinking of him.

Daisy let out a derisive snort. "How do you know what he looks like?"

"Because I met him," Ellie said triumphantly. "Two years ago."

"When?" Tess demanded.

"Do you remember Lady Petworth's ball? The one to celebrate Bonaparte's first exile?"

Tess wrinkled her nose. "I didn't go. That was the week before my wedding. Father was keeping me under house arrest."

"Oh, hell, I'd forgotten about that. I hope he's rotting in his grave," Ellie muttered vehemently.

Daisy nodded in agreement, and Tess felt a flash of gratitude for their unwavering support.

"Well, anyway," Ellie continued, "*he* was there. Half the girls fell in love with him, even with absolutely no encouragement."

"Probably *because* he gave them no encouragement," Daisy drawled. "There's something so appealing about a challenge."

Tess laughed.

"As I was saying . . ." Ellie gave the paper she held a theatrical flourish that would have been perfect for a case-winning courtroom revelation. "His name is Justin Thornton, and he's just returned from the wilds of Canada. He's in London right now, to answer his writ of summons."

"How do you know all this?" Daisy demanded.

"Because I happened to overhear a conversation between my father and Josiah Turnbull at dinner the other night. And when I say 'happened to overhear,' I mean 'shamelessly eavesdropped the minute I heard the name Wansford.'" Ellie grinned.

"I appreciate the spying on my behalf," Tess said. "What else did you hear?"

"Turnbull said there's no doubt he's found the right man, but that Thornton was waiting for it to be made official before he called on you. It *is* quite a delicate situation, after all. It's not often the new duke needs introducing to the old duchess."

"Who are you calling old?" Tess gasped in mock outrage. "I'm twenty-one."

"*Current* duchess," Ellie amended with a laugh. "I should have said current. Or Dowager."

"Dowager duchess is even worse. It makes me sound like a ninety-year-old hag."

"Do you think he knows how old you are?" Daisy mused. "If not, he'll be in for quite the shock."

"Oh, I'm sure Josiah's filled him in," Ellie said. "Which means Thornton's being discreet."

"A mark in his favor, I suppose," Daisy sniffed. "At

least he hasn't barged into Wansford House and ordered you to start packing."

Tess bit her lip. "If he really *is* the new duke, I'll have to move out of the Hall and into the dower house. And find somewhere else to live here in London."

"You own *this* building," Daisy reminded her. "You can stay here if you have to. It's not Portman Square, I grant you, but it's still a lovely part of town."

Tess considered that suggestion. The great collector Sir John Soane lived just down the street, at Nos. 12 and 13, and although much of the fashionable world had moved west, to Mayfair, the neighborhood was still filled with wealthy lawyers and respectable barristers, who enjoyed the proximity to the Inns of Court.

"It may come to that," Tess said. "And honestly, living here would be quite nice."

Daisy opened her mouth to reply when a tentative knock on the back door made the three of them exchange a glance. The back door, leading in from the mews, was used by clients who wanted the greatest secrecy.

Tess and Ellie peered around the doorframe into the corridor as Daisy went to answer it.

It was almost dusk. A carriage with no identifying crest on the panels waited in the cobbled courtyard, and a cloaked figure stood on the back step.

"May I help you?" Daisy asked.

"I wish to speak to Mr. King." The speaker, an older female, had a distinctly foreign inflection. German, perhaps, or Swiss. Her wish sounded like "vish."

Daisy swung the door wide in invitation, revealing Tess and Ellie, and gave the standard response they gave to everyone who wished to speak to their "employer."

"I'm afraid Mr. King's out investigating a case at

present, but do come in and explain your situation. As his assistants, the three of us are in his strictest confidence."

The figure nodded and followed Daisy into the front room, but when she pulled back her hood Tess bit back a gasp.

All three of them dipped into deep formal curtsies. "Your Majesty!"

Tess straightened, trying to hide her shock at seeing England's very own Queen Charlotte—the wife of "mad" King George and mother of the prince regent—*here*, in their front room.

The queen removed her cloak and seated herself regally in the armchair Daisy had just vacated.

All three of them leapt into action.

"It is an honor to have you visit us, Your Majesty," Tess said.

She'd seen the queen on numerous occasions at social functions, starting with her own debut presentation at court, just weeks before her wedding to the duke. But apart from a few brief social niceties, she'd never actually *conversed* with the woman.

"Can I get you some tea, Your Majesty?" Ellie queried.

Queen Charlotte waved her hand. "Please, no 'majesty.' And no tea, either, thank you. Tonight, I come to you as plain Mrs. King." Her gray eyes twinkled. "A name I suspect is as fictional as your employer."

Ellie and Daisy shared a startled glance, but the queen only gave them a maternal smile. "Oh, fear not. Your secret is safe with me. I have no vish to meet your 'Mr. King,' provided I can engage his services. I have a sensitive matter that needs to be handled with the utmost delicacy."

Tess seated herself behind the desk and pulled forward a piece of paper to take notes. "Of course, Your Maj— ma'am. How can we help?"

The queen frowned. She was a handsome woman of over seventy years, and her gray hair had no need of its powder, but the quiet force of her personality was evident in the direct look she gave each of them. She nodded, as if they'd passed some unspoken test.

"As you know, in less than a month my dear grand- daughter, the Princess Charlotte, is to marry her beloved Prince Leopold."

Daisy smiled. "The whole country is eagerly awaiting that happy event, ma'am."

"It is a love match, it is true"—the queen smiled fondly—"which is why nothing can be allowed to inter- fere with it going ahead."

Ellie raised her brows. "*Is* there something that might cause that to happen?"

"Indeed. A most unfortunate situation has arisen, and because of the gossiping at the court—and the indiscreet nature of official channels—there is no one I can entrust to deal with it."

Tess nodded, intrigued, but trying to remain cool and businesslike. "You can be assured of our discretion."

"That is what I have heard. If, as I suspect, the three of *you* are the ones responsible for 'Mr. King's' success, then I hope you will be able to help me with this little problem, too."

The queen settled lower in her chair. "My grand- daughter, you must understand, has lived an incredibly sheltered life. The prince regent was, I am ashamed to say, a rather neglectful parent. He allowed Charlotte very little freedom, and left her in the dubious care of his estranged wife, Caroline, the Princess of Wales, and a series of strict chaperones.

"Three years ago, aged just fifteen, Charlotte embarked on a foolish and youthful flirtation with a young captain in the hussars, a handsome rogue named Charles Hesse. The relationship was *encouraged* by her mother, probably out of spite for poor George—they hate each other quite passionately."

Daisy nodded. The dislike of the prince regent, George IV, and his wife, Caroline, provided the satirical caricaturists with endless fodder. It was entirely possible that the princess had promoted the match to enrage her unfaithful—and possibly bigamous—husband.

The queen continued. "Unfortunately, Charlotte and Hesse entered into a correspondence, and exchanged a series of ill-advised, and extremely embarrassing, love letters before the affair petered out. When the princess fell in love with Leopold, she had her friend Margaret Mercer Elphinstone write to Hesse—who was away fighting on the peninsula—and demand the return of the letters, some trinkets, and a portrait miniature she had given him."

"He didn't return the letters?" Ellie guessed.

"Hesse claimed he burned them, and gave his word as a gentleman that the portrait would never leave his possession, and we were satisfied. We thought the danger had passed, until last week, when the prince regent's office received this."

The queen reached into her cloak and withdrew a folded letter, which she handed to Tess. "A blackmail demand!"

Chapter Six

Tess unfolded the note, as Ellie and Daisy came to read over her shoulders.

> *Sir, I have in my possession four letters of a most embarrassing and personal nature concerning The Princess Charlotte and Captain C—H—of the Dragoons. If you wish the return of these items, I will require payment in the sum of five hundred pounds, at a date and location chosen by myself.*

Tess studied the neat copperplate. "It's unsigned. There's no way of knowing if this was written by a man or a woman."

"My money would be on a man," Ellie said. "Based on court records at the Old Bailey, I've calculated that around seventy percent of crimes are perpetrated by men, as opposed to thirty percent by women."

The queen looked a little bemused, but Tess and Daisy were used to Ellie's encyclopedic knowledge of random legal facts.

"It is not beyond the realms of possibility that the

Princess of Wales herself is behind this," the queen said, with a pained look. "She is currently residing on the Continent, but I have heard reports that this Captain Hesse was, in fact, *her* lover, too."

"Surely she wouldn't want to disrupt her own daughter's wedding?" Tess said.

The queen gave a very un-regal sniff. "She might. She will not be invited to attend, after all, and it would embarrass the regent. But even if Caroline is *not* behind it, this blackmailer must be dealt with. We cannot have Leopold calling off the wedding in a fit of pique, or the princess's suitability for marriage called into question."

"It seems to me that either Hesse lied about destroying all the letters he received, or that someone managed to steal some before he burned the ones he had," Ellie said.

"Sounds reasonable," Daisy agreed.

Tess looked at the queen. "I take it you would like us to try to find this blackmailer and retrieve the letters?"

"Indeed. The prince regent has passed the matter to me. He hasn't the funds to pay the blackmailer, and while I *do*, I refuse to be held hostage in such an impertinent manner. You may use whatever means you deem necessary, short of murder, to get those letters back."

The queen tilted her head, assessing them. "I can understand why you three are such an asset to 'Mr. King.' You are all well connected. You're invited to all the social events. And you, Lady Wansford, have a freedom as a widow that the others do not. My own ladies are too well known to make discreet inquiries, and I do not wish my involvement to become common knowledge."

"I understand," Tess said soothingly.

"Has the blackmailer sent another letter, describing a place to meet?" Daisy asked.

"Yes. Here." The queen handed over a second missive.

Sir. You will send a female representative to attend
Lady Iveson's costume ball this Thursday evening
with the sum to be paid. The lady will wear a red
dress, with a matching reticule and fan, so that I
may identify her. I will issue instructions on where
the exchange will take place.

"Good choice of location," Ellie said begrudgingly.
"Lady Iveson's parties are always a terrible crush. It's one
of the most popular events of the season."

Daisy nodded. "Perfect place to hide in a crowd."

"Do you think we're looking for someone in the *ton*?"
Tess wondered.

"Not necessarily. It would be relatively simple for
someone to gain access to the ball, provided they're wearing an elaborate costume. A chimney sweep could go
dressed as himself, and still not look out of place."

"True."

"Why ask for a woman?" Ellie frowned.

"Whoever it is, they probably think a woman will
be easier to overpower, if it becomes necessary." Daisy
snorted. "I'd like to see someone try it with me. They'll
feel the kiss of my blades."

The queen looked a little shocked at Daisy's gusto, but
managed a weak smile. "How terribly bloodthirsty, Lady
Dorothea."

Daisy inclined her head in proud acknowledgment. "I
grew up with three older brothers, ma'am. Learning self-
defense was the only way to avoid being thrown in the
lake or having an eyebrow shaved off while I slept."

Tess leaned forward. "You can leave the matter entirely
in our hands, ma'am. We will attend the ball, intercept
the blackmailer, and have the letters returned to you forth-
with."

The queen smiled. "Excellent. Now, about payment. What is your usual fee for something like this?"

Ellie stepped forward. "Oh, we couldn't possibly charge you, Your Majesty. It would be our honor to assist you."

Behind her back, Daisy pinched her arm in protest and Tess bit back a smile. Daisy would have *doubled* the sum.

"Your dedication is admirable, Miss Law, but I insist on paying something. I will give you a hundred pounds. Moreover"—Queen Charlotte's eyes settled on Tess—"I have an added incentive for you to succeed. It has come to my attention, Your Grace, that your marriage to the late duke was precipitated by your father's lack of funds. I heard that your father lent money to the king, and it was never repaid."

Tess's brows rose in surprise. "Yes, ma'am. But my father couldn't find the document needed to reclaim the loan. I searched high and low after he died, but had no luck." Her face heated with an embarrassed flush. "I suspect he hid it somewhere 'safe' in a drunken moment and forgot where he put it. He might even have used it for kindling, for all I know. Or gambled it away."

"Do you know the amount?"

"He always said it was for a thousand pounds, but I'm not sure that was true. Knowing my father, it could have been something he dreamed in a drunken delirium."

The queen's face softened and she sent Tess a look of understanding. "I, too, have experience of dealing with someone who is not always of sound mind. It can make life very difficult."

She was talking of her husband, poor "Mad" King George, whose bouts of delirium had forced her son to take over as regent.

"I have a proposition for you," the queen continued. "*If* such a loan were made, I assume there would be a copy in the king's personal papers. If you succeed in this task, I shall ask one of my secretaries to look into it."

Tess opened her mouth to thank her, but the queen held up a silencing hand. "I make you no promises, Lady Wansford. But I will do what I can."

Tess leaned on the desk to support her suddenly weak knees. The queen had no idea of the significance of such an offer. To be financially independent of the duchy would open up the possibility of marrying again. For love.

"Thank you, Your Majesty. I would be forever grateful if you would."

The queen stood, clearly ready to leave, and Tess did the same as Ellie ushered her toward the door.

"I shall leave it in your capable hands, then, ladies."

Tess could only nod as the queen pulled up the hood of her cloak and waited for Ellie to open the door for her. The unmarked carriage was still waiting outside. A footman wearing plain black livery let down the steps and held out his arm for the elderly monarch to ascend.

When the carriage finally rattled down the street, the three girls returned to the study.

"Somebody pinch me to make sure I'm not dreaming," Tess said faintly. "That really was *the queen*, here?"

Daisy gave the end of her nose a playful tweak. "She was real, all right. And *we* have our next case." The excitement in her voice was clear. "Do you think if we get those letters back, she'll let us display the royal warrant?" She waved her hands in an arc in front of her, as if reading an invisible sign. "King & Co., by appointment to the Royal House of Hanover. No job too big. Discretion assured."

Tess smiled. "Hardly. She wants to keep it a secret, not tell the world."

"Shame," Daisy pouted. "Because this is a high-pressure job. If we don't get those letters back, it'll be our necks on the chopping block. We'll be locked up in the Tower and they'll throw away the key."

"Stop being so dramatic," Ellie chided.

Tess sank into her chair behind the desk. "Can you imagine if she manages to find proof of my father's loan? If that debt's repaid, I'll have money of my own. I wouldn't be reliant on anything to do with the duchy."

"You mean if this new duke decides to make your life difficult, you'll have something to fall back on?" Daisy said shrewdly.

"Precisely."

"We'd better get on with it, then," Ellie said. "I assume you received an invitation to Lady Iveson's?"

Tess and Daisy both nodded.

"But which of us will be the contact?"

"You should do it, Tess," Daisy said. "You can wear the red dress you wore to Careby's."

Tess bit her lip, oddly reluctant. She'd worn red with *him*, her handsome stranger. What if he recognized her? Or the dress?

No, there was no chance of seeing him here in London. She had to forget him.

"I only wore that dress because nobody knew who I was," she countered. "If I wear it to Lady Iveson's, as the Duchess of Wansford, it'll be a public declaration that I'm back on the marriage mart. I might as well take out an advertisement in *The Times* saying I'm looking for my next husband."

"That's true," Daisy said with a grin. "You'll be inundated. But that might not be a bad thing. Being surrounded by men will make it easier for the blackmailer to approach you."

"She has a point," Ellie said. "He can hide in the crowd."

Tess sighed. "Fine. But what if there's another lady at the party with a red dress and fan? The blackmailer might approach the wrong person."

"I suppose if he does, he'll realize his mistake when they don't know what he's talking about."

"Actually," Tess mused aloud, "what if Daisy and I *both* wear red? That will double our chances of being contacted. If he speaks to Daisy first, she can feign ignorance, and we'll have identified the target before he approaches me."

"Good idea," Daisy said. "I'll dress as Anne Boleyn. Ready to get my head lopped off."

"Why are you suddenly so obsessed with execution?" Ellie gave an exasperated laugh.

Daisy grinned. "Just reminding myself of the stakes."

"Whoever's contacted second can arrange to meet the blackmailer somewhere private, like the garden, or an empty room, to make the exchange," Ellie said.

"Any sensible blackmailer's going to want to see the money before he hands anything over," Daisy said. "Are we each going to have five hundred pounds in our reticules?"

"I suppose you'll have to," Ellie said. "But the blackmailer won't get to keep it. As soon as you've got the letters, we'll force them to give the money back—at knifepoint and pistol point, if necessary. We'll all be armed."

"The crook might be planning to do the same. They'll certainly be wary of being arrested. And also armed."

"It'll be three against one. The odds are in our favor."

"It could be a trick," Tess said. "What if they don't even have any letters? It might just be a ploy to lure us somewhere secluded and rob us."

"Probably why they wanted a female to make the exchange," Daisy muttered. "We're always seen as an easy target."

Ellie smiled. "Well, they'll soon learn their mistake. Alone, we're good. Together, we're a force to be reckoned with."

Daisy chuckled. "Oh, this is going to be fun."

Chapter Seven

Justin glanced around Lady Iveson's crowded ballroom and decided he'd rather be anywhere else.

Not one for social niceties, he hadn't bothered pasting a fake smile on his face, but his brooding expression hadn't deterred the hordes clamoring for an introduction.

It was just as he'd predicted. An audible ripple of speculation had risen up when he'd appeared at the top of the steps with his old school friend Edward Hussey, and Lady Iveson's majordomo had announced him as His Grace, the Duke of Wansford, in bellowing tones.

The crowd had surged forward. He'd spent the past half hour parroting the same answers.

Yes, he was surprised, honored, and delighted to have been named heir.

Yes, he'd received his letters patent and been accepted by Parliament.

Yes, he planned to take his seat in the House of Lords.

No, he was not married, nor engaged.

That last answer had induced flutters of ill-concealed delight from the assorted females in attendance. Mothers with eligible daughters had showered him with invitations to take tea, walk, and ride in the park with their universally charming progeny.

The daughters themselves—the more forward ones, at least—had batted their eyelashes and fluttered their fans whenever he glanced in their direction.

And the older women, those with inattentive or deceased husbands, had made all manner of thinly veiled suggestions, including one offer to ride *him* at the park at his earliest convenience.

He'd politely declined.

The men had been little better. Those wanting to ingratiate themselves had offered him a season box at the opera, theater tickets, and a seat in the Royal tent at the races.

Beside him, Edward caught his eye.

Justin scowled. "What?"

"You know, for someone who just walked into a dukedom, you could look a little happier, you lucky bastard."

"Lucky bastard, *Your Grace*," Justin corrected dryly. "And on the contrary, the only good thing about this whole situation is that dukes can do as they please. Scowling is my ducal prerogative."

Edward chuckled. "There's nothing *grace*ful about you. I remember that time at school when you smashed me in the mouth with a cricket ball."

"You never could catch." Justin allowed himself a brief smile. "I told Careby it was a mistake to put you at mid-off."

"Well, it's still good to have you back. London hasn't been the same without you."

"It looks remarkably similar to when I left: overcrowded rooms, deafening chatter, mind-numbingly dull gossip."

"Well, true. But we've had the odd scandal to liven things up."

"Not interested," Justin said.

"Not even if it concerns you?"

"*Especially* not if it concerns me. Tell me about the duchess instead. I'm going to have to call on her. I saw the old duke at White's a few times, but I never met his wife."

"That's because they married just after you set off for the frozen wastes of Canada." Edward's brows rose toward his hairline. "Wait. Do you mean you don't *know*?"

"Know what?"

"About the duchess? She's the most eligible woman in the *ton*."

Justin's lip curled. "I suppose there's always some young fool willing to be a rich old woman's plaything."

Edward shook his head, a devilish smile in his eyes. "It's not her money they're after. They'd want her if she were a penniless dairymaid."

"What *are* you talking about?"

Edward scanned the room, clearly looking for someone, and his face broke into a smile of anticipation as he apparently located them. "Prepare to lose your wits and your breath."

"You always were one for hyperbole," Justin scoffed.

Edward motioned toward the far side of the room. "She's over there. In red. On the right."

Justin turned. "No woman has ever had the power to—"

For the first time in his adult life his breath cut short.

"Bloody Hell," he wheezed faintly.

Edward gave a low chuckle. "Told you."

Justin frowned as recognition hit him like a punch to the chest. "Wait a moment. Isn't that Tess Townsend?"

"It is indeed."

Justin's heart began to pound. He'd seen her before, two

years ago, across a crowded ballroom just like this, and the memory was burned into his brain.

Back then she'd been wearing white, like every other debutante; some shimmering fabric shot through with silver thread that was the perfect foil for her dark hair. Her luminous beauty and infectious smile had drawn every eye in the room.

She'd been surrounded by suitors, all richer, older, laughing. Justin hadn't even bothered asking for an introduction. She was clearly destined for a brilliant match—an earl, at the very least. Such youth and beauty would inevitably marry wealth and a title. The *ton* had operated that way for centuries.

As a merchant with a single ship, no fortune, and no aristocratic title, he wouldn't stand a chance. And that was probably for the best, because his skin was clammy and his heart was pounding and he was suddenly filled with the dreadful conviction that here was a woman he could easily fall in love with.

Love was what had wrecked his father. Marrying for it was a recipe for disaster—and entirely avoidable.

So he'd stayed where he was, watching her from the shadows like a dog salivating at the door of the butcher's shop—desperate to enter, to steal whatever scraps he could, but knowing he'd be chased away by the shopkeeper's broom if he dared.

Ever the pragmatist, he'd dismissed her—at least, the *reality* of her. She was the epitome of unattainable. But he'd still allowed himself to dream. In the privacy of his mind, she'd become his fantasy woman, a reason to succeed, a glittering ideal for which to strive, if never actually attain.

He soothed his suddenly dry throat with a healthy gulp of claret.

"Are you telling me that *Tess Townsend* married the eighth duke? That *she's* the duchess of Wansford?"

Edward nodded. "Hearts broke in the gentlemen's clubs that week, I can tell you." He shook his head. "And who would have put money on the old bastard cocking up his toes on their wedding night?"

Justin shook his head in amazement. "Turnbull never told me this."

"Probably assumed you already knew. It was the talk of the town for months, especially since it took so long to find a living heir. Every time they found a candidate, they died. Until you." Edward frowned. "Her own father died only a few weeks after the duke, so she stayed in the country for at least six months of mourning, then returned to town. She's been fighting off potential suitors ever since."

Justin studied her again, drinking her in with his eyes. His memory hadn't done her justice; if anything, she was even more attractive than he remembered. Her hair was still a riot of silky waves, the color emphasized by the deep claret of her dress. She exuded a subtle sensuality that was both alluring and, he suspected, completely unconscious.

"Does she have a lover?"

"Not that I know of. If she has, she's been astonishingly discreet."

"Shown any inclination to remarry?"

"Again, no. She's wonderful company, universally liked, but she never lets a man get too close." Edward glanced at him. "Not thinking of adding your suit to the mix, are you?"

Justin took another swallow of wine and considered the idea. "Perhaps."

He shook his head at the perversity of Fate. Even in

his wildest dreams he'd never have predicted that within two years he'd have become richer than most men in this room, and have a dukedom thrust upon him. That he would now be considered a suitable match for a woman like *her* was incredible.

For a brief moment he considered the wisdom of approaching her, considering how dangerously attracted he'd once been. But he was older now, wiser. He wasn't some callow youth to lose his heart at the drop of a hat. He was perfectly capable of controlling his emotions. He could be attracted to her, but in no danger of succumbing to anything more serious. More foolish.

Edward gave his shoulder a playful nudge. "Come on, I'll introduce you. She's with my cousin Ellie, and that hellion Dorothea Hamilton. The three of them are as thick as thieves."

Chapter Eight

Tess scanned the crowd, idly searching for her handsome stranger.

She was wearing the same red dress she'd worn to Careby's, with an extra froth of lace tacked to the top of the bodice to make it slightly less indecent. The bold color imbued her with confidence. No wonder monarchs wore this shade; it made her feel invincible.

People were definitely looking. They were noticing Daisy, too, who'd raided Drury Lane's costume room and found a Shakespearean costume of burgundy velvet, complete with an oversized neck ruff.

Tess snapped her fan shut, then flicked it open again. Her nerves were jittery tonight, not just in anticipation of meeting the blackmailer, but also thanks to the secret hope that her mystery man could be here, at this very ball.

Which was a stupid thing to wish for. She didn't want him—whoever he was—to recognize her in real life. She might not have stopped thinking about him, but having him suddenly appear in front of her would be very awkward indeed.

She'd told Ellie and Daisy all about her countryside

"adventure." Ellie had been scandalized, Daisy delighted, and the two of them had spent a pointless hour pondering his identity.

Daisy was convinced he was a highwayman, a spy, a smuggler, or all three. Ellie, far more prosaically, thought he was an acquaintance of Careby's who never visited London. A provincial solicitor, perhaps, or a land agent.

Whoever he was, Tess felt as if she'd been awakened after years of being asleep. The man had shown her a glimpse of a whole new world of sensuality, and it was impossible to forget that it existed.

If they met again, would she tell him to stop?

She gave herself a mental shake. She should be looking at the men in attendance with the view to choosing a potential lover, not mooning over lost opportunities. Her "adventure" had clearly proved that she was attracted to *some* men. All she had to do was find another one who made her stomach somersault and her body glow, as her stranger had done. How hard could it be?

"Tess, are you with us?"

"Sorry, what?" Tess forced herself to focus on Ellie.

"I said, assuming the blackmailer really *does* have some of Princess Charlotte's letters, how do you think they got them?"

"You don't think it could be Captain Hesse himself?" Tess suggested.

"Unlikely. His regiment is still over on the Continent. Plus, he was badly injured at Waterloo last year—my cousin Reg says he damaged his wrist and had to learn to write all over again."

"It could be someone writing the blackmail demands at his request," Daisy suggested. "A coconspirator based here in London."

Ellie's ringlets bounced as she shook her head. "I think

we can rule Hesse out. I spoke to Princess Charlotte's friend, Margaret Mercer Elphinstone. Her father, the admiral, was the one who interviewed Hesse about the letters, and he was apparently satisfied that Hesse had destroyed the ones he had in his possession."

"What if someone stole some from Hesse before he burned them, then? Someone in the same regiment? A friend, or ex-friend," Tess said.

"That was my thought, too. Hesse was in the Eighteenth Light Dragoons, a cavalry regiment. I'm going to compile a list of men who served with him, using information from dispatches, muster rolls, and pay records."

"You do know how to have fun," Daisy drawled.

Ellie glared at her. "If you have any better ideas, Dorothea Hamilton—"

Daisy held up her hands in mock surrender. "I don't! But surely there's no need to go to such trouble when we're about to meet whoever it is tonight. We'll find out who they are when we catch them, won't we?"

"*If* they make contact," Tess reminded her. "Which shouldn't be difficult, since we both stand out like two red shipping beacons."

Ellie seemed to have become distracted. She was staring at something across the far end of the ballroom and shaking her head.

"I've said it before and I'll say it again: there's no justice in this world. None whatsoever."

"That's quite the statement, coming from the daughter of one of England's top barristers," Tess chuckled.

Daisy frowned. "What are you talking about, El?"

"The new Duke of Wansford."

Tess whirled around, her heart in her throat. "He's here? Right now?"

"Where?" Daisy demanded.

"Over there, by the orchestra. I'm sure that's him."

Both Tess and Daisy looked in the direction Ellie had indicated. Tess craned her neck and Daisy tried to peer unobtrusively over the ridiculous expanse of her Elizabethan ruff.

"What does he look like? Ill tempered? Irascible? Disapproving?"

"You're just thinking of your *own* father, Daisy."

"True. But he's typical of the breed."

"Well, this new duke doesn't fit the mold at all. Which is why I was saying it's unfair. What kind of universe furnishes a man with sinful good looks, grants him a brain so clever he can amass a fortune to equal a small European principality, and *then* makes him the long-lost heir to a dukedom?" Ellie shook her head. "As Shakespeare would say, it beggars belief."

Daisy nodded. "You have a point. Any one of those attributes would be quite enough on their own. And because I truly believe life has a way of maintaining balance, you just know that somewhere in the world there's a nun who's devoted her whole life to helping orphans and kittens, who's about to be struck by lightning."

"I'll tell you what's unfair," Tess grumbled. "The fact that the old Duke of Wansford is *still* the only man I've ever seen naked."

Ellie's brows rose. "Well, this new duke certainly looks like an improvement in *that* department."

"I heard he didn't want to be duke," Daisy said. "That he tried to turn it down."

Ellie rolled her eyes. "Pfft. Even if it were possible, only an imbecile would do that. And from what I've heard, Justin Thornton is *far* from being an imbecile."

"It would be better for me if he was," Tess muttered. "Still, I suppose I have to meet him sooner or later. I would have preferred to do it out of the public gaze, however. *Where* is he, Ellie?"

Tess was still searching, when a tall figure in a dark coat caught her eye. Her heart missed a beat, and she reached out and clutched Daisy's arm.

"Dear God, it's him! The man from Careby's."

"Where?"

Tess sent what she hoped was a subtle nod in his direction. "Over there. Navy blue jacket. With Ellie's cousin."

Ellie frowned. "You must be mistaken. The man with Edward is Justin Thornton. The new duke."

The room seemed to tilt sideways. A cold sweep of dread was immediately followed by an unpleasantly hot flush on Tess's skin.

"Are you sure?"

She was not wrong. Even across the room, there was no mistaking the man who'd kissed her so thoroughly.

Daisy's eyes widened in dawning horror and amusement. "Wait, are you saying that the new duke is the same man who ravished you against Careby's library door? Your mystery highwayman?"

Tess let out a sound that was half choked laugh, half groan of dismay. She blinked, praying this was a dream, but nothing changed.

"Yes."

Daisy let out an unladylike snort. "What are the odds?"

"Incalculable," Ellie breathed.

Tess was caught between incredulity and a terrible sense of impending doom. Perhaps Daisy's theory about the universe demanding balance was correct, and this awful cosmic joke was her punishment for having lied about her wedding night?

She didn't know many obscenities, but the ones she did know raced through her brain.

Shit. Bloody. Buggering Hell.

Thorn. Thornton. She should have made that connection.

"It's bad, but not *that* bad." Ellie's calm, reasoned voice cut through her panic.

Daisy snorted again. "How could it be worse, exactly?"

"You might recognize him, Tess, but he won't recognize you."

"He might recognize this dress, though."

"Pfft. Men don't pay any attention to dresses, unless it's to imagine removing them. He probably only remembers you wearing something red, not the specifics."

Tess took a deep breath and forced her pulse to slow. Ellie was right. And she'd been wearing a mask at Careby's. There was no way the new duke—handsome stranger—could know they'd met before.

She would be cool. Calm. She would greet him politely and show no reaction whatsoever. Her shameful secret was safe.

"I hope you're ready, because he's coming this way."

Chapter Nine

Justin pushed his way through the crowd, and as he neared the three women, he heard a ripple of throaty laughter that made his stomach clench. Tess Townsend turned, clearly sensing his approach, and there was something about the swirl of her red dress, the angle of her jaw, that made him stop in his tracks.

A barrage of images assaulted him. Red dress. Dark hair. Pale skin. Images of two different women overlaid in his mind.

He frowned. She was familiar. From more than just one distant memory and a swathe of lustful fantasies over the years. His heart began to pound even as his brain struggled to make the connection that eluded him.

No, it was just a coincidence. She was not his scarlet woman from Careby's. A woman like Tess Townsend wouldn't be so short of lovers that she'd need to find one at a house party. His mind was putting two and two together and making five.

And yet he found himself studying her chin, the shape of her mouth, looking for similarities.

He started forward again, staring with an intensity that

was probably making her uncomfortable. She'd definitely spotted him; her eyes widened as she looked him full in the face.

With recognition?

He closed the gap between them. Her eyes were an astonishing hazel brown, her dark brows neatly arched. Her nose was small and straight, and her mouth—

Justin sucked in a breath.

Her mouth was Scarlet's mouth.

Her lips were the same, pink and full, and there—his heart stuttered—there was that same telltale mark near her top lip. The freckle he'd kissed at Careby's.

When her perfume reached his nose, he was left in absolutely no doubt. That same floral scent had infiltrated his dreams for the past week. He hadn't stopped thinking about her, wishing he'd taken more time. To savor. To explore.

Scarlet.

Tess, and the two women flanking her, all bobbed a curtsey. Edward bowed and turned to him.

"Your Grace. May I introduce *Her* Grace, the Duchess of Wansford." He turned back to Tess. "Your Grace, this is *His* Grace."

Edward chuckled, appreciating the ridiculousness of the situation.

Justin bowed and took her gloved hand. He raised it to his lips, exactly as he'd done by the card table at Careby's, and her lips parted in surprise. A delightful spurt of amusement shot through his veins. Surely she must recognize him? *He* hadn't been wearing a mask. But would she acknowledge the fact?

"Your Grace, I am . . . speechless," he murmured. "You are not at all what I was expecting."

"Oh, really? How so?"

Her voice was Scarlet's, throaty and soft. It tightened his gut.

"It was my mistake. I assumed you would be a woman of advanced years."

"I married young," she said faintly. "You must have heard the story. My husband, the eighth duke, died on our wedding night."

"You have my condolences."

She inclined her head and tried to remove her hand from his. He tightened his grip.

"We clearly have a great deal to discuss."

A pink flush was spreading across her cheeks at his deliberately loaded words.

"Of course. You're welcome to call at Wansford House at your earliest convenience."

He shook his head. "Why wait? We're both here, after all. Come, we should dance."

Without giving her a chance to refuse, he tugged her hand. Wisely realizing she couldn't escape without making a scene, she sent him an airy smile and allowed him to lead her toward the dance floor.

"Of course. I'd be delighted."

∽

Tess quashed her instinctive foreboding at the echo of the words he'd used at Careby's. Surely their encounter hadn't been as memorable for him as it had been for her.

But her skin prickled in awareness as she settled into his arms in preparation for the dance, and she deliberately kept her gaze fixed at a point on his shoulder to avoid looking him full in the face.

They swirled into motion.

"Your Grace?"

The hint of amusement in his deep voice made her look up. God, he was even more good-looking than she remembered.

"Tess," she breathed, willing her pulse rate to calm. "You may call me Tess. I think we can dispense with the formalities, given the circumstances."

Those circumstances being your mouth on my breast. My hand on your cock.

She thrust away those unhelpful memories and tried not to blush.

His lips twitched in a smile, as if he could read her scandalous thoughts. "And you should call me Justin. Given the circumstances."

She cast around for something sensible to say. "My friends and I were just discussing your good fortune."

"In being named the new duke?"

"Yes."

"Ah. Yes, I suppose I have been fortunate. The previous incumbents seem to have been a remarkably accident-prone bunch."

The way he was scrutinizing her face was making her hot, as was the delicious scent of his cologne. She swallowed again.

"Ellie says you've been successful in your business ventures, so it's the duchy's good fortune, too. With your skills, you can make the estate more profitable and improve the lives of all its dependents."

His brows rose. "That's very democratic of you. I'm not sure many other landowners care about the prosperity of their dependents, as long as they don't threaten to revolt."

"I've spent almost two years at Wansford Hall, Your Grace, and I've become very fond of the tenants and staff. It's a relief to know they won't suffer because of an incompetent overlord."

Tess knew she was babbling, but she couldn't seem to stop. "But you needn't worry that I'll be in your way when you decide to go there. If you'll give me a week, I'll have my personal belongings transferred to the dower house."

His flint-gray eyes bored into hers. "Oh, I don't think that will be necessary."

"Why not?"

The corner of his eyes crinkled in amusement and his lips curved in a wicked smile. "Do you really have to ask, Scarlet?"

Her heart missed a beat. "What?"

"You're Scarlet. The woman I met at Careby's house party."

His certainty quashed her automatic reaction to deny it, so she tilted her chin up and tried to stay calm. One thing she'd learned as an investigator was knowing when the game was up.

"How did you know?"

His eyes flashed with appreciation that she hadn't tried to continue the subterfuge. He leaned closer.

"Your body. Your scent. But most importantly, that charming freckle to the left of your mouth. It was visible beneath your mask. I enjoyed kissing it immensely."

Tess's stomach swooped in dismay. God, she'd forgotten that distinctive feature. When her whole face was visible it was just one of several freckles she possessed.

A few years ago, Ellie had found an antique print that showed where ladies of the previous century had worn their patches; the one Tess had was called *la coquette*—the tease.

Justin Thornton clearly had an eye for detail, curse him. His gaze flicked to the incriminating spot before he captured her eye again. "Interesting that you should be wearing this dress again, too. Is red your signature color?"

"Not at all. I rarely wear it."

"You should. It suits you." He tilted his head, assessing her. "It's almost as if you *wanted* to be found."

The kernel of truth in his statement made Tess's cheeks flush even more, but she rallied gamely. "You flatter yourself, Your Grace."

He chuckled. A glance to her left made her acutely aware that people had begun to remark on their dancing together. Heads were turning in their direction, fans covering mouths to hide the inevitable gossip.

"I believe we're becoming the latest *on dit*," she said evenly.

He guided them both into another graceful turn. "Of course. The two of us coming face-to-face is the most exciting thing to happen all season, I expect."

Being the center of attention didn't seem to bother him at all, and Tess was struck by the thought that being impervious to what others might think of him made him a perfect fit for a duke.

"We seem to have found ourselves in an unusual situation," he murmured.

She resisted the impulse to snort. "That's certainly one way of putting it."

"I'll speak plainly. I regret that our little interlude was cut short."

A shameful wave of gratification swamped her at his admission. *He'd enjoyed it as much as she had!*

"Oh?"

"I assume from your attendance at Careby's that you're a woman with a healthy, passionate nature."

It was Tess's turn to raise her brows. How had the conversation taken such a personal turn? "I, um—"

"And because of your position," he continued, "you need to be discreet in selecting your lovers."

Tess was sure her cheeks were aflame, but she forced herself to hold his gaze. "Indeed."

"Do you have a lover at present?"

"I do not."

He nodded. "I do not have a mistress."

"Am I supposed to commiserate, or congratulate you?"

He ignored her quip. "I think it's fair to say that we are attracted to each other. Certainly, I'm attracted to you. And since you saw me without a mask at Careby's, I can only assume that you find me attractive, too."

Tess felt as if she'd stumbled into some bizarre dream. Her limbs seemed able to follow the motions of the dance on their own, but her brain was a jumble of confusion.

"What's the point in this conversation, Your Grace?"

"I've thought of a solution that will benefit both of us. As the new duke I'm expected to court someone in the *ton* and make her my wife. But my business affairs consume much of my attention, and I have neither the time nor the inclination to deal with such nonsense. I do, however, appreciate that having a wife would be useful for keeping the matchmaking mammas at bay."

"Perhaps you should consider a personal bodyguard?" Tess joked weakly.

"I *also*," he continued, ignoring her levity, "require a mistress, to satisfy my physical needs. I don't have time to find one of those, either. I dislike going to brothels, and opportunities such as the party at Careby's are both risky and infrequent."

Tess's pulse was pounding in her throat. "I'm not sure I understand. What exactly are you proposing?"

Chapter Ten

Tess tried not to quail as Thornton's gray eyes bored into hers.

"It's clear you didn't marry the old duke for love," he said. "You're obviously a pragmatic woman, in the same way that I'm a pragmatic man."

They completed another graceful turn.

"I don't care if you're a fortune hunter. In fact, I rather hope you are. It will make this even easier."

Tess couldn't decide if she was amused, insulted, or outraged. "I—"

"I understand why you would have married for money and position. I applaud it, actually. It's precisely the kind of thing I might have done, given the same circumstances. As distasteful as bedding an old man might have been, a little unpleasantness in exchange for a life of ease was a calculated risk that in your case paid off handsomely."

Tess drew herself up and tried to sound worldly and sophisticated, instead of shocked to the core at his directness. She'd never met anyone who spoke quite so bluntly.

"You make me sound like a whore, who sold myself to the highest bidder."

He didn't deny it, and she crushed a feeling of disappointment at his low opinion of her. In his defense, he didn't know that she hadn't slept with the duke. He was only saying aloud what the rest of the *ton* doubtless whispered behind her back. In his eyes she was little better than a prostitute, and her behavior at Careby's would only have confirmed her loose morals.

Such a conclusion was so far from the truth it was almost laughable, and Tess felt her lips curve up in amusement.

Thornton was still looking down at her, but his expression held neither condemnation nor disdain. If anything, he appeared impressed. *Intrigued,* even.

"It was a good business bargain," he said. "You had few things to negotiate with, save your youth and beauty. And your virginity, of course."

"Of course," Tess managed faintly.

"The duke's advanced years meant that even if he'd lived past the wedding night, you'd have been unlikely to spend much time with him. How did he die?"

A wicked desire to tease him for his high-handed assumptions seized her. He was rude and abrasive and unforgivably attractive. She wanted to discompose him as much as he was discomposing her.

"His heart gave out. When he saw me naked."

His fingers tightened on hers, and his hot gaze made her feel as if she were bare again.

"Let's hope I don't have the same reaction."

Tess almost swallowed her tongue. "To seeing me naked? What makes you think that will ever happen?"

"Because I wish to be your lover. And your husband."

The dance ended on a triumphant twinkle of notes. Tess made to draw back from his embrace but he held her fast.

"Please, just listen."

"We can't dance two dances in a row. We'll cause a scandal."

His teeth flashed white as he laughed. "Oh, I think we're already doing that, Scarlet."

Tess sent a glance over to the side of the room where Ellie was watching them with eyes wide with speculation. Daisy, she discovered, had found herself a dance partner and was only a few couples away, presumably trying to eavesdrop. She caught Tess's eye and flashed her a wicked smile of encouragement.

Since resistance was clearly futile against an object as immovable as Thornton, Tess acceded with good grace, and as the next dance began—a waltz this time—she returned her attention to the enigmatic man in her arms.

"Go on, then. Let me hear it."

"I would like to propose a marriage of convenience. From a purely practical standpoint, you're already used to being the Duchess of Wansford. As my duchess you will retain your position, and spare me from the tiresome process of having to woo other women."

He bent his head, and his warm breath fanned the wispy hair at her temple. Her belly quivered. Awareness of him made her skin prickle; she knew to the inch how close his chest was to her own, the heat of his hand at the small of her back.

"On a physical level, it's clear we're compatible. This arrangement will provide us both with satisfaction, for the least amount of effort and risk."

Tess tried to corral her thoughts. "That's very . . . efficient. But not terribly romantic."

He gave her a look that suggested she'd disappointed him. "Romance has nothing to do with it. This is a business proposition, nothing more."

"I don't know what to say."

"Say yes. Don't let emotion rule you. Use logic. It makes sense."

"But we're strangers."

His lips gave that devilish curl. "Strangers who've already been intimate."

"Physical intimacy isn't the same as emotional intimacy."

"Emotional intimacy isn't necessary here. A good marriage in the *ton* is a successful partnership. You can do all the things expected of a society wife—entertain as my hostess, accompany me to parties, and so on. I will provide the financial and . . . amorous support."

His dark eyes held hers captive. "We can set a time limit, if you like. The end of the social season, three months from now. We can live together as man and wife here in London, but after that I'll return to Bristol and you'll be free to stay here and do exactly as you wish."

Tess's mind was racing, along with her heart. "But we would stay married? There would be no divorce?"

He shook his head. "No divorce. Just an amicable separation. You will remain the duchess, exactly as you are now, for the rest of your life. And I will remain the duke."

The room swirled around them, a blur of color and faces.

Dear God, what a proposition!

At first, she'd been sure he was joking, but the intensity of his expression indicated that he was quite serious.

His physical attraction to her was immensely flattering—and definitely reciprocated—but his emotionless attitude to marriage was disheartening. Tess had never thought of herself as particularly romantic, but perhaps she was, after all.

Still, she was tempted. Thornton was the first person

she'd ever met who said exactly what he wanted, directly, with no subterfuge. His honestly was refreshing. The *ton* was a quagmire of elisions and half-truths, of people saying one thing in public, and secretly thinking another.

"Are you always this impulsive?" she asked, genuinely curious.

"Not impulsive. *Decisive*. And yes, on the whole. Why waste time, when a good idea presents itself?"

"To think of all the ramifications?" she suggested wryly. "To weigh up the pros and cons?"

The muscles of his shoulder rippled under her palm as he shrugged. "There are a million variables. It's impossible to predict them all. All I know is that life's too short to worry about them. You just have to move in the direction you wish to go and deal with any obstacles as they come."

His closeness was distracting. Tess had to look away from him to clear her head.

What he said made a lot of sense. Here, unexpectedly, was the opportunity to take a lover without the risk of any social repercussions.

"What do you say, Scarlet?"

She glanced up at him. "You can't expect an answer now. I need to think about it."

A muscle ticked in his jaw, and she wondered if he was impatient at her stalling, or satisfied that she was considering his offer.

"Very well. When can you give me an answer?"

"Today is Thursday. You can call on me on Saturday. At Wansford House."

The waltz came to an end.

Tess took a step back. His hand slipped from her lower back to the curve of her waist and she was assaulted by the sudden memory of him pressing her against the door in the darkness, his mouth on hers. Everything inside her seemed to quiver.

She could have that again. And more.

He retained her right hand and led her off the dance floor toward Ellie and her cousin. Tess realized she was short of breath.

Edward shot them an amused glance. "You two seem to have become better acquainted."

Tess snapped open her fan and used it to cool her flushed face. "Yes indeed."

Ellie's fascinated gaze snapped from Tess to Thornton and back again. She opened her mouth to say something, then clearly thought better of it, and closed it again.

Daisy bustled up with a new partner, an aging roué who couldn't seem to take his eyes off her décolletage. She dismissed him with a charming smile and sent him off to find punch, then flashed Tess a look that clearly said *We need to talk.*

"Tess, my love, you look a little flushed!" Daisy's tone was all solicitude. "Are you feeling quite well?"

Ellie took the cue. She peered closer at Tess. "She's right. Perhaps you should sit out the next dance?"

Tess almost rolled her eyes at their unsubtle maneuvering, but grasped the chance to escape Thornton's unsettling presence. She could feel his gaze on the side of her face. She touched her hand to her hot cheek.

"It is rather warm in here." She sent the two men a dismissive nod. "If you'll excuse us, gentlemen, I think we'll visit the gardens for some fresh air."

"Would you like us to accompany you?" Edward offered his arm.

Ellie sent him a fond look but shook her head. "That won't be necessary, but thank you."

As soon as the three of them were safely out of earshot,

Daisy pinched Tess's arm. "Out with it! What were you and Thornton talking about that required *two* dances in a row?"

Ellie, on her opposite side, elbowed her in the ribs. "You should have seen the way he was looking at you, Tess! He couldn't take his eyes off you. He looked completely transfixed. Half the women in the room nearly expired with jealousy."

"We can't discuss it here," Tess murmured. "I'll tell you when we're alone."

"But we can't leave yet. We haven't made contact with the blackmailer."

Daisy glanced at an ormolu clock on a nearby pier table. "It's nearly the end of the night and we've been here for hours. I don't think they're coming. Or perhaps tonight was a test, and they never intended to actually meet. Perhaps they just wanted to see which women turned up in a red dress, to narrow the field of potential contacts."

"That's what I would have done," Ellie mused. "And if it's true, then they have the advantage of us."

"I'm too tired to think straight," Tess said truthfully. "I'm going home. Daisy, are you coming with me, or will you get a ride home with Ellie?"

As a widow Tess had more leniency than the others when it came to requiring a chaperone. Despite the fact that Daisy was six months older, and possessed far greater worldly experience, it was Tess who was seen as an appropriate companion for her unmarried friends. Ever since she'd returned from Wansford, either Daisy or Ellie had been her guest at the ducal mansion in Portman Square, in addition to a house full of servants.

Daisy yawned. "I'll come now. This ruff is making my neck itchy."

"Don't you dare talk about Thornton without me,"

Ellie warned. "Promise you'll wait until we're all at King & Co. tomorrow."

Daisy scowled at having to wait for the gossip, but Tess rubbed Ellie's arm. "Of course we'll wait. We'll see you tomorrow."

Chapter Eleven

Despite Daisy's relentless barrage on the journey back from Lady Iveson's, Tess managed to escape to her room without saying anything. She hadn't thought she'd be able to close her eyes, considering the magnitude of the evening's revelations, but she fell asleep almost as soon as her head hit the pillow.

She refused to answer any of Daisy's questions in the carriage to Lincoln's Inn Fields the following morning, and it was only when the three of them sat in the front office, each with a cup of hot tea, that Tess finally told them everything.

"You should say yes," Daisy said, practically vibrating with excitement. "A thousand times yes. At least to the mistress part. The man's better looking than Byron, not half as mad, and ten times as rich. If you don't say yes, I will."

Tess rolled her eyes at her friend's impetuosity. "It's not as simple as that. One reason I haven't taken a lover yet is because if I do, they'll realize I'm a virgin. Thornton's only making this offer because he thinks I've had a score of lovers. He's expecting me to be as experienced as he is. What do you think will happen when he realizes I have no idea what to do?"

Daisy snorted. "It'll probably be too late, by then. And if it really bothers him, he'll just go back to Bristol early, and you'll be no worse than you are now. I say it's worth the risk."

Ellie took a sip of her tea. "It's quite a contradictory offer, when you think about it. More like two separate offers, really."

"What do you mean?"

"Well, on the one side he's suggesting a cool, business-like arrangement, for you to marry him and be his wife. And on the other, he's making an offer based purely on passionate desire."

Tess dipped a shortbread biscuit into her tea and nibbled on it. "He said they're both logical solutions to our mutual problem."

Daisy snorted again. "Logical, my arse. He's fooling himself. He might be using his brain for the first option, but his cock's definitely responsible for the second. Men always claim they're being logical when they're trying to talk you into bed."

Ellie chuckled.

"I suppose I always thought that, in a perfect world, the roles of wife and mistress would be happily combined," Tess said.

"They are, in some marriages," Ellie said. "Just look at my parents. They're still nauseatingly happy after more than thirty years of wedlock."

"But they're the minority," Daisy countered. "Happy marriages are few and far between, especially in the *ton*. Just look at my family. They're worse than a Drury Lane melodrama."

"Do you *want* to be his lover?" Ellie asked.

Tess flushed, but forced herself to be truthful. "I do. I've met hundreds of other men and never found them attractive. Thornton's the only one who's ever had this effect on me. He makes me all hot and shivery, like I'm both nervous and excited at the same time."

Daisy shook her head with a wry smile. "You've got a terminal case of lust. The only way to stop it from being fatal is to get it out of your system."

"And what do you suggest, Dr. Hamilton?"

"I prescribe a lengthy course of energetic exercise with a handsome male partner, to raise your heart rate and bring a rosy glow to your skin." Daisy wiggled her eyebrows.

Tess laughed. "All right, say I do agree to the physical side of his bargain. There's still the problem of my inexperience. What if I bleed the first time I'm with Thornton, and he finds out that way?"

Daisy set down her teacup. "Actually, we were misinformed on that. Not *every* virgin bleeds. I didn't, the first time I was with Tom. Nor any of the times afterward."

Her face took on a softer cast as she recalled her own "passionate adventure" and Tess sent her a sympathetic look.

Tom Harding had been a handsome rogue, one of the stable hands at Hollyfield. Despite having to keep their liaison a secret, he and Daisy had been inseparable for almost three months, until Tom had been called up to join the army. Tragically, he'd been killed at Waterloo, only a few weeks later.

Despite Daisy protesting that it had merely been a youthful fling, that she'd liked Tom more as a friend than as a lover, she always spoke of their time together with fondness. Tom might not have been the love of her life, but she had no regrets that she'd given herself to him before he'd died.

"Tom said that girls who ride horses don't always bleed. But if you do, just pretend you pricked your finger on a hatpin or something."

"It'll be another lie." Tess sighed. "I'm trying to avoid those."

Ellie took another biscuit. "Even if he *does* discover you're a virgin, so what?"

"He'll be angry with me for lying. He'll probably go straight out and find another, more experienced woman to satisfy his needs."

"Which is exactly what he's going to do after your time together is over, so what difference does it make? You'll still be a duchess with no husband. What have you got to lose? Apart from your virginity."

"If I take another lover, he might divorce me for adultery."

"The legal term is 'criminal conversation,'" Ellie said absently. "And I doubt he'd do that. He seems to be a man who values his privacy. He won't want his name dragged through the courts, or to be mocked as a cuckold in every scandal sheet and gossip rag."

"True, but an absent husband is very different to a dead one," Tess said. "The old duke wasn't around to make my life a misery. If I marry Thornton, I'll lose my widow's jointure and he'll control my finances. He could cut off my allowance and lock me up at Wansford."

"We'd rescue you. And besides, you wouldn't mind living at Wansford. You love it there."

"Beside the point. I don't want to do anything that might threaten King & Co. and steal our independence."

"If the queen finds proof of your father's loan to the king and repays it, you won't need any money from the duchy."

"There's no guarantee that loan even exists." Tess

sighed. "And the queen won't ask her secretaries to look unless we get those letters back."

Ellie sipped her tea. "As long as Thornton puts a provision for you in the new marriage settlement, you shouldn't be any worse off than you are now. You should still get a third of the duchy's income, and life-time use of the dower house if he dies. But you should negotiate a better deal while he lives. You should ask for full use of Wansford Hall, *plus* an extra monthly allowance. If he's as rich as they say, and as keen to marry you for the convenience, he'll have to pay for the privilege."

"Bravo!" Daisy clapped. "And just so there's no chance of him calling off the wedding, you're going to have to stall him until the wedding night."

Tess shook her head. "This is all so strange. I never thought I'd marry again."

"It's an elegant solution," Ellie said. "Thornton's one of the few men in England you *can* marry and not be worse off."

"But he doesn't love me."

"Not *yet*," Daisy said. "But intense physical attraction is a good place to start. Who's to say he won't fall in love with you once you spend more time together? And even if he doesn't, and you part ways this summer, you'll still have had the most wonderful time."

Tess rubbed her forehead. "He's coming to see me on Saturday for an answer."

"You're going to tell him yes?"

"Provided he agrees to my requests, then yes."

Daisy let out an excited whoop. "I love weddings!"

"You love *cake*," Ellie teased. "The fact that there's a wedding attached is just a bonus." She turned to Tess. "Don't worry, we'll help you write a list of demands."

"You make it sound like a kidnapping," Tess laughed. "Or blackmail."

"Speaking of which," Ellie said, tapping the papers on her desk, "I have a potential suspect for who might have stolen the princess's letters."

Tess raised her brows. "How? Did someone approach you after we left Lady Iveson's?"

"No, but I spoke to a friend in the War Office who gave me a list of everyone who served in the same troop as Hesse for the past five years."

"Isn't that a lot of men?"

"About eighty, but the vast majority can be immediately discounted. Most are still serving abroad, and several are dead."

Ellie plucked a piece of paper from the precariously stacked pile in front of her. "There is one man, however, a Richard Case, who bears further investigation. He was with Hesse until he was invalided out on an army pension just before Waterloo. He lives here in London, and according to my cousin Reginald, he's a well-known gamester. Reg says he's a member of a couple of gentlemen's clubs. His latest addiction is horse racing, but he owes money to several other men thanks to losses at cards."

"Sounds like a man in dire need of some funds," Tess mused. "And if he was canny enough to take a couple of Hesse's letters as insurance for a rainy day, he could have decided it's time to cash them in."

"My thoughts exactly," Ellie murmured.

"Do you know his address?"

"Not yet. But Reg says Case will probably be at Lady Greenwood's party on Saturday because the play is always deep."

Tess nodded. "I'll see if we can get an invitation."

Chapter Twelve

Tess was a bundle of nerves by the time Saturday arrived. She'd taken a ridiculous amount of care with her appearance, and even knowing that the pale blue dress she'd chosen flattered her figure, she still felt gauche and ill prepared to face Thornton. A lamb waiting for the wolf.

Daisy, mercifully, had gone riding with Ellie in Hyde Park, so she was alone.

Determined to appear cool and businesslike, she stood behind her mahogany writing desk as Thornton was shown into her study, and the sturdy wood provided a much-needed barrier between them.

Her heart started to pound as he handed his hat, gloves, and cane to Gustav, her footman, with a nod of thanks.

"Your Grace." He swept her a slightly mocking bow.

His white shirt and neat cravat complemented a navy waistcoat and a jacket of the same color that molded to his broad shoulders and tapering waist with loving faithfulness.

Lord, he was beautiful. She wanted to reach out and trace his finely molded cheekbones and sharp jaw. To touch his lips to see if they really were as soft as she remembered.

She sent him a smile instead, and gestured to the chair she'd placed on the opposite side of the desk. "Welcome to Wansford House. I was told the eighth duke rarely stayed here, but I've made a few improvements since I moved in. Including having this room redecorated. Of course, since the house is yours now, you may wish to change it again."

Thornton looked around with interest. "I applaud your taste. And you won't need to vacate the premises if you say yes to my proposal."

Ah. There was that directness she'd come to expect from him. Tess decided to respond in kind.

"About that. I have some questions."

He flicked back the tails of his jacket and sat, so she did the same.

"Of course. Business before pleasure. Go ahead."

Tess had memorized her list. "First of all, if I were to agree to marry you, what living arrangements would you propose?"

"We would live here, together, until I return to Bristol. And we should visit Wansford Hall, too. I need to see the state of it and meet the tenants, and since you already know them, you can ease the introductions."

"Very well." She steeled herself for the next question. "Secondly, since you're suggesting a physical relationship, would there be any stipulations or expectations in that regard?"

Heat rose in her cheeks. How could they be discussing something so intimate in so formal a setting? Thankfully, he didn't seem surprised by her directness, although the corners of his lips curled up.

"Of course there would be stipulations. We should both

know where we stand, going into the agreement." His gray gaze held hers and her stomach did a nervous little flip. "The physical part of our relationship will be limited to a maximum of three months, to prevent either of us from getting bored, and to avoid either party developing deeper feelings which might complicate the situation."

Tess raised her brows. He clearly didn't believe in love at first sight. She wasn't sure she did, either, but did he really think himself immune to it within the next twelve weeks? That was a little disheartening.

He spoke again before she could ask.

"As to *frequency* . . ." His eyes flicked to her mouth, as if he were already imagining kissing her. "You're an incredibly desirable woman. I would hope to make love to you at least three times a week."

Now Tess was sure her cheeks were aflame. Still, she lifted her chin and returned his stare, determined to pretend she was used to discussing such brazen topics. If she'd truly spent the last few months enjoying a string of lovers, as he believed, then she would know how to negotiate an agreement of amorous intent.

She inclined her head like a queen bestowing a great gift. "Agreed. Three days a week."

He nodded. "Except when you're having your monthly courses. I would leave you alone for that week, naturally."

Was it possible to flush even more? Tess doubted it.

"I will, of course, expect you to not take a lover, other than myself, for the time we are together," he said.

"And I would expect the same courtesy from you. I disapprove of infidelity."

His gaze dropped to her mouth again, and lingered. Just to be perverse, Tess bit her lower lip, to see if she could get a reaction out of him, and when he shifted slightly in his chair, she felt a heady rush of power.

She cleared her throat, and his attention snapped back to her eyes.

"Regarding a marriage settlement," she said, injecting some authority into her tone, "I require the same terms as were agreed with the previous duke. Should you predecease me, I would like one-third of the income from the estate, to do with as I wish, and the right to live in the dower house at Wansford for the rest of my life."

"That sounds reasonable. In fact, you can live in Wansford *Hall* for the rest of your life, if that's what you prefer. Once our time together is done, we'll live separate lives. I'll spend most of my time in Bristol. You can have the use of this house, too. I have my own, on Curzon Street, should I ever come to town."

He tilted his head and studied her neck and the skin of her décolletage with slow deliberation. Memories of his mouth there, the faint scrape of his evening stubble, made her shiver.

"You should have a monthly personal allowance, too."

Tess nodded, a little dazed. Ellie had suggested three hundred pounds a year for clothing and other necessities.

"Do you think five hundred pounds a year is reasonable?" he asked.

She couldn't prevent her eyebrows from rising in shock. "Five hundred pounds?"

Her voice came out as an astonished squeak, which he misread as outrage. He shook his head, as if annoyed with himself.

"You're right. It's not enough. An insult. You'll have a thousand pounds a year."

It was a good thing she was sitting down. She gathered her wits and tried to appear only moderately impressed. "For the time we are together?"

"For the rest of my life."

Tess sucked in a quiet breath. God, if she accepted this outrageous proposal, she really would be selling herself. It would be far worse than marrying the old duke. Then, she'd had no choice. Now, the decision was entirely hers to make.

"I'm sure you've considered the fact that we could have an affair *without* marrying," she said.

"I have. But that would still leave me with the expectation of finding a wife. I've come to realize that being married might actually be beneficial to my business. Single gentlemen are rarely invited to intimate gatherings unless there's an unmarried daughter to dispose of. The married men always think we're plotting to steal their wives. If I appear to be besotted with my *own* wife, they'll see me as less of a threat. We'll be invited to events I never had access to before."

He smiled, and her heart fluttered at his ridiculous charm. "This arrangement kills two birds with one stone. Business *combined* with pleasure."

Tess's stomach fluttered at the way he said *pleasure*, but she inclined her head again. Marrying her might make his life easier, but it had the potential to complicate her own quite a bit. She'd have to keep her involvement in King & Co. hidden from him, at least for a while.

"You say this is a logical business arrangement, but what about love?" she asked.

"What about it?"

"Don't you believe in it?"

He frowned, as if giving the matter serious consideration.

"I don't deny its existence," he said slowly. "But 'love' comes in a thousand different forms. A parent's love for their child, for example, or a soldier's brotherly love for his comrade. It's a powerful force. It can make people do extraordinary things." He paused. "But the love you're describing, *romantic* love, ruins everything."

"What do you mean?"

"It's the antithesis of reason and logic. History's littered with fools dying for love, going to war for love. Ruining themselves for love. That's not romantic. It's *imbecilic*. Look at Lady Caroline Lamb, smashing a glass and making a scene when Byron ended their affair." He shook his head. "Ridiculous."

Tess bit back a laugh at his fervency. For someone who claimed to be dispassionate, he seemed to have very strong views on the subject.

"And what about the Trojan War?" he continued. "That all started because Paris thought he was in love with Helen, another man's wife. He wasn't in love, he was in *lust*. And he dragged thousands of men to their death because of his unruly loins."

Tess felt her lips twitch at his phrasing. Poor Paris wasn't the only one at the mercy of unruly loins. Ever since she'd met Thornton, she'd been feeling quite unruly herself.

He glanced up at her, and she sobered at his intense expression.

"You should be under no illusions. This is just two bodies finding physical pleasure. My heart will never be involved."

"A contract for services," Tess said solemnly. "I understand. We should be entirely dispassionate."

He caught the edge of amused irony in her tone and his eyes darkened. "Oh, we won't lack passion, Your Grace. Far from it."

Tess suddenly wished she'd brought a fan. Beneath the desk she wiped her damp palms on her skirts. The way he veered from cool conviction to bone-melting intensity in the space of a few heartbeats was highly unsettling.

Still, she could hardly complain that he was misleading her in any way. He'd laid all his cards on the table.

"Do you think all this haggling makes me a whore?"

She stilled, shocked at herself. She hadn't meant to say that out loud.

"No. It makes you an astute businesswoman, which is something I respect."

He was serious. For some odd reason that made her feel slightly better.

"I asked about love because what happens if you meet someone else in the future, fall in love with them, and want to make *them* your duchess?"

"I believe I mentioned that there will be no divorce between us. Not even if we both take other lovers at a later date." He held her gaze. "Truthfully, I don't believe I will ever love anyone in that way. If I desire someone after we part, I will sleep with them. As long as they are in agreement."

His lips took on a cynical curl. "It will be an interesting experiment, actually. To see who wants me without the possibility of a title."

Tess almost blurted out that she'd want him even if he were a penniless shepherd in a hut, but wisely held her tongue. No need for the man to know just how irresistible she found him. She couldn't believe he'd had any trouble finding willing partners, even before he'd become titled and rich.

"I have more questions."

"I'm gratified you've given the matter such serious consideration."

She couldn't tell if he was being ironic or not.

"What about children? If we are to have an intimate relationship there's always the chance that I might fall pregnant."

He ran his hand over his jaw. "Producing the next heir to the dukedom isn't a priority for me. If I die without issue the title can go to some other poor unsuspecting sod. There's no reason for you to be treated like a broodmare." He frowned. "Do *you* want children?"

"I'm not *against* having them," Tess said truthfully. "But I think it's good for a child to have more than one loving adult in their life. If you're not going to be present, then it wouldn't be an ideal situation."

"I would support any offspring financially, of course."

Tess shook her head, at a loss to articulate her feelings, afraid of sharing too much.

"Financial support is a poor substitute for loving support. I scarcely remember my mother, but I remember wishing she was there. Being brought up by my father was . . . not ideal. I don't want any child of mine to suffer from a lack of affection."

His gaze sharpened in interest and she rushed on, before he could question her further. Millions of people had been raised in worse conditions than hers. She didn't want or need his pity. "So what do you suggest we do?"

"I assume you've taken precautions with your previous lovers. What methods have you been using since the duke died?"

Abstinence, Tess almost said. *And virginity. And talking about truffles.*

She waved her hand in an airy gesture, panicking inwardly. God, he thought she knew every whore's trick to avoid pregnancy. She was going to have to have a serious talk with Ellie and Daisy as soon as he left.

"Oh, you know. There are several different ways."

He nodded, as if he knew what she was talking about. "I dislike the feel of sheaths, personally. They dull sensation. And I hate the lack of spontaneity."

Tess nodded solemnly. *Sheaths? What sheaths?*

"Neither of us have the pox, I assume?"

She tried to hide her mortification. "No."

"Me, neither. So we don't need one to prevent disease."

She shook her head.

"In that case, you must have other feminine ways of preventing it?"

"Of course."

Oh, she was such a liar.

"I'll leave it in your capable hands, then."

Another thought struck her. "What if I take a lover after we part, and get pregnant by him? Any child born in wedlock will be deemed as legitimate."

Like Daisy.

He shrugged. "If it's a boy, then I suppose he'll be the next duke, God help him. And if it's a girl, then she'll doubtless make an excellent marriage. As you have done."

"It wouldn't bother you that another man's child would inherit the dukedom?"

He shrugged. "Why would it? I never expected to inherit it myself."

Tess supposed he had a point. A tiny part of her had expected him to react with jealousy at the thought of her with another man, but he seemed sincere in his assertion that their arrangement would not involve any emotions other than logic and passion.

Business and pleasure.

"One final question. *If* I agree, when would we announce our engagement? There's going to be an absurd amount of gossip and speculation as it is. I think we should wait at least a month, attend the same social events, make sure people see a growing attraction between us and—"

"Tomorrow."

"I beg your pardon?"

"I'd announce our engagement tomorrow."

"That's ridiculous. We've only just met. We've danced twice in public. Everyone will know it's not a love match."

Thornton's brows lifted in amusement but his gaze was hot as it rested on her face. "I thought you prescribed to that love-at-first-sight, thunderbolt-from-heaven, starcrossed lovers stuff the poets spout? Could that not have happened to us?"

Tess narrowed her eyes at his teasing. "It will take three weeks to have the banns read."

Again, that head shake. "I'll get a special license from the Archbishop of Canterbury. We'll be wed this time next week. Here, at Wansford House. After which we'll travel immediately to Wansford Hall."

Her head was spinning.

"But—"

"Nobody who knows me will be surprised. I have a reputation for wanting the best of everything. Why wouldn't people think I'd want the most beautiful woman in England as my wife?"

Despite herself, Tess felt heat rise in her face. She'd heard such outrageous flattery before, of course, but he stated it as if it were a simple, irrefutable fact.

He also sounded as if he truly believed it.

He leaned forward in his seat. "Every man who hears it will understand my desire. Every married man will be seething with jealousy. And every bachelor will mourn that his chance to win you has evaporated."

A ball of disappointment lodged in her chest, but she

tried to keep her tone light. "It seems I'm only ever prized for my beauty."

"Not at all. You'll be praised for your ability to bring me to heel. For capturing not one, but two successive dukes, and quite sensibly securing your position."

Tess let out a slow, steadying breath. "I only have one request left."

"I'm glad to hear it. I've had hard-nosed investors on Threadneedle Street give me less of an inquisition."

She tried to look coy, and not simply terrified.

"I want to wait until we're wed before we consummate the marriage."

A brief frown crossed his face and she braced herself for a refusal.

"May I ask why?"

Tess cast around for a believable evasion. *What would Daisy say in a situation like this?* Inspiration struck.

"I just think that anticipation only increases the pleasure." She sent him her best, most sultry look. The one a baronet had once claimed made her look like Venus and Salome rolled into one, or some such nonsense.

She rolled her shoulder in the faintest shrug, and was gratified when his gaze slid over her collarbone and then wandered helplessly down to her cleavage. For the first time in her life, she was *glad* that someone was admiring her breasts. When she thought of him touching her there again, the hint of roughness in her voice wasn't feigned.

"There's something so delicious about teasing out the moment. After all, anything hard to get always provides the most satisfaction."

Thornton's eyes narrowed in faint suspicion that he was being manipulated, and she prayed she hadn't overplayed her hand. Was she making a fool of herself? How did one flirt?

He sat back in one swift, fluid movement. "I agree."

"To what?"

A muscle ticked in his jaw. "To increasing the pleasure by waiting. Do *you* agree to my terms?"

Did she? Tess plunged headlong. "Yes. I accept your proposal."

Thornton showed no visible sign of relief, nor satisfaction, and for a moment she wondered if she'd made a terrible mistake.

He gave a curt nod and stood. "Excellent. I'll have the documents drawn up. Where shall we meet next?"

Feeling at a distinct disadvantage, Tess stood, too, but his presence still dominated the room.

"I'll be attending Lady Greenwood's party tonight."

"In that case, I'll be sure to be there." A glimmer of amusement seeped into his expression. "Should we seal our bargain with a kiss? Or a handshake?"

Her brain was still swirling with the enormity of what she'd just agreed to. Kissing him again might stop her from thinking at all. She extended her hand across the desk.

His mouth broke into a grin that made her weak at the knees as he reached out and enfolded her fingers in his much-larger clasp.

Instead of raising her hand for a kiss, as he'd done before, he gave it a squeeze and a shake, as he might give a fellow business acquaintance. The gesture was one of appreciation for a worthy adversary, and Tess accepted it with a sense of gratitude.

"I am aflame with anticipation already," he said softly. "I'll see you tonight."

Chapter Thirteen

"Ellie, Daisy, help!"

Tess slid behind her desk at King & Co. in a flurry of skirts. "Thornton thinks I know a hundred tricks for avoiding pregnancy. What are they?"

Daisy twisted her hair up onto the top of her head and stabbed it with a pencil to hold it in place. Ellie took off her reading spectacles.

"You discussed contraception? With Thornton?" Daisy's eyes were glowing with interest. "How very progressive. Most men wouldn't have given it a moment's thought."

"He seems to think of every detail. It's no wonder he's so successful at business. He said he dislikes using sheaths, so he's leaving the task up to me."

Daisy pursed her lips. "Hmm. Well, one way to avoid it is to time your 'amorous episodes' to just before or just after your monthly courses. Those are the times you're least likely to fall pregnant. But it's not terribly reliable. I knew a dairymaid at Hollyfield who—"

Tess shook her head. "That's not going to be possible.

He's expecting us to have an 'amorous episode' at least three times every week."

Her skin grew hot just saying it out loud, and Daisy laughed at her obvious mortification. "At *least*? Tess, you must be the luckiest woman in London."

"Any other ideas?"

"Well, Tom and I prevented it by having him pull out before he completed the act. But again, not really ideal."

Having grown up in the countryside, Tess had a basic knowledge of the physical mechanics of animal mating, and her understanding of what went on between men and women had been greatly increased by the satirical—and often borderline pornographic—engravings that hung in the printsellers' windows around Covent Garden.

"I don't think he'll expect to do that, either. Ellie, any thoughts?"

Ellie breathed on the lenses of her glasses and gave them a thoughtful polish with her shawl.

"Well, I obviously don't have any *practical* knowledge, like Daisy, and you'd be surprised at how little information is available to ladies of an inquiring nature when it comes to books you can borrow from the lending library. But I *did* find some fascinating details when I searched through the records of court cases involving ladies of ill repute."

"You read about trials involving prostitutes?"

"Yes. I thought it might prove enlightening. And it was. Did you know, for example, that some women use half a lemon, inserted inside their—" Ellie waved vaguely at her lap as she struggled to find the appropriate language.

"Personal area?" Daisy suggested with a laugh. "Gates of Venus? Honey pot?"

Tess wrinkled her nose. "Ugh. That sounds uncomfortable."

"One used a sea sponge covered in silk and attached to a ribbon. And another mentioned something to do with honey, oil, and vinegar."

"Sounds more like cookery than contraception," Tess said doubtfully.

"Plenty of women lie with men and don't get pregnant. You might be barren," Daisy said. "Or he might not be able to father a child. That could happen to you."

"It's incredibly risky."

Ellie shrugged. "So what if you *do* get pregnant? You've always loved children. Would it be so bad?"

"They'd be legitimate," Daisy added.

"But Thornton wouldn't play any part in their upbringing, except to pay for their education."

"That's no different to ninety percent of the *ton*." Daisy sniffed. "My father barely even remembers my brothers' names. He's always confusing them. They were packed off to school almost as soon as they could talk. And you know how little interest he takes in me. He pays more attention to his favorite basset hound."

"That's my point," Tess said. "An absent or uncaring parent is a terrible thing to subject a child to."

"But you'd be a wonderful, loving mother," Ellie said. "And we'd be the most spectacular aunts. The child would just have two extra mothers, instead of a father. I call that a good exchange."

"I wouldn't be upset if I *did* end up having a child," Tess mused. "I'd have someone to love when Thornton goes back to Bristol."

Daisy rested her chin on her hand. "Then I fail to see the problem. Go ahead and make fabulously energetic love with one of the most handsome men in London, and leave the rest to Fate. You'll either end up with a child, or be left with a slew of happy memories and a body exhausted by a surfeit of pleasure. There's no bad outcome here."

"There is *one*," Tess said. "He says he'll never fall in love with me. But what if I fall in love with him?"

"Is that a danger?" Ellie asked.

"Of course it is," Daisy said adamantly. "A very real danger. He's outrageously handsome. And from her experience at Careby's, he clearly knows how to pleasure a woman. A girl can fall in love with having climaxes, El. They're like chocolate eclairs—once you have one, you want another. And another and another. If Thornton's as good at lovemaking as I suspect he is, Tess could easily get addicted to him."

"Maybe he'll be terrible," Ellie said brightly. "A huge disappointment."

"Huge, yes," Daisy snickered. "Disappointment, no. Have you seen the bulge in his breeches?"

"Daisy!" Tess shrieked.

"What?" Daisy gave an unrepentant shrug. "No harm in inspecting the merchandise. Men do it to us all the time. Why shouldn't we return the favor? Can I help it if current gentlemen's fashion provides a snug outline? No."

"You can stop your eyes lingering on unsuspecting men's crotches," Ellie scolded.

"Only if I'm asleep. That's like touring the British Museum and averting your eyes from the statues. I'm glad we don't live in ancient Greece. Some of those athletes required *extremely* small fig leaves."

Tess tried to bring the conversation back on track. "I wasn't talking about falling in love with the physical side of things. Nor his looks. What if I fall in love with *him*? As a man. I already know he's clever and quick-witted. What if he turns out to be nice, too? What if he isn't the ruthless, commerce-obsessed cutthroat he seems?"

Daisy sucked in a breath. "You're right. What if he's kind to puppies and orphans?"

"And has a sense of humor?" Ellie added.

"I'll be doomed," Tess groaned. "I'm practically guaranteed to fall in love with him. And then he'll leave me without a second glance and find someone else, and I'll be left a miserable, heartbroken wreck."

"A beautiful, titled, financially secure, well-pleasured wreck," Daisy reminded her dryly. "It could be worse."

Ellie burst into laughter. "You must be the first woman ever to worry about falling in love with her own husband."

Tess groaned again. "Maybe I should tell him I've changed my mind."

"Don't you dare!"

"What if *I'm* the one who's a huge disappointment? I'm going to have to pretend I know what I'm doing."

Daisy rolled her eyes. "It's not hard. Just do what feels nice. Relax, enjoy it, and whatever he does to you, do back at him."

Tess bit her lip. "That doesn't sound too difficult. I can do that."

"Of course you can."

"He's going to pretend he's besotted with me tonight, at Lady Greenwood's, to start rumors of an upcoming engagement."

Ellie replaced her spectacles. "Excellent. Because I've just heard from Reg that our prime suspect, Richard Case, is going to be there, too. We can wait until he's deep in his cups, then question him to see if he knows anything about the missing letters. Agreed?"

Tess and Daisy both nodded.

"It's going to be a busy night."

Chapter Fourteen

Thornton was the first person Tess saw when she paused at the top of the steps that led down to Sylvia Greenwood's ballroom, and her heart leapt as their eyes met over the crowd.

Good Lord, he was devastating in evening clothes.

In an excellent impression of a man deeply enamored, he simply walked away from the group he was conversing with without a backward glance, and crossed the room to meet her at the foot of the stairs. His smile of admiration and the warm look in his eyes made her pulse flutter. Even though it was all for show.

She inclined her head as he gave a neat bow.

"I see you look beautiful in colors other than red, Your Grace." He sent her forest-green evening gown an appreciative glance.

"Tess," she reminded him.

"Scarlet," he murmured, for her ears only.

"Don't call me that!"

His smile widened. "Ready for another adventure?"

"If you mean, am I ready to try to persuade everyone

here that you're falling madly in lust with me, then yes. I am."

She offered him her hand and he drew her to stand at one side of the dancers. Daisy and Ellie were already making their way toward the cardroom in search of their quarry.

"It has to work both ways," he said. "We have to convince everyone you're succumbing to my wicked charms, too."

He stared deep into her eyes and Tess felt an instant of disorientation, as if she were falling through space.

"Look at me as if you're thinking of kissing me," he said softly. "As if I'm the only one you see in the room."

"Is that how you're looking at me?" she countered breathlessly. *It certainly felt that way.* Her lips started to tingle, as if in anticipation of his touch.

His eyes darkened. "No, Scarlet. I'm looking at you with far more wicked thoughts in mind. I'm counting down the hours until I can make you gasp my name."

If any other man had said such things to her, she would have burst out laughing. But when *Thornton* said it, everything inside her seemed to go on a slow boil.

Tess slid a quick glance to the left, where a group of society matrons were watching their every move. "We're definitely setting the rumor mill flying."

He offered her his bent arm. "Shall we dance?"

She nodded.

"Speaking of rumors . . ." He slid his arm around her back and they moved into the first turn. "I've started one of my own. You were worried that you'd be judged for the hastiness of our engagement, so I told Edward *in the strictest confidence* that our 'romance' is long-standing, but secret."

Tess chuckled. "Telling anyone 'in the strictest confidence' is a guarantee that it'll be all over London by midnight. What did you say?"

His eyes rested on her face. "That I fell in love with you the first time I ever saw you, at Lord Ogilvy's two years ago."

Tess frowned. "Were you actually there? We were never introduced."

She'd never have forgotten meeting him.

"No, we were not. You weren't even aware of my existence. I was a country merchant far below your notice. I knew you were destined for a brilliant match. But I never stopped thinking about you. Dreaming about you. About what might have been."

God, he was a magician. His words wrapped around her like a spell, convincing her of his sincerity even when she knew it was just a fairy tale to disguise the true, far less romantic agreement they'd made.

For an instant she wondered what would have happened if they'd truly met back then. No good would have come of it. Still, she played along with his foolish fantasy.

"I suppose I fell madly in love with you, too, after only one dance?"

His lips twitched in appreciation.

"Of course you did. We were both young and ridiculously impulsive. Like Romeo and Juliet."

"And our romance was equally doomed." She added some dramatic flair to her tone. "My father wouldn't hear of me marrying a penniless upstart."

"Penniless *yet irresistible* upstart," he amended. "We were tempted to elope to Gretna Green—"

"But our plan was stopped when I was locked in my room and forced to marry the duke." Tess shook her head with mock gravity, making a joke of what was horribly close to the truth. "We were both brokenhearted. You, poor love-wracked fool, couldn't bear to be in the same country. To see me with another man was worse than death. So you set sail for shores unknown—"

"Canada," he said dryly. "Not entirely undiscovered."

"—vowing never to love again. Every woman you met after me was just a poor imitation, a substitute who never claimed your heart."

"You're very good at this. Have you considered penning a novel?"

Tess bit back a laugh. "Occasionally."

"Which brings us back to last week," he said. "When I saw you across Lady Iveson's dance floor, a vision in red satin. Against all the odds, I discovered that not only were you single, but that the torch of your love for me had never gone out."

"That's rather romantic, for someone who claims not to believe in love."

His smile was bittersweet. "I didn't say I didn't believe in it. I said it was stupid and illogical."

"So, you think people will believe this fairy tale?"

"Some of them already do. Just before you arrived two elderly ladies congratulated me on my unexpected inheritance and asked if I thought I'd be luckier 'this time around.'"

"You think they were talking about me?"

"About us," he corrected. "And yes. The only thing the *ton* secretly loves more than a scandal is a happy ending."

"Even if it's make-believe?"

"Why else do you think Drury Lane's stalls are packed every night? Most people want to dream it's possible. Even if it never happens to them."

His cynicism was a little dampening, but Tess refused

to let it ruin her evening. "Well, I'm glad I won't be seen as quite such an easy conquest."

"I'll be the one everyone thinks is a besotted fool."

Tess shrugged. "Even that's to your advantage. It might dissuade some of those matchmaking mothers from thrusting their pretty daughters at you."

"It hasn't happened yet."

His gaze never left her face, and Tess couldn't help but be warmed and flattered by his attention. Men had looked at her admiringly before, but Thornton stirred something inside her, a desire to look *back*, just as closely. He was a fascinating creature; a mysterious, beckoning unknown. She wanted to know everything about him.

He blinked, and she realized she'd been staring deeply into his eyes. Flustered, she cast around for another topic of conversation.

"So, what's it like being the duke?"

His lips quirked. "Expensive. The prince regent's been trying to convince me to buy one of his racehorses, a stallion called Fool For Love."

"Did you buy it?"

"God, no. I might not know much about horses, but I know a bad investment when I see one. I watched the creature race at Newmarket yesterday. It might have been a good horse once, but it's long past its prime."

"Considering the rumor you just started, it's rather perfectly named. If you bought it, it would add fuel to the fire. People would be speculating about the significance for weeks."

"That's true."

"Maybe you should buy it just to get in the prince regent's good graces?"

"And be stuck with a horse that would be better off going to the knacker's yard?"

"Oh, be kind. You can put the poor thing out to pasture. Or use it for stud."

Tess blushed. A lady shouldn't be speaking of horse breeding on the dance floor. Or anywhere else, for that matter. And speaking of copulation while being held in Thornton's arms was an even *worse* idea.

He noticed her embarrassment and laughed. "I'll think about it."

She was immensely relieved when the dance came to an end. "If you'll excuse me, there are a few other people I wish to speak with tonight."

He relinquished his hold on her with every evidence of reluctance. "Very well. I think we've done enough to sow the seeds of gossip for tonight. I'll see you tomorrow. When I announce our surprise engagement."

Tess nodded and took her leave.

She found Daisy in the room next to the cardroom and forced herself to concentrate on the task at hand, rather than remembering the sensual promise in Thornton's eyes whenever he looked at her.

"Have you found Richard Case?"

Daisy inclined her head toward the open doorway. "Yes. He's in there, playing vingt-et-un with Lord Greenwood. Ellie and I have been plying him with brandy, so he's already bleary-eyed. We've primed him for you, Tess."

Tess took a quick glance at herself in the mirror to the left of the door and realized she looked even more glowing than usual. Flirting with Thornton had brought a sparkle to her eyes and a rosy flush to her cheeks.

"You're irresistible," Daisy assured her wryly. "As usual. Case doesn't stand a chance." She turned Tess's shoulders and gave her a gentle shove toward the cardroom. "He's the blond in the green coat. Go bedazzle him into telling you everything."

Chapter Fifteen

Richard Case was not unattractive, but not to Tess's taste. His straw-colored curls and ruddy complexion made him look almost cherubic, but there was nothing childlike about his stocky frame. He looked like a country farmer. She vastly preferred Thornton's dark elegance.

Case's inebriation was evident in the way he slouched, and the careless way he disposed of his cards. As Tess approached, the game came to an end, and Lord Greenwood vacated his seat. Tess took his place, sliding into the empty chair opposite Case as he scowled at the small pile of winnings in front of him. When he glanced up and noticed her, however, his sullen expression changed to one of lecherous interest.

Tess sent him her widest smile, and leaned forward with her elbows on the table to give him a teasing hint of cleavage. It was a cheap trick, but it never failed. Thankfully, the table was tucked in the very corner of the room, partly shielded by a large potted fern.

"Good evening, handsome," she purred. "Are the cards not falling your way tonight?"

Case's answering smile oozed confidence. "Not particularly, but you know what they say. Unlucky at cards, lucky in love."

Tess almost rolled her eyes at such an unoriginal line, but she pretended it was the wittiest thing she'd ever heard. She gave a breathy little laugh.

"I'm Tess."

His bleary gaze slid over her, dropping to her breasts for a long moment before returning to her face.

"I know who you are. You're the Duchess of Wansford. How come you never introduced yourself before?"

"A shocking oversight. I recently heard tales of your bravery on the battlefield, and I knew I had to hear more." She traced her finger in a slow scrolling figure-eight pattern on the green baize. It seemed to mesmerize him. "*So* impressive."

Flirting like this made her feel absolutely ridiculous, but Case seemed to be lapping it up. He didn't even notice when Ellie appeared at his shoulder and refilled his glass. He just reached down and took a long drink while studying Tess's neckline with a hooded, sleepy gaze.

Her skin prickled unpleasantly at his lazy inspection.

"Thought you had every man in London panting after you," he slurred. "Including the new duke."

Tess gave a dismissive shrug and dropped her voice to a whisper. "Well, between you and me, the new duke's rather dull. He's spent his whole life balancing books in a gloomy office in Bristol."

In between sailing to Canada and back, she added silently. It felt cruel to malign Thornton to another man, but Case was so drunk he was unlikely to remember what she'd said. "He's nothing but a boring accountant."

She leaned closer. "I've always preferred military men,

myself. *Real* men, who've seen the world, and know how to treat a woman."

Case took another swig of his drink and eyed her with even more interest. "Like a bit of rough, do you? Tired of those pretty dandies bowing and scraping? Well, well."

He was practically preening. Tess sent what she hoped was a secretive-looking glance over her shoulder.

"Do you know the best thing about being a widow? It's the freedom. I don't have a silly chaperone watching my every move and following me everywhere. I can do what I like. With *whomever* I like." She fluttered her eyelashes. "As long as I'm discreet, of course."

Case hooked his finger in the top of his cravat and tugged, as if it were too tight. He was practically dribbling at her suggestive tone.

"Discretion. Of course." He took another deep drink of his brandy, as if he needed the strength.

Tess bit her lower lip with her teeth and a bead of sweat glistened at his hairline.

"I'm tired of this ball. Maybe we could go to your house to become better acquainted? You can tell me all about your adventures with Wellington in Portugal."

He straightened in his chair, his cheeks flushed. "Absolutely. I have lodgings near the Strand. It's less than five minutes away."

"Is it private? You don't have a roommate, do you?"

"Very private. We won't be disturbed."

Tess straightened. "Wonderful. Just let me go and freshen up in the ladies' room. Meet me out the front with your carriage."

Case's ruddy face flushed even more. "Ah. I don't actually have my own carriage at the moment. Had a bad loss at Newmarket a while ago and had to sell it."

Tess feigned interest. "Oh, really?"

He nodded. "Lost a monkey on a horse called Fool For Love."

She tried to look commiserating. "Owned by the prince regent?"

He seemed surprised and impressed at her knowledge of the turf.

"That's the one! My friend Croxton swore it was a surefire winner, but I've never seen a more miserable nag in my life. A three-legged donkey could have beaten it." He sat up a little straighter in his chair. "But you needn't worry that my pockets are to let now. I've had a windfall. I can still treat you to some pretty baubles and fripperies."

Tess gave an airy wave. "I'm not interested in gifts. But we can't use my carriage; it has the Wansford crest on the side. We'll have to get an unmarked hackney. You go and summon one while I get my cloak."

Case lurched tipsily to his feet, and Tess made her escape.

Daisy and Ellie were both waiting for her in the room set aside as the ladies' retiring room. Daisy pretended to be repinning her hair until the only other occupant, one of the elderly Montgomery aunts, left the room.

"Case has rooms near the Strand," Tess said quickly. "He had a recent loss at Newmarket, but says he has funds now."

"If he just inherited some money, perhaps he isn't our blackmailer," Daisy mused.

"Or perhaps he got that money by selling the princess's letters to someone else," Ellie countered.

"He's worth investigating," Tess said. "Unfortunately, he didn't tell me his full address, so I can't stall him here while you two go and search his house."

"I don't feel comfortable letting you go with him alone."

"Nor I. Thanks to my father, I'm well-versed in the various stages of intoxication, and Case is tipsy, but still sober enough to be dangerous." She held up her reticule. "My little pistol won't provide much protection against a man his size."

"You're going to have to put him to sleep," Ellie said briskly. She opened her own reticule, pulled out a silver flask, and unscrewed the top.

Daisy took a tentative sniff. "What have you got in there?"

"Brandy laced with laudanum. My father just tried a case where a washerwoman drugged a blacksmith with it and robbed him while he was asleep. I thought it was an excellent idea."

Tess shook her head. "I'm so glad you haven't decided to pursue a life of crime, El. You'd run rings around Bow Street."

Ellie grinned at the compliment.

"So you think I should get Case to drink this? What if he takes too much, and it kills him?"

"I've spoken to several doctors, and they all quoted an ancient chap called Paracelsus, who said, 'Only the dose makes the poison.' Since Case is already drunk, he'll only need a tiny bit of this to make him sleep. I put ten drops in this whole flask."

"What if ten drops is enough to fell a horse?"

Daisy shook her head. "One of Father's friends regularly has *thirty* drops in his wine. He is a poet, though."

"Is his profession relevant?"

"Could be. I suspect poets have an unusually high tolerance for opiates. Shelley definitely does. And having read that new poem Coleridge just published, the one about Xanadu, it's quite clear *he* was under the influence, too."

Tess frowned at the flask. "Can you taste the laudanum?"

"No idea," Ellie said. "I haven't tried it."

"Give me that." Daisy took the flask, tilted her head back, and took a sip. Her nose wrinkled. "Ugh. Well, it's got a slightly bitter aftertaste, but it's hardly noticeable when mixed in with the brandy. Case probably won't even notice."

Tess replaced the cap. "Fine. I'll see if I can get him to take a few sips while we're in the carriage, or when we arrive at his house. If not, I'll make my excuses and leave."

"I wish we could follow and linger outside, in case you need help," Daisy said. "But my stupid brother's here tonight. He'll insist we go home with him."

"Which brother is this?" Tess asked, momentarily diverted. "You call all three of them stupid."

"True," Daisy admitted. "It's Dominic this time. I don't know where David and Devlin are. At a brothel in Covent Garden, probably. Or at a cock fight. Wherever there's trouble, that's where they'll be."

Tess swirled her cloak around her shoulders and pulled up the hood. "Right. Wish me luck."

Chapter Sixteen

Case lounged on his side of the carriage as it bounced over the uneven cobbles, watching Tess with undisguised lechery as she pretended to drink from Ellie's little flask.

He'd tried to sit beside her, but she'd held him off with a playful plea not to crush her skirts, and he'd slumped onto the opposite squab with a low grunt. The scent of brandy clung to him, and she thought fondly of Thornton's delicious woodsy scent. If only she were in a carriage with *him*.

"A little something for the road?" She offered the flask to Case.

"Don't mind if I do."

He took a good mouthful, and she waited with bated breath for him to comment on the taste, but he swallowed it down with a deep sigh of contentment.

For the next few minutes, she dodged his clumsy attempts to press his knees against hers as he spread his legs wide and took up most of the space. He made a show of unbuttoning his waistcoat and untying his cravat, which she assumed he meant to be suggestive, but only proved his increasing lack of coordination.

He took a second gulp from the flask, then handed it back, and she sent him a flirtatious smile as she slipped it into her reticule.

"No more for me." She feigned a delicate hiccough and covered her mouth with a giggle. "Oops! I fear I'm a little tipsy myself."

Case's head dropped to one side and for a delighted moment she thought he was going to sleep, but he jerked upright again with a start and peered blearily out of the window. The hackney rocked to a stop.

"Ah, here we are!" he slurred. "Home sweet home."

Tess was relieved to see a row of small but relatively neat town houses, tucked into a narrow side street. At least he didn't live in a hovel.

With the hood of her cloak pulled up to hide her face, she debated whether to ask the driver to wait for her, but decided against it so as not to rouse Case's suspicions. She would summon another as soon as she was finished here.

She paid the driver while Case fumbled through his pockets for his key.

Thank goodness he was still on his feet. He was too big for her to move if he fell over.

After three abortive attempts to unlock the door, he finally pushed it open and gestured her into a hallway with a black-and-white tiled floor.

"Do you have any servants?" she asked.

He shook his head and steadied himself with a hand on the wall. Movement clearly made his head spin.

"No. Just a char lady who comes once a day." He sent her a lopsided smile. "We'll be completely undisturbed, my sweet."

"That's good to hear," Tess purred.

He leaned forward in a clumsy attempt for a kiss,

but she ducked his lunge with a light laugh. "Someone's eager!"

He chuckled and waved his hand toward the open doorway to her right. "Parlor's through there. Make yourself comfortable. I'll be back in a minute."

To her great relief he turned and staggered off down the corridor, using the walls on either side for support, as if he were on a swaying ship. Perhaps he needed to relieve himself?

Glad of the temporary reprieve, she entered the parlor and looked around with interest. Did she have time to search it before he came back? How long would the laudanum take to have an effect?

A small bow-fronted sideboard held some glasses and a half-empty wine bottle with the cork wedged in the top. She poured herself a glass, and emptied the rest of the contents of her flask into the second glass for him.

A series of shuffles and bumps suggested Case was bumbling around somewhere upstairs, so she made a brief search of the mahogany desk in the corner, and rifled through the drawers of a small dresser. She found nothing useful, except the stubs of betting slips from various racecourses and a handful of bills, most of them from wine merchants.

A sound in the corridor made her grab her glass and sink quickly into one of the brown leather armchairs that flanked the fireplace, in an attitude of casual relaxation.

"Ta-da!"

Tess tried not to gasp, or burst out laughing.

Case stood in the open doorway, his arms spread wide in an attitude of triumph. He was wearing what appeared to be nothing but an open shirt and a silk banyan robe, and for an awful moment she was flooded with memories of her wedding night.

Case was stockier than the old duke. The sash of the robe strained around his waist and the front gaped to reveal a chest furred with a thatch of curly blond hair.

"Thought I'd make myself a little more comfortable," he said with a tipsy smile. "Perhaps *you'd* like to take some things off, too?"

Subtlety was clearly not this man's forte.

"I'm still a little cold, from the carriage," Tess lied.

"I'll warm you up."

"Let's have another drink," she temporized. "And why don't you sit down?" She patted the seat next to her invitingly.

Case took the glass she offered. He was swaying, and his lids were beginning to droop.

"Might sit down, actually," he said with a nod. "Do you know, I can see two of you. Twice as nice." He fell heavily into the chair, dropped his head on the backrest, and patted his knee with the hand that wasn't holding the glass. "Why don't you come sit on my lap?"

Tess raised her wine. "I'll just finish my drink."

He took a sip of his own, and let out a long exhale.

"So," Tess said sweetly. "Tell me about your time in the Army. A friend of mine said you were in one of those dashing cavalry units."

Case's chest puffed out with pride. "The Eighteenth Hussars. Under General Sir Henry Murray."

"Did you see any action?"

"Every battle between Vittoria and Tolouse."

Tess widened her eyes. "That must have been very dangerous."

"Very," he said with a nod.

She pretended to take another sip of her wine. "Perhaps you knew an acquaintance of mine? A Captain Hesse?"

Case snorted. "Charles Hesse? Why, yes. He always

was popular with the ladies." His lip curled in a slight sneer.

The laudanum was clearly starting to take effect—his lids had started to droop, and his pupils had narrowed to pinpricks.

Tess swirled her wine in the glass. "I heard a rumor that he was the illegitimate son of the Duke of York."

"Could 'ave been. But I couldn't say for sure."

She leaned in conspiratorially. "I *also* heard he had a secret affair with Princess Charlotte."

Case let out a low chuckle. "Ah, now that I know to be true. The princess wrote 'im love letters."

Tess feigned astonishment. "No! How terribly indiscreet! Did he ever show them to you?"

"No. He kept 'em close. But I read them, just the same."

"You didn't! Oh, you naughty boy. How?"

Case let out a jaw-cracking yawn. "Charlie kept 'em in a cigar box under his mattress." He wrinkled his nose. "Full of girlish nonsense and silly love-talk, they were."

Tess leaned closer. "What happened to them?"

"He burned 'em. At the princhess—princhesses—" His words slurred, and after several more attempts to say *princess's* he switched to, "Because she told him to."

Tess pouted. "Oh. What a shame. I would have loved to read them. I *adore* gossip."

His blurred gaze focused on her protruding bottom lip. "You and the rest of London, love. The scandal rags would have given a pretty penny to get their hands on 'em." A crafty look crossed his face. "Lucky for me, Hesse didn't have 'em all to burn."

Tess gave a scandalized gasp. "What do you mean? You stole some?"

He preened. "Maybe I did."

Bollocks. He was still being cagey, despite his inebri-ation. Trying not to let her frustration show, she reached out and stroked his arm.

"I *do* love a man who uses his own initiative. You know, we're not so different, you and I. I wasn't born with money. I only married the old duke because I saw an easy route to a fortune."

Case yawned again. "Can't say I blame you. A body's got to do whatever it takes to get ahead in this world."

He was so drowsy now that his head was drooping toward his chest. He jolted his chin back up with a jerk. "What were you saying, my pretty?"

"The princess's letters. Do you have them here? I'd *love* to see them!"

He shook his head. "Sold 'em a couple of weeks ago to a chap over in Covent Garden."

Tess bit back a groan of disappointment. Ellie's hunch had been right. "What was his name?"

He closed his eyes again, barely able to keep them open. She shook his shoulder, and he roused with a snort.

"Come here and give me a kiss, you little tease."

"The name of the man you sold the letters to?" she pressed.

He frowned, as if struggling to recall. "Stockton? Think that was it. He gave me fifty pounds and threw in a couple of naughty prints, too. Do you want to see 'em?"

Tess gave him a brilliant smile. "Oh, yes, absolutely."

"They're upstairs, in my bedroo—"

He finally succumbed to the sedative. His head rolled back and he started to snore gently.

Triumphant, Tess stood and placed her glass on the sideboard, then headed out into the hall.

Should she leave? She had a name, after all. But Case

hadn't seemed all that certain, and Covent Garden was home to hundreds of print sellers. His muddled brain could easily have given her the name of his tailor, or his barber.

She shot another glance at Case, then swiftly ascended the stairs.

His bedroom was simple enough to find. Where would she keep naughty drawings, if she were him?

A quick search of his clothes drawers yielded nothing, nor were the engravings tucked under his bed. She checked behind all of the paintings on the wall, and then her eye fell on a small drop-front bureau in the corner.

Her father had owned something similar, and she'd been thirteen the day she spied him hiding something in the secret drawer.

Sure enough, the top section of this one opened to reveal the usual assortment of letter compartments and cubbyholes. Tess slid open the top drawer of the lower section and turned her palm upward, searching on the underside of the writing shelf for a metal spring.

There!

She pressed upward, and a hidden drawer slid out of the top section with a satisfying little click.

She peered inside, and gasped.

Case hadn't been joking when he'd called them naughty prints. Her cheeks grew hot as she shuffled through them, marveling at the acrobatic, and surely anatomically impossible, groupings. One in particular showed a mythological scene, with a handsome satyr doing something rather shocking to a nymph, and Tess felt her heart pound as she realized the satyr reminded her of Thornton.

The name at the bottom of the print confirmed she'd been right to check. The printer was Stock*dale*, not Stockton.

Horribly tempted to steal all the drawings, Tess took just the one with the satyr. She rolled it up, slipped it into the pocket of her skirts, and went quietly back downstairs.

Case was still sprawled in his armchair, head lolling, and she grinned as elation coursed through her. Poor Case. He reminded her of a golden retriever: blond, eager to please, but not overly blessed with brains.

Satisfied that he would wake with a terrible headache and very little memory of what they'd discussed, she donned her cloak and slipped out into the street.

A dark-painted carriage was coming toward her. Hackneys were often carriages that had been discarded by the nobility, and since there were no identifying crests on the side panels, she raised her arm to flag it down.

It was only as the vehicle drew closer, and began to slow, that she realized her mistake. The carriage was no shabby castoff; the paint was neat, and the horses that pulled it were of prime quality. Their black coats glistened in the light that escaped from Case's partly open door.

She lowered her arm and, as expected, the carriage passed her by. She caught a glimpse of a dark-haired occupant.

And then she heard a shout, and the carriage clattered to an abrupt halt. Before the horses had even stopped protesting, the door swung open and a dark male figure leapt down onto the pavement. He started toward her, purpose in every long, impatient stride, and Tess was entirely certain her heart stopped beating.

Shit. Bloody. Buggering Hell.

It was Thornton.

Chapter Seventeen

Tess's first impulse was to duck back inside Case's house and hide, but Thornton was upon her before she could make her escape. He caught her by the shoulders and spun her around to face him, angling her face toward the light.

"It *is* you," he growled. Incredulity burned in his eyes as he studied her face. "What in God's name are you doing here?"

"I could ask you the same thing," Tess countered, battling an awful combination of frustration and guilt.

Damn it. What were the odds that he'd be driving past at that precise moment? She must be cursed.

His brows lowered ominously as he glanced at the half-open door, and then back at her, clearly arriving at the correct conclusion that she hadn't just been walking down the street. His fingers tightened on her upper arms, but the anger that seemed to have propelled him from the carriage had been replaced by a cool calm that was even more intimidating.

"Whose house is this?" he asked softly.

She raised her chin. "A friend's."

"A male friend?"

"As it happens, yes. Not that it's any business of yours."

A muscle ticked in his jaw. "Oh, Scarlet, we made a deal. That makes it very much my business."

His tone made it clear that he thought she'd been with a lover. Tess rolled her shoulder and he released her arm, but then caught her hand instead.

He was not wearing gloves. The touch of his skin was like a static shock.

"I must admit, I'm curious to see who could have drawn you here."

To her horror, he tucked her hand against his side, and pushed open the door. She had no choice but to go along with him, pulled along in his path.

Shit. Shit. Shit.

It took him three strides to reach the open door of the parlor, and he took in the scene with a single, devastating glance.

It did look horribly incriminating. Two half-drunk glasses of liquor. Case, half dressed, his shirt and robe hanging open as he dozed in apparent postcoital exhaustion in the chair. He didn't even rouse as Thornton strode forward and stood looking down at him.

"You told me you didn't have a lover." His voice was almost a growl.

"He's not my lover," Tess hissed, keeping her own voice low to avoid waking Case. "This isn't what it looks like."

He shot her an incredulous, cynical look. "I find it hard to believe you were seized by a charitable impulse to escort him home and put him to bed. Is he your brother?"

"No."

"A relative of any kind?"

Tess shook her head. "No."

"Then it's *exactly* what it looks like, Scarlet."

He sent a scathing glance at the blissfully ignorant

Case, then shook his head, as if her choice was inexplicable.

"Really? A drunken sot like him? You're going to have to explain the attraction. I'm amazed he could even perform, in that state."

Tess tugged her hand from his. "I'm leaving."

He followed her back into the hallway. "Are you breaking it off with him? Was this one last goodbye fuck?"

The deliberately crude word shocked her, despite the fact that she'd heard it plenty of times in the rougher parts of town. She strode through the open door.

What could she say? *He's like that because I drugged him, looking for the princess royal's love letters.*

Absolutely not. Her case, her profession, was none of his concern. Still, the unfairness of him thinking that she'd lied to him scalded her, as did the fact that he thought her a light-skirts.

Furious—with herself, and life in general—she set off down the street. How had success turned to disaster so quickly?

Behind her, Thornton closed Case's door with an efficient click, then strode after her, easily catching up with his longer strides.

"You must have had a good time. He looked exhausted."

Tess stopped by his carriage and glared at him.

His brows rose in gentle mockery. "But *you* look a little frustrated, my sweet. What's the matter? Was he too drunk to give you what you wanted?"

His teasing was beyond irritating.

"I wasn't there for pleasure," she snapped. The stolen print rustled in her skirts, and she grasped the inspiration it provided. The best lies always had an element of truth, after all. She let her mouth curve upward. "At least, not from *him*. I came for this."

She pulled the rolled paper from her pocket and pressed it against his chest.

He opened it, and she tried to look defiant instead of embarrassed as he registered the scandalous subject matter. The thrill of trying to outmaneuver him made her blood pound in her ears.

This was the lesser of two evils. Better for him to think she had a naughty secret, than to start digging into the real reason she'd been there.

His brows rose. "An erotic print?"

She snatched it back, her cheeks flaming, and stuffed it back in her pocket. "Yes, if you must know. I bought it from Case. He has a whole collection of them."

She glanced up at him, but his expression was enigmatic. She couldn't tell if he believed her or not.

And then he lifted his hand and traced her cheekbone with his thumb, and those gorgeous lips of his curved in wicked amusement.

"You have a penchant for naughty engravings? Oh, Scarlet. How delicious."

"Why not? Men seem to like them. Why shouldn't a woman enjoy them, too?"

"No reason at all. In fact, I love that you seek your own pleasure."

His eyes were all pupil in the shadows and her breath caught as he stepped closer, filling her vision, sending her senses into a frenzy. For an instant she thought he was going to kiss her, but he merely reached around her and opened the door to the carriage.

"Get in. I'll take you home."

She didn't have the will to argue. She climbed in,

unsurprised by the understated luxury of the interior. Unlike the hackney she'd taken earlier, there was no cracked leather or musty smell in here. A subtle masculine scent, like cedarwood and smoke, greeted her as she settled on the navy velvet cushions, and her belly fluttered.

She moved her skirts aside, expecting him to sit across from her, but instead he took the place beside her. His shoulder pressed against hers and his muscular thigh brushed her own.

His nearness made her body hum. Danger and excitement seemed to hover in the air; an expectant hush, like before a thunderstorm. She stared straight ahead as the carriage jolted forward, but she knew he was watching her.

"I'm intrigued by the print you chose," he murmured. His voice curled around her in the darkness. "Does the thought of a man doing that to you appeal, Scarlet? Is that why you chose it? Does looking at that picture make you burn?"

Yes. Yes, it does.

She'd never even imagined a man kissing her there, between the legs, but now that the idea had formed in her brain she couldn't seem to dismiss it.

Her cheeks were burning, that was for certain. Damn it, why had she shown him the cursed thing?

"It amused me," she managed haughtily.

"There's a certain irony in looking at it alone," he purred. "Because that particular activity requires more than one person."

His warm breath tickled her ear, and the musky, delicious scent of him filled her nose. She wanted nothing more than to turn her head and put her mouth on his.

"I'd be more than willing to provide you with the same service, Scarlet."

Chapter Eighteen

Tess's heart stuttered at his scandalous suggestion. She opened her mouth, but no words came out.

He gave a low laugh at her confusion. "I still can't help feeling that I owe you a climax."

She tried to school her unruly pulse. "You can write me a voucher—an IOU to be redeemed at a time and place of my choosing."

He shook his head. "I don't think that will do. Seeing that print has given me all manner of wicked thoughts."

His finger traced her ear as he brushed a lock of her hair from her face. Her skin tingled.

"I thought we agreed to wait until our wedding night?" Even to her own ears she sounded flustered, breathless.

"For full consummation, yes. But this doesn't count." He pressed a kiss to the outer corner of her eye. "Let me give you a glimpse of how good it's going to be."

Tess forced herself to keep looking forward, even as he trailed a teasing line of little kisses across her cheekbone and then lower. She should tell him to stop, but his scent filled her lungs, and her whole body went weak.

He kissed the freckle at the corner of her mouth and

she sucked in a breath, almost shaking with the need to kiss him back.

"I've wanted you all evening, Scarlet."

The carriage wheel hit a rut. Without thought, she reached out to steady herself and accidentally grasped his thigh. His long fingers came up to cup her face, and the world tilted as their lips met in the darkness.

Tess almost groaned in relief. His mouth claimed hers with lazy insistence, and it was exactly how it had been at Careby's: slow and deep and delicious. She kissed him back, meeting his tongue with her own, loving the bone-melting intensity of it.

God, she could do this for days.

She'd never thought much about kissing, until she'd met this man. Now she wondered how she'd ever gone without.

His low hum of pleasure reverberated through her as his chest pressed hers, pushing her back against the soft velvet cushions. Tess closed her eyes as he kissed his way down her throat. His hands molded her body, shaping her curves, sliding over her ribs and breasts with the perfect amount of pressure.

And then he slid lower, off the seat, onto his knees and between her legs. His clever hands slid to her ankles, and she gasped as he pushed her skirts up over her knees in a flurry of silk and petticoats.

She grabbed the leather strap by the window as the carriage hit another jolt. "What are you doing?"

He sent her a wicked smile. "Exactly what you've been thinking about since you looked at that print."

His warm lips pressed a kiss to the inside of her leg, on the bare skin just above her garter, and Tess let out a strangled gasp. Her free hand settled on his head, her fingers threading through his hair, but whether it was to push him away or pull him closer she wasn't sure.

His broad shoulders crowded the space between her legs. The cool night air raised goose bumps on her bare skin.

She was wearing the most scandalous pair of drawers, purchased from Madame Lefèvre on Bond Street. The heat of his palms seeped through the silk as he caressed higher, and she gasped again as he caught her hips and pulled her forward until her bottom rested at the edge of the seat.

He pressed a kiss over the silk, high on the inside of her leg, and her blood turned molten as his fingers tightened on her thighs to hold her in place.

"You shouldn't—!" She tugged ineffectually at his hair. "Not here!"

Her pulse was beating so wildly she was finding it hard to breathe.

"I really should." The look he sent her was hungry, carnal. "Have none of your other lovers made good use of a carriage? Poor Scarlet. No wonder you came looking for me at Careby's."

He exhaled; a soft huff, like a dragon. The heat of it warmed the damp silk between her legs, flattening it against her throbbing flesh and making her squirm with mingled nerves and anticipation.

She felt as if she had a fever. Was he really going to put his mouth *there*, like the satyr in the drawing?

He leaned closer, his lips pressing the silk against her most private parts, and Tess's eyes almost rolled back in her head. The material was so sheer it was hardly a barrier at all, and her cheeks flamed as she realized she was wet.

Dear God, what a sensation!

Desperate to ease the jumbled knot of confusion in her belly, she tightened her fingers in his hair. The carriage bounced on the cobbles, nudging him against her in thrilling, erratic little jolts, and she gasped as he found the slit in the silk.

He licked her. A slow, delicious swipe with the flat of his tongue, and she nearly bucked off the seat in pleasure. And then he flicked the sensitive bead at the top of her curls, and a jolt cut through her like sharp lightning.

Her astonished gasp mingled with his own low hum of pleasure.

"Christ, you taste so good."

She was almost beyond thought. Her body was liquid, boneless, and yet racked with an exquisite tension that only increased as he teased her with lips and tongue. Dazed, she leaned farther back on the seat, scarcely able to believe that she'd let things get this far.

Flashes of illumination from the streetlamps outside cast him in alternate stripes of light and darkness, and she was seized by just how primitive this was, how utterly uncivilized. He was claiming her, tasting her, taking her scent inside him.

And it was glorious.

The most wonderful vibrations were shooting through her body. Tess heard a moan, and realized it had come from her.

Thornton slid his arm under her thigh, tilting her bottom off the seat to give him even better access. The velvet tugged at her skirts as they were pulled against the knap.

She bit her lip, determined not to cry out and alert the coachman to what they were doing, but it was impossible to stay quiet. Thornton reacted to her every sigh, every groan. He seemed to note every time she squirmed closer or away, learning her responses, sucking and licking with a soft insistence that was devastating.

The tension inside her was almost at a fever pitch. She

grabbed his head with both hands, trying to push him away to stop the torment, but he mumbled something incomprehensible against her thigh. And then his fingers joined his mouth, his thumb sliding in her wetness, around and around, slipping over that little bundle of nerves just as his wicked tongue stabbed *into* her.

Tess rolled her hips, but his arm held her firm against him. She was burning up, but escape was impossible.

"Come for me, Scarlet. Now."

She didn't know what he was talking about. Every muscle was taut, straining for release, and she gripped his hair in her fist, punishing him as he was punishing her.

He didn't seem to mind. She closed her eyes, pushing against his tongue, beyond shame, beyond everything but the need to end this pleasure-pain torment.

And then the world exploded behind her eyelids. Her thighs tightened around his head as her stomach clenched and wave after wave of pleasure rolled over her, as unstoppable as the tide.

She was still dazed and panting when he pulled back, drawing her skirts down demurely over her legs. In an easy movement he sat back onto the seat opposite her and straightened his long legs.

Tess slowly pushed herself upright. Her limbs seemed to be made of melted wax. Her heart was hammering in her throat, her body glowing and damp, and her brain seemed to be slow to restart.

Good God. So *that* was a climax. No wonder Daisy said women could get addicted to them. Who wouldn't want this tingly, wonderful sense of well-being again and again?

Unfortunately, embarrassment was swiftly following in pleasure's wake. Too mortified to look at Thornton, she stared blindly at the world outside. Dark shapes of buildings flashed past, and then the familiar iron railings of Hyde Park.

What on earth had she been thinking? They were almost at Portman Square! She'd been blissfully debauched while half of London carried on oblivious outside.

She braved a glance at Thornton, and found him watching her in that intense, burning way he had that turned her limbs to jelly.

What was he thinking? Could he tell she'd never had anyone do that to her before?

The corner of his mouth turned up. "You look delightfully disheveled, my love."

Tess put her hand up to her hair and found it partially unpinned. Loose tendrils cascaded over her shoulders, but it was impossible to say how bad it was without a mirror. She cleared her throat and sent him an arch look. "As do you."

It was true. His hair was a mess, ruffled as if he'd been in a fight, and she blushed as she realized it had been her hands that were responsible. She clenched them into fists in her skirts.

He ran his palm over his chin and jaw. "I trust that was adequate?"

She bit back a snort at that understatement. "You couldn't tell?"

He shrugged. "You seemed to enjoy it, but women can feign pleasure far better than men. I didn't make you scream my name, after all."

"Perhaps I forgot it?" She couldn't resist the teasing barb; his confidence deserved a little deflating. "Or perhaps I've made it a rule never to say a name, in case I get it wrong."

His lips twitched at her cheek. "You have so many lovers you're worried about confusing them?"

She sent him an arch smile and refused to be drawn. Let him think he had plenty of competition.

"It's Justin," he reminded her softly. "And you *will* say it. I promise you."

His arrogance was breathtaking, but she couldn't deny the shiver of anticipation at his vow. "We'll see."

"I'll work on my technique."

Tess tried to look wholly indifferent, but she was burning up inside. *Good God. If his technique improved any more, her heart would give out.*

She was saved from having to answer as the coach turned into Portman Square and rocked to a stop in front of Wansford House. She made her escape, but couldn't resist a glance back up at him through the open carriage door.

His dark beauty made her catch her breath. How on earth had she become entangled with such a man? She was out of her depth, but drowning was *not* an option.

Thornton leaned forward. "I still plan to announce our engagement tomorrow, but I have some business that will require my full attention for the next couple of days. You're going to have to face the *ton*'s inevitable speculation alone, I'm afraid."

Tess shrugged. "It's nothing I haven't done before. But are you so sure you'll be able to get a special license?"

"I don't foresee a problem. Charles Manners-Sutton, the Archbishop of Canterbury, was a good friend of my father's. In fact, he's my godfather."

"How convenient," she murmured faintly.

"Indeed. So I suspect the next time I see you will be at our wedding ceremony on Saturday. Make sure you sign the marriage documents I will send you. And spend whatever you like for the wedding. Send the bills to me."

Tess nodded.

"You were right," he said suddenly.

"About what?"

"Waiting. It only increases the desire." His gaze ran over her in a searing caress, then he rapped on the roof of the carriage to tell the driver to move on. "Good night, Scarlet."

"It's Tess," she countered. "And I'll make *you* say it, too."

The humor returned to his gaze, and she felt a ridiculous surge of pleasure that she could make this stern man smile. Despite his enviable position, the successes he'd had in life, she had the feeling that he didn't smile enough.

"Challenge accepted."

∾

Justin sank back in his seat with a soul-deep sigh as the carriage sprung forward.

He resisted the urge to watch Tess through the window as she turned and mounted the steps in front of Wansford House. Resisted the urge to stop the carriage, bound up the steps after her, carry her up to bed, and make love to her until they were both sweaty and thoroughly exhausted.

God, he was like a man possessed. He could still see the image of her in the seat opposite, her hair mussed from the velvet, her lips puffy and pink from his kisses. It was burned in his memory like a brand.

His cock throbbed insistently and he readjusted himself in his breeches with little hope that it would subside any time soon. The scent of her clung to his fingers, the sleeve of his shirt where he'd wiped his face after pleasuring her. A man could get addicted to that scent.

To *her*.

He took a perverse satisfaction from the fact that he'd given her pleasure but denied himself. She'd cared for him at Careby's, and he'd returned the favor tonight. It made them equal. Although why, precisely, that was important, except perhaps to assuage his natural preference for order, he was at a loss to explain.

He was satisfied that *she'd* been satisfied, he supposed.

Still, teasing her felt like the most delicious of games, with each of them trying to gain the upper hand. Tonight had probably ended in a draw, and he couldn't wait for the next turn of the cards.

If all went well, she would be his duchess by the end of the week, and he could dedicate himself to pleasuring them both to the utmost.

He was not looking forward to the next few days without seeing her. No woman had ever filled his thoughts to such an extent, and he wondered, briefly, if he ought to be alarmed. He'd had beautiful women before, but there was something about Tess Townsend that attracted him in other, more inexplicable ways. Despite her undoubted experience with men, there still was an air of innocence, of sweetness, about her that called to both his protective instincts and his need to possess. And beyond her beauty there was a quick wit and a slyly subversive sense of humor that matched his own.

He hadn't lied when he'd told her he could respect her. It was a compliment he'd rarely given anyone, male or female, but in her case it was true. She was much more than just a pretty face, but the majority in the *ton* were so shallow they could never imagine her hidden depths.

Her willingness to spar with him, and the fact that she clearly had intriguing secrets of her own—a penchant for erotic sketches being one of them—excited him beyond measure.

Chapter Nineteen

Ellie and Daisy were waiting for Tess when she entered King & Co. late the following morning.

Ellie tapped the open newspaper in front of her. "Tess, you're in *The Times*! Thornton's placed an announcement, although it's very brief. It just says 'Justin Thornton, ninth duke of Wansford, to marry Tess, née Townsend, relict of Sir Archibald Thornton, eighth duke of Wansford, this Saturday, at Wansford House, Portman Square, by special license.'"

Tess removed her gloves and sank into her chair. "Relict! That makes me sound even more ancient than dowager duchess! Like some prehistoric artifact."

"You're in *The Courier*, too," Daisy said. "And *La Belle Assemblée*. Although that one's more an article about what you might wear. Apparently, silver is all the rage this season."

"He certainly doesn't believe in wasting any time," Ellie chuckled. "He must be quite desperate to make you his wife."

Tess felt heat rise in her cheeks, and Daisy pounced. "Tess Townsend, you're *blushing*!"

There was no hiding anything from Daisy, but Tess tried to divert the conversation. "Last night he said he wouldn't see me until the wedding because he has work to do. That doesn't exactly imply desperation."

"Absence makes the heart grow fonder," Ellie pointed out.

Daisy snorted. "Ha! In *this* case, it's 'absence makes the cock grow harder.'"

"Daisy Hamilton!" Tess scolded, torn between laughter and shock. "Whoever would believe you're the daughter of a duke? Miss Burnett would wash your mouth out with soap and water!"

Daisy chucked, utterly unrepentant.

Ellie replaced her spectacles. "It seems like we sent you on a wild-goose chase with Richard Case last night, though. Sorry."

Tess frowned. "Why do you say that?"

"Because just after you left Lady Greenwood's with Case, the real blackmailer tried to talk to Daisy."

"I feigned ignorance, as we agreed," Daisy said. "So he'd think he had the wrong woman."

"What did he look like? Did you recognize him?"

Daisy shook her head. "Never seen him before in my life, unfortunately. He was a few inches below six feet, with dark hair."

"So we don't have any way of discovering who he is," Ellie grumbled. "We tried to follow him, but we lost him in the crowd."

"I suppose we'll have to wait until he sends another demand," Daisy said.

"Not necessarily." Tess gave an enigmatic smile.

"What do you mean?"

"Richard Case might not have been our blackmailer, but he *is* the one who stole the letters from Charles Hesse."

Daisy lifted her brows.

"He told you that?" Ellie said wonderingly. "Tess, you're amazing. You could make a Mother Superior confess to murder."

"I think it was the laudanum and brandy that loosened his tongue, but thank you."

Tess reached into her satchel and pulled out the print she'd retrieved from Case's bureau. She smoothed it flat on the desk, trying to control her flush at exactly *how* it had become so crumpled. It had been smooth when she'd left Case's house. It had been crushed in her skirts when Thornton had done those disgracefully debauched things to her in the carriage.

Ellie gasped in shock.

Daisy tilted her head to get a better view. "Well, she certainly seems to be enjoying herself."

Ellie made a face. "It doesn't *look* very enjoyable."

Daisy gave a lusty sigh. "Oh, it is, believe me. Tom did it to me once, in the stables. I thought I'd died and gone to heaven."

Ellie didn't look convinced, and Tess prayed the others would interpret her pink cheeks as embarrassment, and not guilt.

At any other time, she would have told them exactly what had happened after she'd left Case's house, but for some reason she didn't want to share. It was her secret, something she wanted to keep to herself.

"Why are you showing us this?"

Tess pointed to the bottom of the print. "See that? Joseph Stockdale. He's our blackmailer. Probably the man you saw last night. Case sold the letters to him for fifty pounds a couple of weeks ago."

"He's a print seller?" Daisy asked.

"Yes. If the queen doesn't pay the ransom, I expect he'll publish the letters himself. Case said he has a print shop over in Covent Garden."

Daisy leaned on the edge of the desk. "Would it be so terrible if they *were* published? If Leopold is as smitten with Charlotte as everyone says he is, then surely he's not going to call off the wedding just because of some years-old indiscretion." She wrinkled her nose. "It's such a double standard. Nobody expects *him* to have a spotless reputation."

"It's always been that way," Ellie grumbled. "Women are held to a completely different standard."

"That's what I hate about the *ton*," Daisy said. "Nobody really believes the princess is a virgin, or cares, but they all like to *pretend* she is. It's a mass conspiracy."

"True. They'll turn a blind eye to youthful folly when there's no hard evidence, but if explicit details of the letters come out it will be very hard to dismiss it as rumor and spite."

"So what should we do? Head over to Covent Garden and pay this Stockdale a visit? Or wait for him to issue another demand?"

Tess pursed her lips. "Neither. We should turn the tables and send *him* a demand. It will put him on the back foot. He'll realize we know who he is, and the fact that he hasn't already been arrested will make him think we're prepared to continue dealing with him discreetly. He'll think he still has a chance to get the money."

"An excellent plan."

Tess pulled out a pen, paper, and ink from her desk and started to write.

Sir,

*Your attempt to contact me at Lady Greenwood's
last night was unsuccessful, but as you can see,
your identity has been deduced.*

*My client requires proof that you do, indeed,
have the letters you claim to possess. You will have
one delivered to King & Co., No.7 Lincoln's Inn
Fields, as a gesture of goodwill. If we are satisfied
that it is genuine, we will arrange a time and place
for you to exchange the rest.*

"Should we sign it?" Daisy asked. "He might already
know who you are, Tess, if he saw us together last night."

"True." Tess smiled. "But in case he doesn't, I'll just
sign it 'Scarlet.'"

Chapter Twenty

The following day Tess, Daisy, and Ellie took a trip to Covent Garden and found the print shop owned by Stockdale.

It was impossible to see inside from the street: each pane of the lopsided bow window was filled with a scurrilous print, although none so scandalously erotic as the one Tess had stolen from Case.

The three of them were chuckling over unflattering portraits of the prince regent and the Duke of York, when Daisy let out a snort.

"Lord, Tess, it's you!"

"What?"

"Look." Daisy pointed, and Tess's mouth dropped open as she recognized a figure that was unquestionably herself, depicted in a scandalously low-cut red dress. She was dancing with a man who bore an obvious resemblance to Thornton; he was gazing down at her with a hungry, besotted look on his saturnine face. Even in caricature he was handsome.

In hideously bad taste, a closed coffin with a plaque reading "No. 8" on the lid was propped up on the ballroom wall behind her, presumably a reference to the old duke, and behind Thornton stood a long list of other dukes, including Wellington and the Duke of Clarence, all apparently waiting their turn.

The title beneath read, "Her Grace, the Duchess of W—hopes that the Second Duke's the Charm. Or: If at first you don't succeed . . ."

"How rude!" Tess fumed, torn between outrage and amusement.

"It's an excellent likeness," Ellie said reasonably. "He's even got that freckle by your mouth."

"Your bust is bigger, though," Daisy noted. "He's given you melons, instead of oranges."

"I expect melons sell better," Tess scowled. "At least he hasn't put me in a see-through dress."

She peered at the illustrator's signature in the bottom corner of the print, and sure enough, it said *Stockdale*. "I suppose I got off lightly. It could have been worse."

Daisy straightened her bonnet. "I'll go inside and make sure he's the same man who approached us at Lady Greenwood's."

Tess and Ellie lingered on the street, and a few minutes later Daisy reemerged with a rolled paper in her hand.

"Definitely our man," she said. "A clerk served me, but I caught a glimpse of him in the back room." She thrust the rolled paper at Tess. "Here. I bought you a copy of your print. You should give it to Thornton, as a wedding present. I'm sure he'd appreciate it."

"Daisy! I can't believe you gave that scoundrel a single penny! This is encouragement."

"Aiding and abetting." Ellie nodded solemnly.

Daisy laughed. "How many other women can boast they've been immortalized in print? It's like having a sonnet written about you. It's an honor."

"A dubious honor. This basically says I'm a shallow strumpet, desperate for money and a title. That's exactly what Thornton thinks of me."

"Only because he doesn't know you," Daisy said stoutly.

Ellie gave her a quick hug. "*We* know it's not true, and that's what matters. Besides, why do you care for his opinion?"

"I don't," Tess protested, but she knew she lied.

She wanted Thornton's respect, his admiration. Which she *shouldn't*. She'd agreed to a union based on logic and physical pleasure. There was no room for feelings, for emotions other than desire. Gaining his good opinion shouldn't matter to her.

But it did.

She pushed the matter aside, and when the three of them returned to Wansford House it was to find a packet of papers waiting on the silver tray in the hallway.

Tess took them to her study—the same one in which she and Thornton had first discussed his outrageous plan—and started to read.

True to his word, the contract contained every one of the stipulations she'd asked for. Ellie and Daisy read every line closely, to make sure there were no surprises hidden in the small print.

"A thousand pounds a year?" Daisy spluttered. "Bloody Hell, Tess."

Tess shrugged. "One can't deny he's generous."

"Or ruthless in getting what he wants."

"That, too."

Tess's hand shook only slightly as she signed her name at the bottom of the final sheet, next to Thornton's own. His signature was strong and confident, just like the man, and her stomach fluttered in anticipation of their next confrontation. Matching wits with him was a delightful challenge.

"It's so much better agreeing to my own marriage settlement, instead of simply reading the one my father arranged for me."

And if anything went wrong, she'd have only herself to blame.

She gave the ink one final blot, then refolded the papers and called for Gustav to have them sent back to Thornton.

Ellie slouched in her comfy leather chair. "So, now that's done, we need to discuss underwear."

"We do?" Tess wrinkled her nose.

"Your underwear, to be precise. You didn't have any new clothes for your first wedding, but this time you definitely need a trousseau. Specifically, undergarments that look like they belong to a pleasure-loving harlot."

"She's right," Daisy said with a nod. "Apart from that one set of silk drawers I bought you last Christmas from Madame Lefèvre—"

The one's she'd mercifully been wearing the night Thornton debauched her in the carriage, Tess conceded silently.

"—your underwear is all practical cotton and boring linen. There are hermits in caves with more seductive drawers than you."

"You need impractical lace. Delicate ribbons. Silk and damask so sheer you might as well be wearing nothing at all."

"Then what's the point?" Tess countered.

"*Seduction* is the point," Ellie said forcefully. "Reducing a grown man to a stammering, gibbering wreck, willing to obey your every command is the *point*. With the right underwear you can achieve total annihilation."

"Good God," Tess laughed. "It's my wedding night. Not a battlefield."

"It is both," Daisy said sternly. "And you can gain the early advantage by looking the part, even if you don't have the faintest idea what to do. Distraction is an extremely effective tactic. Men are perverse, and very visual creatures. A partly naked woman is almost more exciting to them than a completely naked woman. Don't ask me why."

Ellie nodded vigorously. "With the right underclothes, Thornton might be so befuddled he might not even notice you're a virgin."

"That's highly unlikely," Tess scoffed. "*He's* not a virgin. And he'll have seen plenty of naked and half-dressed women before."

"But none as beautiful as you," Ellie said loyally. "And he didn't want any of them enough to offer them marriage, did he?"

"I suppose not."

"So it's decided." Daisy clapped her hands in excitement. "We're going shopping. For the most scandalous, impractical, man-befuddling garments we can find. If Thornton's willing to pay you a thousand pounds a year to dress well, the least you can do is comply."

Tess threw up her hands in good-natured defeat. "Fine. I suppose I could buy a new gown for the wedding."

"That's the spirit."

⌒

Tess didn't hear a word from Thornton for the rest of the week, nor did Stockdale make contact regarding the princess's letters.

On Friday, the day before the wedding, a package

containing a flat leather box arrived at Wansford House, bearing the illustrious name of Rundell, Bridge & Rundell, one of the prince regent's favorite jewelers.

Tess read the accompanying note first, and her heart beat a little faster when she realized it was from Thornton.

Scarlet,

In anticipation of our wedding tomorrow, please accept this small token of my regard.

J

The box contained the most beautiful pearl necklace Tess had ever seen: three strands of graduated pearls, each one longer than the last. A pendant comprising a single large diamond, a delicate bow of smaller diamonds, and a huge pear-shaped pearl droplet hung from the center of the lowest strand.

Daisy gaped when she saw it. "Lord, Tess, that's beautiful! It must have cost five hundred pounds at least."

"But why does he address you as Scarlet?" Ellie frowned, reading the card over her shoulder.

Tess tried not to blush as she stroked her fingers over the smooth globes. "Oh, it's just a silly joke. A nickname he's made for me because of my red dress the first time we met."

"How sweet."

Tess nodded, but she wasn't quite sure how to feel about the gift. She had a niggling sense that she was being bought, but perhaps that was being unjust. After all, Thornton was so rich that five hundred pounds to him was the same as another man spending fifty pounds on her.

It *was* a sweet gesture, even though he probably thought she expected such gifts as her due.

Had he chosen it himself? Or merely had one of his minions select something for her? Either way, it was lovely. Perhaps she should tell him that the eighth duke hadn't given her a single thing for her wedding, apart from the title of duchess. It was her father who'd pocketed the two thousand pounds.

A shiver of excitement, or perhaps apprehension, ran through her as she imagined Thornton placing the necklace around her neck himself. His long fingers would brush the skin at the nape of her neck while the pearls would warm to her skin. Perhaps he would kiss her shoulder.

The thought of him kissing her again—anywhere at all on her body—made her pulse flutter. She might be dreading the wedding night, but there was no denying there was an element of anticipation there, too.

Her reply was equally brief.

J,

I thank you for the gift. It is beautiful.

Regards,
Tess

She refused to call herself Scarlet. As tempting as it would be to go into her wedding night with that shield, it would be too easy to hide behind the sobriquet. She was not a coward. She would face him unmasked, as Tess.

Even if she still had plenty to hide.

Chapter Twenty-One

Ellie and Daisy were her only guests at the wedding.

Thornton, too, had only invited a couple of his old school friends as witnesses: Ellie's cousin Edward, and Thomas Careby. Tess supposed Careby deserved an invitation, considering it was his party that had precipitated this unlikely turn of events.

The six of them stood in the powder-blue drawing room at Wansford House—one of Tess's favorites, since she'd redecorated it to her own taste—as Charles Manners-Sutton, the Archbishop of Canterbury, conducted the ceremony.

The general public, and indeed most of the *ton*, seemed to think it their right to be included in the wedding of a duke, but Tess was extremely grateful that Thornton hadn't wanted a huge, public wedding at St. George's, Hanover Square. She had no desire to be gawked at. There would be enough gossip as it was.

Her first wedding had been an equally low-key affair, but that had been due to the eighth duke's miserly desire to save money, rather than any particular preference for privacy. They hadn't even had a wedding breakfast. At least this time her father wasn't hovering by her side, scowling when she tripped over her words or sent desperate, longing glances at the door.

She didn't want to escape today. Rash and inadvisable it might be, but the choice was entirely her own. Thornton stood at her side looking impossibly handsome in a navy jacket so dark it was almost black. A diamond stickpin glimmered at his throat amid the neat folds of his white cravat.

He was beautiful in profile, so different from the wrinkled, powdered old duke. His voice, when he said his vows, was deep and sure, and his hand, when he took hers, was warm and steady.

To have and to hold, for better, for worse, for richer, for poorer, in sickness and in health.

Tess paused slightly on *to love and to cherish*, but when no lightning flash interrupted her, she rushed on to *until death do us part*.

It passed so quickly, almost like a dream. In less than no time he was slipping a plain gold band on her finger, and they were pronounced man and wife.

When Thornton finally turned to her, her stomach flipped at the hot satisfaction in his gaze and the irresistible curl of his lips as his face broke out into a smile.

He raised her hand to his lips and looked deep into her eyes. "My duchess."

He straightened and pressed a chaste kiss to her cheek, and she quashed a ridiculous feeing of disappointment that he hadn't broken all sense of decorum and kissed her on the lips instead.

Everyone crowded round to offer their congratulations.

The men shook hands, and Daisy and Ellie hugged her tightly, taking care not to crush the delectable cream-and-silver dress she'd purchased at vast expense from Madame Lefèvre.

Impatient for cake, Daisy ushered them all toward the wedding breakfast that had been laid out on the sideboard, but Tess was too nervous to do more than nibble at a bread roll.

"Not wearing the necklace I sent you?" Thornton's quiet voice at her shoulder made her jump.

"It's not really something one wears at eleven o'clock in the morning," she protested. "But I'll be sure to wear it for the next dinner or ball we attend."

It felt strange, saying *we* instead of *I*.

Thornton nodded. "If you're not hungry, we could make an early start to Wansford Hall. The weather is fine, but it will take several hours to get there, and I'd like to arrive before dark. I've already sent my majordomo, Simms, ahead to liaise with the staff for our arrival."

Tess nodded and went to say her goodbyes.

"Want us to follow you to Wansford and pretend the dower house is on fire?" Daisy joked quietly. "We can, you know."

"Not this time," Tess laughed. "And I've packed my pistol, in case of a real emergency."

Ellie gave her another hug. "If you need us at any time, just send word."

"And don't worry about tonight," Daisy whispered. "Just enjoy yourself. It will be wonderful."

"We'll write if we get another demand from Stockdale," Ellie added.

Daisy nudged her in the ribs. "Stop talking business! It's her wedding day, for goodness' sake."

"Sorry. But hopefully we won't hear anything from him

until you're back here next week. It would be a shame to cut short your honeymoon."

"Definitely a shame." Daisy grinned. "And don't worry about us. I'll take care of this poor, lonely cake in your absence." She took another huge bite from the slice in her hand.

Tess hugged them both and made her way out to the carriage, and her cheeks heated as she realized it was the same unmarked one Thornton had used the night he'd discovered her at Case's house.

Thornton obviously preferred discretion over conspicuous display. Considering the alarming number of coaches reportedly being held up by highwaymen on Hampstead Heath, not having a crest painted on the panels was probably a wise move.

Tess had thought he'd travel in the carriage with her, so she was a little deflated when she saw a groom holding a fine black stallion by the reins.

Thornton handed her into the carriage.

"You're not coming in here with me?"

"I prefer to ride and avoid temptation. Someone once told me that anticipation is good for a man." His lips twitched in good humor.

Tess couldn't help but laugh. "I suppose I deserve that."

"Yes, you do."

He pointed at a wicker hamper on the floor between the seats. "There's a hot brick for your feet, blankets if you get cold, and food in that hamper if you're hungry."

"You seem to have thought of everything."

"Oh, not me. Simms. I must admit that food and hot bricks have been quite far from my mind this past week."

Tess lifted her brows, and a delighted flush warmed her. His tone suggested he'd been thinking of her. Just as she'd been thinking of him.

"Busy at work?" she taunted.

"No." His gaze traveled to her mouth and lingered. "I've been distracted by all the things we're going to do when we get to Wansford Hall."

Her stomach somersaulted, but she sent him a teasing smile. "You mean meet the tenants, explore the house, that kind of thing?"

He growled low in his throat. "Amongst other things."

He shut the carriage door, and mounted his horse in one fluid movement. The carriage driver snapped his whip, and Tess waved goodbye to Ellie and Daisy, who were hovering on the doorstep.

They soon left London, heading up the Great North Road, a trip Tess had done many times over the past year. She passed the time by reading one of her favorite novels, *Pride and Prejudice*, and catching occasional glimpses of Thornton whenever he drew parallel to the carriage window. He looked just as attractive on horseback as he did in a drawing room, and the closer they got to their destination the more her nervousness increased.

Tonight they would share a bed, but whether it would be for just one night, or the beginning of a whole series of nights, depended entirely on her performance.

They stopped once, at a coaching inn to rest the horses, and she heaved a sigh of relief as the honey-colored stone of Wansford Hall finally appeared through the rippled glass of the window.

Despite her disastrous first wedding night with the old duke, she had no bad memories of the place. It felt far more like home than the house she'd shared with her father, and she'd grown to love the staff and tenants. During her months of mourning she'd kept herself busy by familiarizing herself with the running of the estate, and redecorating many of the musty, outdated rooms.

With a start, she realized Thornton would be the first person to stay in the newly refurbished master suite, which shared an adjoining sitting room with her own chamber.

Would he come to her room? Or was she expected to go to his?

The staff had all lined up on the front steps to welcome them by the time the carriage reached the end of the long drive, and Tess smiled as she introduced Thornton to everyone.

"Welcome, Your Grace!" Mrs. Jennings, the housekeeper, bobbed a deferential curtsey to Thornton, then turned to Tess with a wide smile. "And welcome home, my lady. The staff would like to extend their warmest felicitations on your wedding."

"Thank you, Mrs. Jennings."

Mrs. Ward, the cook, stepped forward. "I know you must be tired from your journey, but I hope you'll still partake of the dinner we've prepared for you both."

"Of course," Thornton said smoothly. "I'm famished. I can't wait to sample whatever you've made."

Tess watched in awe as the usually unruffled sixty-year-old cook blushed like a schoolgirl under his warm regard.

"Mrs. Ward and Mrs. Jennings are sisters," she explained.

When Thornton moved on to greet the footmen and the grooms, Mrs. Ward sent her a subtle, congratulatory wink. "An *excellent* choice, ma'am. If he's as good-natured as he is 'andsome, you'll be a lucky lass indeed."

The only person Tess didn't recognize was a tall, neat man, whom Thornton introduced as Simms, his major-domo, and she bit back a smile as she saw the irritated look her own head footman, Withers, shot this interloper.

Withers vastly preferred the delights of London to the rural calm of Cambridgeshire; no doubt he was relishing the appearance of this newcomer as a chance for some much-needed entertainment.

Thornton was waiting for her at the top of the steps and Tess assumed he was merely being polite.

"Would you like me to give you a tour of the house now?"

He sent her a sly, sideways smile. "One moment. There's something we have to do first."

Before she could ask, he bent, slid one arm around her waist, placed the other around the back of her knees, and scooped her up into his arms.

"*What are you doing?*" Tess shrieked.

"Carrying you across the threshold," he said with a grin. "I believe it's customary at times like this."

Chapter Twenty-Two

The assembled staff let out a rousing cheer as Tess was swept through the open doorway, her skirts swishing against Thornton's legs, her head cradled against his muscled shoulder. For a split second she marveled at his strength as he carried her with long, easy strides, then she remembered where they were.

She whacked him on the arm. "Put me down!"

He strode into the arched hallway and obliged, but when her feet touched the marble, he kept his arm around her waist. She was pressed against him, full length, a little out of breath. He, on the other hand, didn't appear to have expended any energy at all. He wasn't even breathing heavily.

"You look flustered, my love." He smiled down at her, looking more lighthearted than she'd ever seen him. "I assume the previous duke never did such a thing?"

Of course he hadn't. The old duke had been so decrepit his legs would have buckled if he'd tried to carry her anywhere, but Tess felt it disrespectful to say so. She sent Thornton a stern look instead, aware that the staff had entered behind them and were avidly watching their by-play.

"He did not."

She had no doubt that Thornton had just increased his standing with all those present. The women would think his grand gesture sweepingly romantic, and the men would be congratulating him for taking the manly initiative when it came to his new wife.

Tess stepped back, out of the shelter of his arms. Her whole body felt hot and bothered.

"Perhaps that tour can wait?" he suggested easily. "I'd like to bathe and change, after so long in the saddle."

"Of course."

His man, Simms, stepped forward. "I have arranged fresh clothes for you in the master suite, Your Grace."

Hannah, the undermaid who'd sent Tess such commiserating looks on her first wedding night—and who now acted as Tess's personal maid—bobbed a curtsey. "And I've done the same for you, ma'am."

Tess glanced at their still-smiling audience. "Very good. Shall we say dinner in an hour, then, Mrs. Ward? And a hot bath for his grace, and one for myself, in fifteen minutes."

"Yes, my lady."

The staff all set off to do their bidding, and Tess led Thornton up the wide staircase to the upper floors. The steady click of his boots echoed next to hers as they strode toward the west wing.

"So, are your first impressions favorable?" She was genuinely interested to hear what he thought.

"Extremely. You can't imagine how relieved I am to find the place isn't sinking into a swamp."

"What? Why on earth would you think that?" Tess spluttered.

He shrugged. "Call it my natural cynicism. I just assumed it would be as ancient and crumbling as its previous owner."

"You knew the eighth duke?"

"I'd seen him a few times in London, before I sailed for Canada. My father always told me we were distantly related, but I never gave it much thought."

"Well, I'm glad we've exceeded your expectations," Tess said dryly. "However low they may have been."

His answering smile was wolfish. "Oh, you've certainly exceeded my expectations. I only hope I can return the favor tonight."

Heat rose to her cheeks, and she hastily opened the door to the master suite.

"Here's your room. The door on the left leads to a shared sitting room, and my chamber is beyond. That door on the right leads to a private bathing room."

He nodded. "I'll see you at dinner."

Tess entered her own suite, relieved to be somewhere comfortingly familiar. With Hannah's help, she quickly bathed and re-dressed her hair, then donned one of the numerous new gowns Daisy and Ellie had insisted she buy. The beautiful amber satin rustled as she descended the stairs and made her way to the dining room.

Thornton was already there, sipping a glass of brandy, and her heart pounded at the intimacy of the scene. Instead of seating them at opposite ends of the vast eighteen-seater table, two places had been laid at one end, opposite each other, with a branched candlestick and a flower arrangement creating a romantic tête-à-tête.

Thornton raised his glass in a jaunty salute. "Good evening. You look beautiful, as ever."

"Thank you."

He pulled out her chair for her, then sat down himself,

and Tess smiled as Withers poured her a glass of wine. She needed a little Dutch courage to steady her nerves. Was every woman this jittery before their wedding night? She surely had more reason than most to be on edge.

Mrs. Ward bustled in, accompanied by two further footmen who placed a series of covered dishes on the table and removed the silver domes with a flourish.

"What have we here, Mrs. Ward?" Thornton asked.

Tess bit back her smile as the elderly cook blushed in pleasure that he'd remembered her name.

"Well, Yer Grace, there's asparagus in butter, roast parsnips and carrots, a pie of pheasant and woodcock, roasted potatoes, and peas. And for dessert, almonds, candied ginger, and a gooseberry fool. Plus, cheese with shaved truffle."

Tess smiled. "It sounds perfect."

The servants withdrew, but as soon as they were out of earshot Thornton gestured toward the food.

"Your staff seem to be in favor of our marriage."

"How so?"

His lips curved up. "Asparagus. Parsnips. Ginger. All believed to be beneficial to the male circulatory system, as it were."

Tess frowned. "What do you mean?"

"They're all aphrodisiacs," he chuckled. "I'm surprised they haven't served us oysters, too. And strawberries."

Tess gasped. "You're right! Oh, the cheeky bunch!"

She put her hands up to cool her heating cheeks, as he snorted at her mortification.

"It's a sign that they care for you." He grinned, apparently unoffended by their well-intentioned meddling. "And they clearly don't dislike me, either, which is a relief. They'd probably be serving me something laced with laudanum or some terrible laxative if they wanted me to leave you alone on your wedding night."

Tess flushed even more as she remembered serving poor Case his laudanum-laced brandy. She'd stooped to such underhand tactics herself.

The staff's attitude toward her had certainly changed since her *first* wedding night. Then, they'd all thought she was a fortune-hunting harlot, and it had taken the past eighteen months to prove to them that she was more than just another pretty, empty-headed aristocrat intent on her own enrichment. It was rather nice to know that she was so appreciated.

Unfortunately, the man sitting opposite her still thought of her as a seasoned seducer, but she longed to change his mind, too.

She'd eaten so little that morning that hunger overrode her nerves. Thornton made easy conversation about the business that had kept him busy in London that week—problems with a supplier, and a near-miss with a brewery cart that had almost knocked him down—and Tess began to relax.

When the main course was removed, he leaned forward and inspected the thinly sliced truffles that curled like dark wood shavings on top of the cheese.

"I've never actually tasted a truffle, you know."

It was Tess's turn to raise her brows. "You haven't? They're quite an acquired taste. Some people love them, while others can't stand them. These ones are harvested right here, on the estate."

"Really?"

"Yes. The locals used specially trained dogs to find truffles here for generations, but the old duke refused them access to the grounds a decade ago. He claimed they'd disturb the game birds he liked to shoot. After speaking to some of the tenants, I agreed to open up the woods again, and now the estate gets fifty percent of the profits from every truffle that's found. It's a nice source of income for everyone involved."

"That's very enterprising."

Tess felt a warm glow of satisfaction at gaining his approval. He hadn't been horrified by the thought of a woman taking an active interest in the running of the estate, which was a good sign that he might be equally accepting of her work for King & Co., but it was too soon to introduce that subject just yet.

"If you like, we can go truffle hunting sometime this week," she offered tentatively. "It's a little late in the season, but we might still be lucky."

His eyes glowed as he studied her. "I'd like that very much."

She speared a small piece of truffle with her fork. She'd grown to like the musky, pungent flavor. The smell reminded her of tramping through damp autumn leaves with Ellie and Daisy, or the scent of bonfires.

Or pressing her nose to the fabric of Thornton's jacket and inhaling his cologne.

Her stomach tightened at the memory.

When he took a piece, along with some cheese, she watched for his reaction. "They don't actually taste that strong, it's more the scent that people enjoy."

He took a tentative bite. "Hmm. It's savory, almost meaty. It pairs well with the cheese. It's a fungus, is it not? Like a mushroom?"

"Yes. They grow as lumps on the roots of other trees."

Tess finished her wine. Thornton drained his own glass, laid his napkin on the table, and rose. Her pulse fluttered as he came around the table and took her hand in his to help her rise. The touch of his skin made her jump.

"It's been a long day, and I'm sure you're ready to retire."

He kept hold of her hand as they ascended the wide stairs, and her skittishness increased with every step. When they reached the door to her chamber, she forced herself to speak.

"Will you be coming to my room later?"

His mouth curved up as he released her hand. "Not that much later. I think we've had enough anticipating, don't you?"

Tess nodded, dry-mouthed.

"Go on. I'll join you in a few minutes."

Chapter Twenty-Three

Hannah was waiting in the bedroom, and sent Tess a smile as she helped her out of her dress and into the scandalously sheer silk nightgown and equally flimsy dressing robe she'd chosen from Madame Lefèvre.

Red, of course.

Tess tightened the sash at her waist, hoping the garments would give her a much-needed boost of courage. *Dress like a seductress, feel like a seductress.*

Hannah caught her eye in the mirror as she brushed out her hair. The girl was almost buzzing with excitement.

"Oh, ma'am, I can't tell you how glad I am to see you with such a handsome new husband, after all you've done for us here."

Tess blushed, touched by her sincerity. "Thank you, Hannah."

The maid sent her a cheeky grin. "And since I'm a married lady myself now, I can wish you the *very best* of wedding nights this time! I hope you don't sleep a wink!"

Tess laughed at her bawdy humor and shooed her toward the door. "I'll see to the rest myself, thank you."

Hannah winked. "I'll 'ave Mrs. Ward cook a hearty

breakfast for the morning. You'll need to keep up yer strength."

When the door closed behind her Tess rose, willing her heart rate to calm. Ellie or Daisy would have distracted her with a silly joke, or an obscure legal fact, but neither of them were here. This was her own hill to conquer.

The door to the shared sitting room opened, and she tensed as Thornton's footsteps crossed the room and paused outside her door.

When would she start thinking of him as Justin, and not Thornton? Would physical intimacy effect the change?

She took a steadying breath, and then he was there, in her room, looking as breathtakingly handsome as ever.

Whenever she was away from him, she could almost convince herself that he wasn't as attractive as she remembered, but then he'd appear, and prove her wrong all over again.

She could only pray she had the same effect on him.

He'd removed his jacket, cravat, and shoes, but unlike the old duke, he wasn't wearing a hideous dressing robe. His white shirt lay open in a deep V that showed an inviting sliver of tawny skin, and his buff breeches conformed to the muscles of his thighs with loving faithfulness.

Daisy was right: it was impossible not to admire the masculine bulges so perfectly outlined by the soft fabric. Tess raised an imaginary glass in salute to Bond Street's tailors, and whoever had decreed that form-fitting breeches should be the masculine garment of choice. Fashion occasionally had its benefits.

Light from the lamp by her bed warmed the angles of his face as he came toward her with slow strides, and his heated perusal of her own clothing certainly suggested he liked what he saw.

A muscle ticked in his jaw as he stopped less than a foot away.

"Red." His voice was low, almost a croak, as if he were parched for water, but his lips curved in that self-mocking way he had. "I should have known. I'm beginning to see why the last duke didn't live until morning."

He reached up and touched the silk at her shoulder, then followed the exquisitely fine lace down across her clavicle toward her breastbone.

"Are you trying to kill me, Scarlet? Because you rob a man of breath."

Tess shook her head. His nearness was making her dizzy; she was almost trembling with need. How could she want something so badly, and yet dread it simultaneously?

"There's something I must tell you." She said it quickly, before she lost her nerve. She'd come up with this plan of action while she was alone in the carriage.

"Go on."

"My experience with the first duke was . . . not the most pleasant."

"I'm sorry to hear that. But hardly surprised. The man was old enough to be your grandfather. Believe me when I say that I will do everything in my power to make *this* time pleasurable for you."

He cupped her face and smoothed his thumb over her cheekbone. "I'm sure you've had far more agreeable lovers since, but I must admit to being rather competitive. I like to be good at whatever I do."

Butterflies seemed to have taken up residency in her stomach, but she managed to send him a teasing smile. "I have a request. Well, more of a suggestion, really. How do you feel about playing a little game?"

His brows rose, but whether it was in interest, or suspicion, she couldn't tell.

"What kind of game?"

"A make-believe game. Like a play, almost."

His thumb was still stroking her jaw, his palm warming her cheek, and she had to force herself to concentrate.

"Since I'd rather forget my first wedding ever happened, what if we . . . pretend that *this* is my first wedding night?"

"Pretend you're a virgin, you mean?"

She nodded, breathless with worry that he'd say no.

He frowned. "Have you done this with your other lovers? Because I can't say I've ever cared overmuch about being the first. I'd much rather be the *best*." His gaze held hers. "But if that's what you want, then I'll play along."

Tess almost sagged with relief. It was clear from his expression that he thought this some bizarre kind of seduction technique, but at least he hadn't said no outright.

He didn't believe she was a virgin for one minute, but the fact that he was willing to suspend his disbelief and accommodate her request made her respect him even more.

His mouth curved up. "So, what exactly does this fantasy entail?"

"Let's pretend that I have no idea what to do. That my education has been sadly limited to that single, naughty print I bought the other night."

"A shameful omission," he said with mock solemnity. "Your mother should have prepared you for the duties of matrimony."

"My mother died when I was a child," Tess said, with perfect honesty. "My governess blushed at the word *copulation*, and none of my close friends are married."

His brow cleared. "Makes sense."

She almost laughed at his need for logic, even when he was sure they were deep in the realm of fantasy.

"Which means you have to tell me exactly what you're doing," she continued, "so I don't get nervous."

"Very well."

"And . . . you have to say what you want *me* to do . . . to you."

"Understood." Heat, and a faint amusement filled his eyes. "In that case, allow me to inform you—suitably in advance—that I'm going to kiss you."

His thumb stroked the corner of her lip, and hot and cold shivers chased over her skin. He bent until she could feel his tickly warm exhale.

"This freckle is the most provocative thing I've ever seen. It just sits there, begging to be kissed."

Tess smiled. "You know, historically, the placement of a lady's patch just there was called *la coquette*."

"The tease," he translated. "Very apt."

He kissed it, and she sucked in a shaky breath. He pressed a line of soft kisses up her cheekbone until he reached the freckle at the outer corner of her eye.

"And this one?"

"That one's *la passionée*, I think. The passionate one." Tess could hardly think. She was almost shivering with nerves and excitement.

"Interesting. Now, brace yourself, because I'm going to kiss you again. Most ardently."

Tess closed her eyes, and his lips met hers in a kiss that started out soft but almost immediately degenerated into something hotter and darker. His tongue stroked hers, a slow delirious tasting, and she pressed closer, loving the feel of his body against hers.

Yes! She'd dreamed of this ever since Careby's!

Her silk robe and nightgown were so thin that the heat of him seeped into her, and her nipples tightened as she rubbed against his chest. The cotton of his shirt provided a delicious friction.

She returned his kiss with equal fervor, and slid her arms around his waist. He caught her hips and pulled her up against him, then ran his palms up her ribs to cup her breasts.

Tess breathed a sigh of happiness against his mouth.

Growing bolder, she slid her hands under his shirt, exploring the smooth, warm skin and strong muscles that bracketed his spine. He made a low growl of pleasure, and when she reached down and squeezed the firm mounds of his bottom, he smiled against her lips.

"Vixen! Get on that bed."

His words shocked Tess out of her sensual haze, and she pulled back, but Thornton registered her wide eyes and let out a wry chuckle.

"Oh, right, I forgot. Virgin." He seemed to be reminding himself of the plan, but his playfulness made her heart swell with affection. "Let's try that again."

He pressed a gentle kiss to her lips, then stroked down her arm until his fingers threaded through hers. "As fetching as this robe is, I'd very much like to remove it. Would that be acceptable?"

Tess nodded. "Yes. But only if I can remove your shirt."

"For a virgin, you're very curious," he teased.

"A girl can be curious as well as inexperienced, can she not?"

"True. I just hope your maidenly sensibilities can cope with such an excess of stimulation."

Tess laughed. "It's a risk I'm willing to take."

Chapter Twenty-Four

He untied the sash at her waist and eased the robe over her shoulders. It dropped to the floor with a silken hiss. Determined to keep things equal, Tess tugged at his sleeve.

"Come on, off with it."

He reached over his head and removed his shirt, tossing it carelessly aside, and her senses reeled at the sudden expanse of his chest, so close. He was so beautiful it made her a little dizzy. He looked like one of the Greek athletes she'd seen carved in plaster at her neighbor Sir John Soane's house.

"How are you feeling, little virgin? A bit faint?" The amusement in his voice showed he was enjoying the game, and his eyes held nothing but admiration. "Breathing helps, you know."

Tess sucked in a shaky breath.

"Since this is all quite new," he said dryly, "I should tell you that you're allowed to touch me." He held his arms out to the sides. "Anywhere you like. I'm yours to explore."

Tess didn't need telling twice. Fascinated, she pressed

her hands to the flat planes of his chest, testing the hardness with her palms. His skin was warm, almost hot, and he had an intriguing line of hair running from his belly button down into the waistband of his breeches.

The scent of his skin made her stomach flutter, and she skimmed her fingers along the bumps of his ribs, then back up to circle his tawny nipples. He hissed in a breath, as if she'd caused him pain, and she paused.

"Does that hurt?"

"Not at all. It feels good. Are you ready for the next step?" His fingers toyed with the ribbon of her nightgown at her shoulder.

"Yes."

He gave the little bow a tug, and it started to untie. "This may shock you, but the next bit requires the removal of this very un-virginal nightgown."

"Should I have worn my plain white cotton chemise?" Tess teased, loving the way his eyes darkened as he stroked her collarbone.

"Absolutely not."

He released first one ribbon, then the other, and the silk slid down her body to pool at her feet. Hot and cold flashed across her skin, puckering her nipples as he gazed at her in silence. Instinctively, she moved to hide her nakedness, but he shook his head.

"Don't," he murmured. "You're beautiful. So beautiful. God. My imagination didn't do you justice."

There was no mockery in his tone, and the way he was looking at her was almost reverent. It gave her some much-needed confidence.

"So, what comes next?"

He shook his head, as if to clear it. "Now I touch you. And kiss you. Everywhere."

"Shouldn't you be naked, too?"

"Not if you want this to last longer than five minutes," he said wryly. "Remember the last time you touched me? At Careby's? I was like a virgin myself."

Tess bit her lip, amused at his self-deprecation. Most men made a point of insinuating their endless stamina in the bedroom, but Thornton was confident enough to joke about the exact opposite.

"I don't care how long you last," she said, with perfect honesty. "I just want you to touch me."

"Your wish is my command. If there's anything you don't like, just tell me and I'll stop. Agreed?"

"Agreed."

She'd barely completed the word when he cupped the back of her head, threaded his fingers through her hair, and pulled her in for a kiss. Her breasts squashed against his chest and she groaned at the extraordinary sensation of skin against skin. Her bare toes curled into the Aubusson rug.

Every inch of her was sensitive to his touch as he skimmed his free hand along the dip of her waist, then around, to mold the curve of her bottom. She went up on tiptoe, trying to get closer still, stroking his back and shoulders in return.

The soft edge of the mattress bumped the back of her legs, and she vaguely registered that he'd turned them both around. And then he was lowering her down, onto the cool, smooth coverlet, covering her with his big body.

Tess squirmed against him, pleasantly surprised that his weight was thrilling, and not threatening. He was unquestionably stronger than her, but despite the ardency of his passion, it was clear he was showing some restraint.

Just to be sure, she panted, "Wait!"

He stilled instantly, lifting himself up onto his forearms

above her so that she lay caged beneath him. She felt like a feast, laid out on the bed for his delectation.

"What?" He seemed a little out of breath, which she took to be a good thing. It wasn't fair that she was the only one panting.

"Nothing. Just checking to see if you meant what you said about stopping."

"You like what I'm doing?"

"Absolutely. Carry on."

"Thank God."

He lowered himself and kissed her again, his bare chest pressing hers, his breeches-clad thighs settling between her legs. She slid her fingers into the front waistband of his breeches, loving how the muscles of his stomach tensed at her touch. And then she stroked lower, cupping the hard bulge of him through the cloth, and he ground against her hand.

"Wicked girl. Yes."

Tess bit her lip, delighted by his praise. She would have explored more, but when she tried to slip her hand into his falls, he moved away with a chiding sound.

"A virgin like you isn't ready for the sight of an erect cock just yet."

"I think I am."

He shook his head. "You're going to have to curb your maidenly curiosity a while longer. I'm not done with you." He hovered over her breast and the teasing play of his breath made her skin pebble. "Fair warning. I'm going to kiss you here."

He flicked her with his tongue, then sucked her nipple into his mouth, and she bit back a groan of pleasure. Her blood was pounding, thick and slow like treacle, and a yearning ache was gnawing at her insides.

He sent her a wicked glance. "Like that, little virgin?"

She could only nod.

"Now, you've admitted to owning a naughty print, so perhaps you can guess where I'm going to kiss you next."

His hands stroked her waist as he slid lower, his shoulders pushing between her knees, and she fought a hot wave of embarrassment. In the carriage it had been dark, but here the light played over her body, illuminating the curves of her belly, breasts, and thighs. There was no hiding in the shadows.

"Your skin is so soft," he murmured. "Like peaches and cream. I want to eat you all up."

He pressed a kiss to her stomach, and her muscles quivered in reaction. His hand moved to the inside of her thigh, and then his clever fingers slid between her folds, and she pressed the back of her head into the covers in desperation.

Oh, that felt so good!

Ever since he'd pleasured her in the carriage, she'd been dreaming of the bliss he'd given her, and when his tongue joined his fingers, she was unable to stop her sharp exhale of delight.

"In case you were wondering," he said softly, his breath tickling the inside of her thigh, "this wetness is your body getting ready for mine." His finger circled, rubbing and sliding in the most frustrating manner possible.

Tess ground her teeth. "Stop teasing!"

He chuckled. "What a demanding thing you are. But since you've never done this before, I have to explain it to you."

His tone was one of patient, superior martyrdom, and she bit back a laugh. How could he make her smile, even as he held her body on a knife-edge?

"My cock—the one you haven't seen yet—is going to fit perfectly in here."

He slid the very tip of his finger inside her, and Tess gasped at the extraordinary sensation. A heavy ache, like a heartbeat, throbbed where he touched.

"I know it seems unlikely," he continued in a conversational tone, "but you're just going to have to trust me. I'm the one with all the experience here."

He pressed again, and Tess dug her heels into the sheets as pleasure tightened her skin.

And then a flash of panic jolted her. Surely he'd encounter the physical proof of her virginity at any moment?

She held her breath, waiting to be denounced, but his finger just slid smoothly in and out, building the same maddening pressure he'd conjured in the carriage. There was no pain, no tearing sensation.

Would that only happen when he put himself inside her? God, she hated being so ignorant. She should have asked Daisy far more questions.

When she'd imagined her first time with Thornton, she'd expected a blur, a frantic coupling in the dark. She should have known better. He wasn't a man to rush things. This slow seduction was less hot desperation and more deliberate slide into pleasure.

Just as the tension between her legs was becoming almost unbearable, he pulled back, and Tess almost hit him in frustration.

He chuckled. "Oh no. Not without me. This time we're doing it together."

Chapter Twenty-Five

In one smooth move he rolled off her and made quick work of the buttons of his falls. Her eyes widened as he lifted his hips and stripped his breeches down his thighs, releasing an impressively erect manhood.

She must have made a sound, because he turned his head and looked at her with a cheeky smile. "I warned you. At least now you're lying down if you faint."

Tess couldn't seem to look away. His body was long and lean and gloriously muscled, every line running seamlessly into the other. His cock jutted up toward his belly, and his thighs and lower legs were covered in a smattering of dark hair.

"How's your heart?" he chuckled. "Able to bear the strain?"

Tess pressed her palm to her breastbone, and discovered it pounding. Her skin was hot, glowing, as if she had a furnace inside her.

"Now I'm going to put myself inside you," he said. "And I'm going to make you say my name."

Her stomach somersaulted at his confidence, but she rallied gamely. "What is it again?"

He rolled on top of her, covering her with heat and glorious muscle.

"Vixen," he scolded with a laugh. The head of his cock slid into the notch between her legs and she squirmed with mingled anticipation and excitement.

"Josiah!" she squeaked, mainly to distract herself.

He pressed forward. She was tense, but her flesh yielded with only the slightest resistance.

"No," he growled. "Try again."

He slid a little deeper. There was pressure, a strange new sensation of fullness, but no pain. Still, she waited for him to pull back in shock and angry confusion and call her a cheat, a liar. But he merely rocked his hips again, and she almost cried with relief when she felt nothing but pleasure.

"John?" It was hard to keep the delight out of her voice. *Daisy had been right! Her secret was safe!*

He pulled out then pushed forward again, the most delicious punishment imaginable. "Again."

"Jeremy."

"No." He slid fully into her and groaned deep in his throat. Pleasure shimmered along her veins as she absorbed the astonishing sensation.

"I'm fairly sure your name is Joseph," she panted.

He nipped her earlobe lightly with his teeth and she shivered. Every new slide of his body provided the perfect combination of friction, and she lifted her hips, trying to magnify the thrumming, throbbing ache that was growing inside her.

"Scarlet," he growled, a clear warning. "Say it."

It was becoming harder and harder to think of names beginning with *J*, but Tess was ludicrously lighthearted.

"Jonah?"

He threaded his fingers through her hair and kissed her,

hard, his tongue probing her mouth in the same wicked rhythm as he pumped his hips. Tess closed her eyes and captured his head in return, pulling him into her, drowning in pleasure.

Here was the passion she'd expected, this heat-slicked frenzy of delirium.

He tore his mouth from hers. "Who's your husband, Scarlet? Say my name."

"Tess," she gasped stubbornly. She was almost there, almost at the highest peak, but she was determined not to cave. "It's Tess. Not Scarlet."

Each thrust touched a spot inside her that drew her tighter, higher.

"Say it," he demanded. An order, a curse.

So close. So close she could barely think.

"*Please,*" he groaned.

She hurtled over the edge. Her muscles contracted as pleasure pounded through her, pulse after pulse, beating against the inside of her skin like a million butterfly wings, and she gave him what he'd asked for.

"Justin!"

Her climax seemed to trigger his own. His body tensed as rhythmic shudders racked his frame and he made a muffled sound of pleasure against her neck.

His weight seemed to increase as he fully relaxed, pressing her deeper into the bed, and she was struck by an odd wave of affection at his vulnerability. She doubted he let his guard down very often.

She stared up at the ceiling in mingled wonder and relief. *A virgin no more!* And he hadn't seemed to notice. *Thank God.*

He was still pressed inside her, but when she lifted her hand and stroked his shoulder he seemed to come back to his senses.

"God, that was perfect."

He pulled away and rolled to the side, and she winced at the unfamiliar soreness between her legs, and the wetness.

She turned her head to look at him. His eyes were closed, and a faint flush warmed his cheekbones. Her heart gave an odd little patter.

Her limbs felt like lead. She wanted to sink into the bed and sleep for a week, but the cool air was starting to make her feel chilly.

Would he join her under the covers? Would he sleep with her all night?

She rolled onto her side, toward him, and he opened his eyes and fixed her with a sleepy stare. His lips curved upward.

"Now what?" she whispered.

His gusty sigh made his chest rise and fall. "Now we sleep. For a little while."

"Are you staying in here? With me?"

He rolled onto his own side to face her, and she tried not to flush at the reminder that they were both naked. He reached out and stroked a strand of hair away from her temple.

"I know it's not usual for a married couple to share a chamber, and I certainly don't plan on joining you every night, but I would like to do so tonight."

Tess nodded, trying to look as if she was well versed in postcoital etiquette. Was she supposed to get up and clean herself? She needed to use the chamber pot. Embarrassment heated her cheeks. How should she suggest—?

"I'll give you a moment to clean up, and then I'll join you." He rolled off the bed and she almost kissed him in relief for anticipating her needs.

"Thank you."

He didn't bother to pull on his shirt as he strode back to the connecting door and she couldn't help but admire the musculature of his buttocks and back. Her fingers itched to touch him.

He must have spent some time without his shirt—maybe on board ship?—because there was a distinct demarcation between the darker tanned skin of his upper body and the level that would indicate the waistband of his breeches. For some reason it made her smile. It made him more human, more approachable.

Less perfect.

She made quick work of using the chamber pot and used a handkerchief to wipe the evidence of his pleasure from her skin. She still expected to see a hint of blood on the white cotton, but there was nothing to betray her secret and her heart soared with relief.

This must be how jewel thieves or criminals felt after a successful heist: this heady sense of delight at getting away with something utterly improbable. She quashed the urge to giggle like a madwoman.

To give Thornton his due, he might not have reacted as badly as many men if he *had* guessed her secret. He had a pragmatic sense of self-preservation himself. He might have understood. Still, she was glad she didn't have to put it to the test.

She retrieved her silk nightgown from the floor and slipped it back on, which was probably a pointless gesture, since he was doubtlessly only going to remove it again, but she might as well get her money's worth. She slipped beneath the covers moments before he reentered the room.

He was still naked, and she studied him, unashamed by her curiosity. He, in turn, seemed perfectly at ease with his nakedness. Not that he had any reason to be ashamed—he was gorgeous.

He stopped a foot from the side of the bed, and since she was already lying down, his privates were almost at eye level. Heat filled her cheeks as she realized he was becoming aroused again, and she bit her lip to stop a smile as she remembered Daisy's old complaint about Greek statues and small fig leaves. Thornton certainly wasn't in *that* category.

"Looked your fill, Your Grace?"

Tess pulled the covers up to her chin and tried to sound bored and sophisticated. "You'll do, I suppose."

He tugged back the covers and she squealed as he slid in beside her. "Cheeky wench. Come here."

He slid an arm around her waist and pulled her into his embrace, and she shivered in pleasure as their bodies met. The musky scent of him, of them, filled her nose and made her stomach somersault.

She flattened her hand against his chest, and smiled up at him.

"What?" he asked, brows raised.

"Whoever said you were lacking a heart was wrong." She leaned forward and pressed a kiss to his warm skin. "I can feel it beating right here. For me."

∾

Justin stared down into Tess's eyes and felt as if he was diving deep into the ocean. Or falling from a height. Some mildly uncomfortable sensation, at least. One that squeezed his lungs and pressed on his chest.

Usually after bedding a woman he felt nothing but blissful exhaustion. A desire to roll over and fall asleep. But with her he didn't want to waste a single minute.

His heart *was* pounding at her nearness, at her touch, and he marveled at the inexplicable jumble of emotions that lodged in his chest even as he attempted to identify them: Triumph? Yes. Satisfaction? Definitely.

Infatuation?

Quite possibly.

He could barely believe that this was real, that she was here, warm and naked in his bed. He'd fantasized about this situation so often that his brain almost refused to believe it was anything other than a dream.

But her skin was smooth and soft beneath his, her gorgeous lips *right there* to be kissed, and he smoothed his thumb over the lower one with a sense of wonder.

She might like to pretend to be a virgin, but he was the one who felt as if he were discovering things for the first time.

He'd lost his own virginity to a flirtatious dairymaid when he was seventeen, and his subsequent lovers had all been women of equal experience. He should have found Tess's "innocence" annoying, a calculated act to rouse his interest, but there was something so refreshing about her, a playfulness and curiosity that made him uncharacteristically lighthearted. He'd allowed himself to be drawn into her illusion willingly.

Making love with her once wasn't nearly enough. He was greedy for all of her secrets, for knowledge no other man possessed. He wanted to know how she liked to be touched, how hard she liked to be kissed. What made her eyelids flutter and her pulse pound in her throat. How her breathing changed when she dreamed.

He wanted all of her.

And tonight was only the beginning.

Chapter Twenty-Six

When Tess awoke, she was alone, but the sheets beside her were still warm, as if Thornton had only just left. She was naked, and her skin heated as she recalled everything that had happened during the night.

The second time he'd made love to her he'd been slower, more methodical. As if he'd been determined to take her to the very edge of madness. He'd kissed every inch of her, both through the silken nightgown, and without. He'd trailed his fingers over her curves, lingering with absolute focus on the areas that made her writhe and buck and sigh.

Tess had joked that if he paid his account books the same close attention as he paid her, then it was no wonder he was so successful. His answering smile had made her glow.

He'd extinguished the light by the bed, and she'd dozed in his arms, luxuriating in a half-waking dream of warmth and lazy caresses.

Dawn had just begun to lighten the edges of the curtains the last time he'd woken her. Tess had been fuzzy-headed, but his rough voice by her ear had brought her back to full wakefulness. He was behind her, close against her back, his hand lazily cupping her breast. His hardness pressed against her bottom.

She should have been shocked, but it seemed so natural, so completely *right* to be there with him that she couldn't summon an ounce of outrage. Her body was perfectly attuned to his embrace.

"Are you sore?" he whispered.

His hand skimmed her hip and a shiver of excitement trickled down her spine.

"A little," Tess answered truthfully, but when he started to draw back, she caught his arm. "But not enough to tell you to stop."

His answer was a low rumble. "Excellent wife."

He pressed a soft kiss to her temple even as his cock slid between her thighs.

Tess let out a little gasp of surprise. "Like this?"

He smiled against her neck. "Are we still playing the virgin game? Or have you never done it this way with anyone else?"

Tess bit her lip. "Never done it."

True. She'd never even *imagined* people made love this way. She really should have stolen more of those erotic drawings from Case's—

Her train of thought dissolved as he slid into her.

"God, you're so sweet. So tight."

His impassioned growl made her body clench around him and she arched her back, instinctively searching for a better angle. He caught her hip and pressed forward. "Don't want to hurt you."

"You won't."

"Tell me to stop if—"

"Just show me."

He seemed to have lost the ability to speak eloquently, and she bit back a smile. She loved the fact that the tightly controlled businessman had dissolved into base, inarticulate male. Perhaps she *did* have the ability to befuddle a man after all. With or without a silk negligee. He still hadn't said her name, but there would be other chances to even the books.

The sound of muted conversation from the adjacent room jolted her from her recollections; Thornton was there with his majordomo, Simms. Tess dressed without waiting for Hannah's assistance, and her stomach fluttered as she descended the stairs for breakfast.

Thornton arrived in the breakfast room only a few minutes later, looking as stern and as perfectly turned out as ever, and she was seized with a disconcerting desire to dishevel him. To ruffle his hair and untie his cravat and tug his jacket askew, so he looked more like the lover who'd ravished her in bed, and less like the starchy industrialist he appeared this morning.

But his forbidding appearance softened as his lips curved up, and she noticed the heat in his eyes. Blood rushed to her own cheeks as she noted the unusually high number of servants who just happened to be hovering around. Everyone clearly wanted to see how the wedding night had progressed.

"Good morning, Your Grace." Thornton's smile was for her alone.

"Good morning." Tess bobbed a curtsey so brief it was clearly a mockery.

How ridiculous was it to be so formal when he'd been *inside her* only a few hours ago? Still, it was a charade they were expected to play.

They both sat.

Withers poured her some tea. Thornton asked for coffee.

Mrs. Ward bustled in with a covered plate and placed it with great ceremony between them on the table. She bobbed a curtsey at Thornton.

"I've made that breakfast you asked for, Your Grace."

Tess raised her brows at him in silent question.

"I requested one of my particular favorites," he said with a smile. "In Canada they call it *pain perdu*. Lost bread. It's bread dipped in milk and eggs, then fried."

Mrs. Ward nodded. "We call it French toast, here." She whipped off the domed lid and Tess inhaled the delicious aroma.

"That smells marvelous, Mrs. Ward. I'm famished."

The cook sent her an amused, congratulatory wink. "I should hope so, my lady."

When the servants had left, Thornton gestured to a small stoneware jug on the table. "I have another present for you. A new experience. Something you've probably never tried before."

Tess bit back a private smile. She'd had a *lot* of new experiences in the past twelve hours.

"What is it?" She removed the cork stopper, and took a tentative sniff.

"It's a syrup, all the way from Canada. It comes from the sap of a certain kind of maple tree. The people there have produced it for centuries, and I must admit I've developed quite a liking for it. It's sweet, like honey, but with an entirely unique taste."

Intrigued, Tess poured a small puddle onto her plate. She was just wondering how to sample it when Thornton rose and came to stand by her chair. He dipped his finger into the amber liquid and held it in front of her mouth.

"Try it."

His eyes twinkled with amusement and the hint of a dare.

Her stomach somersaulted. She was clearly supposed to lick it off.

Never taking her eyes from his, she leaned forward and touched the tip of her tongue to his finger. Her heart pounded with dark delight.

"What does it taste like?" His voice was rougher than before.

"Hmm. It's very sweet, almost like caramel, or burnt sugar. It's a stronger taste than honey."

She took another lick, and a muscle ticked in his jaw.

"The syrup is boiled to increase the flavor. It's wonderfully complex."

Like you, Tess thought. Complex. Strong, almost overpowering. But sweetly addictive, too.

It felt so naughty, to be *tasting* him, in broad daylight. Any of the staff could come in at any moment.

Seized by a wicked impulse, she sucked his fingertip into her mouth, swirling her tongue to remove the last remnants of syrup.

His playfulness vanished: tension arced between them like summer lightning. His eyes darkened, and he let out a groan that warmed her from the inside out.

"Do you like it?" he growled.

Tess released his finger and gazed up at him. "Very much."

His gaze was fixed on her lips, so she licked them, just to be perverse, and relished the way his own mouth parted in a little pant. She flicked a teasing glance down at his falls, and was gratified to see the bulge he couldn't hide. She glanced back up at him with a smile.

"I think you like it, too."

"Very much."

He dipped his finger back into the syrup, but when she moved to taste it again, he shook his head and stroked it over her lower lip instead, anointing it with the liquid like a balm.

And then he bent down and kissed her. His tongue licked away the stickiness, then slid inside, and the smoky taste of the syrup mingled with the heady taste of him and made her head swirl.

Tess kissed him back, despite the awkward angle of her seated position, and it was only the discordant crash of her silverware hitting the floor that broke them apart.

Thornton stepped back and she cursed her clumsy elbow as he retook his seat as if nothing had happened. He clearly had more willpower than she did.

He cleared his throat. "I'm glad it meets with your approval."

Tess managed to nod, even though her lips were still tingling. "It does, thank you."

She racked her brain for a new topic of conversation. As much as she'd have liked to go straight back to bed, she and Thornton couldn't make love *all* day. She was determined to prove that there could be more than passion between them, but to do that they needed to spend time together. To become friends—if that were even possible with a man like him, who guarded his emotions so fiercely he probably thought an elevated heartbeat was a cause for concern, instead of satisfaction.

"Do you have anything planned for today?"

He glanced up from his plate. "I'd like to spend an hour or so looking over the books, to get an understanding of the place."

Tess nodded. Business before pleasure. "You'll find it's

all in order. I've been working with Mr. Arden, the land agent, to ensure the smooth running of the estate. Will you be free this afternoon?"

"Yes."

"In that case, I'll arrange for a surprise for *you*."

Chapter Twenty-Seven

Justin's morning ensconced in the estate office with Arden, the land agent, proved most enlightening. The steward had been full of praise for Tess, and while it was clear the older man was not immune to her beauty, it was her sound business sense that had earned Tess his undying devotion.

"I don't mind sayin', I thought she were an empty-headed bit o' fluff when she first arrived," the older man chuckled in recollection. "But she soon put me to rights. The old duke was barely cold in 'is grave when she came down here and asked to see the books, just as you have, my lord. She read them cover to cover. And then she demanded to know what else she should read to be a better landlord."

Justin raised his brows.

Arden pointed to the rows of leather-bound tomes behind them on the shelves. "She read 'em all. And then she ordered a whole crate more from London, and read those, too. And *then* she came to me with a list of things we could do to improve the estate."

"Did you implement them?"

Arden nodded. "I did. Truth be told, Yer Grace, it was a relief to have someone interested in the place for a change. The old duke barely paid us any mind, as long as the tenants paid their rent and the harvests came in, but he never permitted me to make any changes at all, or agreed to any kind of investment."

"What kind of changes did the duchess make?"

"Well, first she said it was a disgrace that there was no school in the village. The last one closed when old Miss Evans died, see, and the duke never appointed her replacement. Her Grace had the old schoolhouse re-painted, and hired two new tutors to teach the children. She said they'd 'ave better prospects if they knew how to read and write."

Justin nodded. "What else?"

"She found a civil engineer to change the old under-shot design on the watermill to a new breastshot type, which proved twice as efficient, and we added a second pair of stones, so now we grind oats as well as corn."

"An excellent decision."

"She also suggested we change the crop rotations, to improve grain yields, so now we plant wheat, barley, turnips, and clover in successive years, and there's no need for the fields to be left fallow."

Justin nodded. He had as little knowledge of crops and tenants as Tess had when she'd first arrived, but he could read a ledger at a glance. There was no denying her success.

He tapped the topmost account book. "The improvements have almost doubled the estate's profitability in two years."

Arden gave a pleased nod. "Aye. They have. And you have happy tenants to show for it. Poaching is almost unheard of, now people have food in their bellies. Add in the fact that she's brought back truffle hunting, and you'll be hard-pressed to find anyone who doesn't love your duchess. You're a lucky man to have a woman like that at your side. A lucky man indeed."

Justin smiled, not wanting to spoil the steward's romantic misconception about the nature of his agreement with Tess. She was only at his side because of their agreement. They would part when the summer was done.

For the first time that did not feel like the escape he'd envisioned. Not because of her obvious head for business, but because he was beginning to like having her around.

Justin shook his head to dislodge that unacceptable thought. "Thank you, Arden. That will be all."

The older man stood and dusted off his hat. "Good day, Yer Grace."

❧

"Are you ready for your surprise?"

Tess couldn't help smiling as she met Justin in the hallway. She hadn't seen him all morning, and she was eager for his company.

He pulled on his topcoat. "I am. You said to dress for a walk, so here I am. Where are we going?"

"Truffle hunting. I've arranged to meet Mr. Collins, the gamekeeper, who also happens to be one of the county's best truffle hunters, in the woods behind the dower house."

They descended the front steps and set off across the formal lawns.

Justin's stride was longer than hers, but he shortened it to keep pace with her. Tess glanced at the clear blue sky. "We have a lovely day for it."

They skirted the flower beds and passed through the

orchard, and she smiled as the dower house came into view. Built from the same mellow, golden stone as the main hall, it was nowhere near as grand, just a comfortable cottage with a pretty rose arch over the front gate. A thread of smoke floated from the chimney.

"I'd be quite happy living here, if you change your mind and decide to live in the hall," she said.

Justin tilted his chin at the smoke. "Isn't someone living here?"

"It's being let to one of the new schoolteachers at the moment, but she'll be moving to live with her sister, in the village, in a few months to help with her new baby."

Justin shook his head. "I don't plan to live in the hall. I have a perfectly good house in Bristol that serves my needs, and the town house on Curzon Street for when I have business in London."

Tess's spirits sank, but she tried not to show it. She doubted she'd ever get to see his house in Bristol. He seemed determined to keep the different parts of his life neatly compartmentalized.

A lively bark interrupted her thoughts as a pale ball of fur hurtled out of the trees and launched itself at her.

"Oliver!"

The puppy paid no heed to the sharp command of his owner, and instead leapt up at Tess, pressing muddy paw prints all over her cloak and skirts.

She bent to pet the exuberant little creature with a laugh. "Well, hello, Oliver! You must be Mr. Collins's newest recruit."

The gamekeeper emerged from the trees with another, slightly larger dog trotting obediently at his heels. He shook his head when he saw the puppy's leaping.

"Apologies, Your Grace! That's Oliver. He's here to

learn from Nell, but he's the worst pup I've ever tried to train. Always getting lost, chasing squirrels, and biting twigs."

The creature abandoned Tess and went to sniff at Justin.

"Still, he's only young."

"I wonder if it's because he's a male," Tess chuckled. "Short attention span, easily distracted."

Thornton gave her a mock scowl at being so maligned. "He's merely lacking guidance and discipline. He'll learn."

The dog was adorable, like a small poodle, with very curly hair, variegated in patches of brown and white. Just as Justin bent to ruffle its shaggy coat, the little creature cocked its leg and peed all over the front of his shiny leather boots.

Mr. Collins's eyes widened in horror, and Tess froze, waiting to see how Thornton would react. Her father would have grabbed the dog by the scruff of the neck and shaken it in a rage, but Justin merely raised his brows. And then his lips curved up in amusement.

"Hoby uses champagne blacking to polish boots, Oliver. I'm not sure *that* will have the same effect."

Tess let out a relieved laugh, while Oliver plopped down on his round little bottom and stared up at Justin in clear adoration, as if expecting praise for his brilliant trick.

"Naughty boy." Justin smiled, shaking his head. "Go find a tree next time."

The puppy simply stared up at him with his deep brown eyes, tongue lolling.

"Your Grace, this is Mr. Collins, our gamekeeper," Tess said quickly. "He lives near Hollyfield with his wife and six children."

Justin nodded a greeting and the older man touched the rim of his hat in deference.

"And this is Nell." She pointed to the second dog.

"What type of dog are they?" Justin asked as they started walking into the trees.

"They're a poodle mix that originated in Italy, Your Grace," Collins said. "My family have bred them for years."

"The French and Italian truffle hunters often use pigs," Tess added. "But pigs love the truffles so much that they tend to gobble them up as soon as they find them, whereas the dogs can be persuaded to leave the truffle in exchange for another treat."

"Which is why I have a pocketful of cheese, to bribe Nell and Oliver here." Collins patted his coat.

It was a glorious afternoon. The trees were still bare, the ground carpeted in a rusty brown layer of leaves. Rays of sunshine slanted through the branches, and motes danced in the beams. The dogs trotted by their heels, and Tess's spirits soared. She loved being immersed in such a peaceful, natural environment.

"So, what makes this a good spot for truffles?" Justin asked.

"This is a beech forest, and chalky soil," Collins said. "Perfect conditions for truffle growing."

"We might not find any today, though," Tess cautioned. "Autumn and winter are the best time, when it's wetter. We're right at the end of the season."

Collins nodded. "We'll see. You always seem to bring us luck, Your Grace." He glanced down at the dog. "Nell, go find!"

Nell put her nose to the ground and set off, snuffling quickly through the fallen leaves. Oliver bounded after her, clearly enjoying the sport, even if he wasn't precisely sure what he was supposed to be doing. His tail wagged in constant excitement.

"How do you know when she's found a truffle?"

"She'll stop and start to scratch at the ground, then she'll look at my pocket for her reward." Collins smiled. "She's a clever one, is Nell. By the end of the day, if she's found a dozen or so, she doesn't even eat the cheese, but she still expects to receive it."

They ambled along, and Tess dropped back to admire Thornton's broad shoulders and long legs. With a view like that, she didn't really care if they found any truffles or not. He was as irresistible here as he was in an evening jacket in a London ballroom, but it was nice to see him relaxing a little. His intensity seemed to have mellowed a little.

"Look, she's digging!"

The three of them hurried over to where the dog was scrabbling with its front paws. Collins pulled out his tool, a wooden stick with an iron point at one end rather like a spear, and began to scrape away the soil. He had to push Oliver's inquisitive nose away a few times, but sure enough, two or three inches below the surface, he uncovered a small gnarled ball, about the size of a large walnut.

"It's a good 'un!" he beamed. "Well done, Nell!"

Both dogs received a chunk of cheese, while Justin inspected the truffle. It looked like a tiny, knobbly lump of coal, with a texture like a cauliflower.

Tess tried to concentrate on the truffle, and not on Thornton's hands. Memories of them on her skin produced a fluttery sensation in her stomach.

"These are 'summer truffles,'" she said, flustered. "They're very similar to the black truffles that can be found in France, and there are only a few places in England they can be found."

Thornton raised it to his nose and took a sniff. "How much would this sell for?"

"We get half a sovereign per pound, down in Covent Garden," Mr. Collins explained. "On a good day we can find upward of ten pounds of truffles. Then some days we don't find any. That's the luck of the draw."

"The largest one he ever found weighed almost a full pound," Tess added with a proud smile. "It was the size of my fist."

Collins took the truffle, wrapped it in a red handkerchief, and put it in the pocket of his coat that didn't contain the dogs' cheese. "I'll send Harry down to London in the morning."

Tess nodded. "Excellent." She glanced at Thornton. "Shall we return to the house? I know Mrs. Ward is planning something nice for dinner."

"Of course." He held out his hand to Collins and the other man shook it with a smile. "Thank you, Mr. Collins. This has been most instructive."

The gamekeeper and his dogs ambled out of sight, and Tess gave a happy sigh. "That was an incredible find, on your very first ever hunt. You must be one of the luckiest men in England."

"You're not the first person to have made that particular observation," he said. "But this is the first time I've actually believed it might be true."

Chapter Twenty-Eight

Surprised by his admission, Tess glanced over at him, and her heart missed a beat at the heated intensity in his face. It was the way he looked when he was about to kiss her.

She backed up as he stalked her slowly, like a hunter after game, but when she bumped against the trunk of a large beech tree, she made no attempt to escape. She wanted to kiss him, too.

"Your cheeks are pink," he teased, closing the distance. "Are you too warm?"

"I must have caught the sun."

"We've been in the shade all afternoon."

"Wind-chapped, then."

His brows quirked upward in mockery as he cocked his head, listening for the breeze. Damningly, not a single leaf fluttered around them; even the forest seemed to be holding its breath.

"I want to thank you," he murmured.

"For what?" Tess was sure she could hear her heart beating against her ribs.

"For taking care of Wansford so well."

She sent him a dry, cynical look. "For making it more profitable for you, you mean."

"No, for improving the lives of the people who live here. You are an extraordinary woman."

Tess's cheeks flushed even more at the compliment. "There's still so much more to do. Mr. Collins wants you to petition parliament to get the dog tax repealed, and—"

"Tess."

His calm, amused tone stopped her babbling.

"Yes?"

He'd never said her name before. Did he even know he'd done it?

"You can tell me all about the dog tax another time. Right now, I'm going to kiss you."

Tess tried to keep the excitement out of her tone. "Oh. Well. All right, then. Do your worst."

He rested his hands on either side of her head, trapping her against the trunk. He leaned in, pressing himself against her, and a delicious shiver of anticipation raced through her body.

This man. How could he affect her so? It wasn't fair.

His lips quirked. "Oh, I intend to do my very best."

Tess closed her eyes in anticipation, but the fiend paused just before his lips made contact with hers.

"Our first kiss was standing up like this. At Careby's. Do you remember?"

"Yes." She breathed it against his lips. "I thought you were a professional gamester."

He gave a soft snort of derision. "Gambling's for fools. The surest and quickest way to lose a fortune. I never bet on anything unless the odds are significantly tipped in my favor." His lips brushed hers, petal-soft. "I thought *you* were a whore."

She gave his lower lip a teasing nip and he grunted in pleasure. "I know."

"We were both wrong, then."

"Yes."

Tess opened her mouth and he swept inside, fusing them together. The bark of the tree was rough against her back, but she didn't care. She wrapped her arms around his waist and kissed him with an urgency that made no secret of her desire.

His passion was almost overwhelming. She craved him like a drug, needed the rush of intense, heart-bursting joy that he alone could provide.

A deafening crack shattered the silence.

Tess gasped, even as she ducked automatically, flinching away from the sound.

"Bloody Hell!"

Before she could even make sense of what was happening, she found herself flat on the ground, her face pressed into the damp leaves and mud, Justin's heavy body sprawled on top of her.

"Stay down!" His voice was rough and urgent in her ear. "Some bastard's shooting at us."

Another shot boomed through the trees, and a shower of wooden splinters rained down as the pellets of a shotgun decimated the branch above them.

Tess could hardly breathe. Justin was crushing the air from her lungs. She tried to lift her head but he shoved her roughly back down.

They both stilled, listening for any telltale rustle of leaves; and the diminishing crash of footsteps to the east indicated the shooter was rapidly making their escape.

After a full minute of silence, Justin slid off her, and she took a welcome, gasping breath.

"Stay here," he whispered, so softly she could barely hear. "It could still be a trap to draw us out."

Tess nodded, still scarcely able to believe what had occurred.

He crawled forward on his belly and risked a glance around the tree, scanning the area for further signs of life, but when nothing else moved, he slowly rose to his feet and reached down to pull her up.

"Are you hurt?"

"Just a little shaken, that's all."

Tess exhaled deeply and brushed the leaves from her skirts. Her hands were shaking and she felt vaguely sick. She wished he would take her into his arms, but he didn't move.

"Whoever that was can't possibly have meant to shoot at us," she said. "It must have been a poacher, thinking we were deer."

Thornton's narrow-eyed look suggested he didn't share her opinion.

"You don't think so?" she pressed.

"Let's just say a healthy dose of skepticism has kept me alive thus far."

"It must have been an accident. Why would anyone shoot at us deliberately?"

He shrugged. "Any number of reasons. Do you have any disgruntled tenants, neighbors with a grudge?"

"No! The tenants all like me, respect me. The closest neighbor is Daisy's father, over at Hollyfield, and he's hardly ever there. He spends most of his time in London. And I'm on excellent terms with everyone else."

"Arden told me that poaching was almost nonexistent on the estate."

"That's true, but I suppose there could be some itinerant workers making their way through these parts."

Since Thornton clearly wasn't going to embrace her, and she had more pride than to throw herself on him like some needy barnacle, Tess started trudging toward the edge of the woods.

He kept pace easily beside her.

"You might be right." His tone still indicated his doubts. "But I'll have Simms make some discreet inquiries, all the same. One of the villagers might have seen something suspicious." He pulled his pocket watch from his waistcoat and glanced at the time.

She looked sideways at him. "You seem remarkably composed. Is this the first time you've been shot at?"

"God, no. I might not have seen any action against Bonaparte, but I've had plenty of run-ins with rival fur traders up near Hudson Bay. And a disagreement with a silk merchant in Venice a couple of years ago that convinced me of the need for boxing and shooting lessons."

Tess raised her brows. "Well, this was a novel experience for *me*. I need a strong cup of tea."

The humor finally returned to his face. "I think this calls for something a little stronger than tea, don't you?"

They parted ways when they reached the house. Justin went in search of Simms, and Tess retreated to her room.

Between Oliver's muddy paws, and rolling around on the forest floor with Thornton, her cotton dress was completely ruined. She took it off and pulled on her dressing robe, then sat at her writing desk to think.

Despite what she'd told Justin, she'd be a fool to discount the possibility that she might have been purposely targeted.

But who could want her dead? She'd certainly made some unpleasant people very unhappy in her work for King & Co. but none of them were likely to be in a position to threaten her in such a way. The cad who'd tried to kidnap his own cousin for her fortune was safely locked away in Newgate, and he didn't have the funds to pay for an assassin. The woman who'd tried to blackmail a countess had retreated to France.

Tess frowned. Could it be Stockdale? Might he have discovered her identity as the queen's emissary? But even if he had, there was no reason for him to want her dead. He wouldn't get the money he wanted for the princess's letters if he killed the messenger.

She pulled a piece of paper and a pen from her desk and wrote a brief note to "Charles King, Esquire." Ellie and Daisy would receive it at King & Co. in the morning. She warned them both to be on their guard, and asked for news of Stockdale as soon as they heard anything.

That done, she dressed for dinner in one of the new gowns Daisy had insisted she buy, a beautiful forest green silk with a crossover front that made the most of her cleavage, and added the pearl necklace that Justin had given her as a gift.

When she entered the dining room half an hour later it was to find Justin looking as handsome as ever in a dark navy jacket, white shirt, and buff breeches. His eyes lingered appreciatively on her throat.

"I knew that necklace would look magnificent on you."

Tess touched the pearls lightly with her fingertips. "It's lovely. You have exquisite taste."

"I'm glad you like it. I had it made, a special commission." His lips quirked. "The design is similar to one owned by Queen Marie Antoinette."

Tess's brows rose in surprise. So much for assuming he'd sent a lackey to choose something pretty.

He tilted his head. "At first, I considered rubies— Scarlet would definitely wear rubies. Something huge, and wonderfully vulgar." His gaze caressed her as much as his words seduced.

"But Tess?" he continued. "Tess is more subtle. Understated, classically elegant. Hence the diamonds and pearls."

They both took their seats at the table. Tess took a sip of wine, momentarily speechless at the thought he'd put into the gift. The fact that he acknowledged the difference between the fictional Scarlet and the real Tess meant more than she could say.

What would he say if she told him the reason she played those two roles? Would he approve of her work for King & Co.? Or try to interfere? It was still too early to tell.

"My fortune has been built on trading valuable items," he said softly. "On providing things people desire. Most items are prized for their ability to be useful. Because they are hard, or strong, or taste good."

"Like truffles." Tess smiled.

He nodded, studying her across the table.

"A few things are valuable simply because they're beautiful. People crave beauty in the same way they crave air. Pearls, for example, are mainly decorative, but they're also incredibly rare. They start as an accident—a tiny piece of debris on the inside of a shell, that over time develops into something extraordinary, layer upon layer."

His gaze lingered on the necklace, on the pulse beating in the hollow of her throat.

"But the *best* things are valuable because they combine beauty with other qualities. Watchmakers use rubies in their timepieces as bearings for the pivots to reduce friction. Diamonds don't just sparkle; they're strong, so hard they're used for engraving copper and glass."

Tess felt warm, and oddly exposed. Was he only talking about the necklace, or was there a deeper meaning to his words? Did he see her as strong and rare, as well as beautiful? Or was that just wishful thinking?

She raised her glass. "A toast. To things that can't be bought."

Chapter Twenty-Nine

He did not come to her room after dinner. After the dishes were removed, he asked Withers to pour him a glass of brandy and turned to Tess.

"It's been a long day, and since neither of us got much sleep last night"—he smiled faintly at her blush—"I'll see you in the morning."

Tess had been both relieved by his consideration, and slightly disappointed that he seemed to find her so resistible.

Still, she would forge on with her plan to become his friend, as well as his lover. If they were truly to part ways in a few months, she wanted to do so on amicable terms. He might not fall madly in love with her, but there was no reason he couldn't *like* her, at least.

Daisy's probing in Debrett's *Peerage of the United Kingdom* had revealed that Justin's mother had died when he was sixteen, of scarlet fever, and his father was also deceased. He had no siblings, nor close relations, so in that respect he and Tess were similar.

But who did he count as his most loyal companions? He was clearly good friends with Edward, Ellie's cousin, and with Tom Careby, but Tess wanted to be someone he could rely on, too. She wanted to be valuable to him. Not just as a temporary lover, or as a useful social ornament, but as a true friend. Someone he could trust.

"I promised to visit the school in the village tomorrow morning, but if you're free again in the afternoon, perhaps you'd like to go on another outing with me?"

He nodded. "Let's hope it's less eventful than today's excursion."

∽

"Are you sure you remember where it is? We must be half-way to Hollyfield by now."

Tess bit back a smile at Justin's impatient grumbling.

"Of course I do. It's just over this rise. And technically, we're right on the border between our lands and Daisy's father's estate. The river marks the boundary."

She pushed forward, leading him onward through the trees, her skirts billowing about her legs.

It was the perfect day for what she had planned; beautifully warm, with not a cloud in the sky. Justin had driven the open-topped gig, following her directions, but they'd had to leave the horse and conveyance up on the track and continue on foot.

"Ah! Here we are!" Tess stopped and pointed in triumph.

"A swimming hole."

Justin's voice gave nothing away, but Tess beamed at him, willing him to share her pleasure.

"I'm sure you've seen far lovelier ones, in your travels, but it's one of my favorite places in England. I can't tell you how many afternoons Daisy, Ellie, and I spent messing about here when we were younger. It's where I learned to swim."

She'd always thought of the dell as a magical place, a fern-lined fairy bower shielded from the rest of the world by the sloping banks of the stream. A natural bend in the river, and some large boulders, had created the most perfect pool—deep enough to dive into, and wide enough in which to swim.

She pointed to a knotted rope that hung from a tree branch suspended over the water.

"That's not the original rope, of course. It's been replaced several times over the years. We used to see how far out we could swing before we let go."

His lips curved up approvingly. "And here I thought proper young ladies spent their days stitching samplers and arranging flowers. It sounds as if you were complete hellions."

Tess laughed. "Oh, we were. But I must admit, I actually *like* stitching samplers, too. Embroidery is much maligned. I find it quite relaxing."

She bit back a giggle at the memory of the sampler she'd made for Daisy last Christmas. It read, *Life is often a badly stuffed sausage.* Daisy had hung it on the wall of her office at King & Co., and most visitors assumed it meant something very profound, instead of being a joking reference to disappointing male genitalia.

"Are you planning to swim?" Thornton's voice broke into her reverie.

"Goodness, no! The water's absolutely freezing, even in the height of summer. It comes straight down off the hills. But it's wonderfully clear."

She spread out the rug she'd tucked beneath her arm. "I thought we could just have a picnic."

She patted the place next to her and he lowered the basket she'd insisted he carry from the cart. She peered inside, amused to note that Mrs. Ward hadn't abandoned her theme of foods conducive to romance. A bottle of champagne, some strawberries, and a loaf of bread joined a jar of honey, a wedge of local cheese, and a slice of cold meat pie wrapped in a cloth.

Justin let out a snort. "How many people did you tell them you were inviting? You could feed half of Wellington's army with that. In fact, I've sailed across the Atlantic with fewer provisions."

Tess laughed and held out two glasses. He opened the champagne with a pop, and she wrinkled her nose as she took a sip and the bubbles tickled their way down her throat.

She broke off a hunk of bread and ate some, and she was halfway through her second strawberry when she sensed him watching her. She turned her head, and her heart did a little flip as he sent her that wicked smile she'd come to recognize as trouble of the finest sort.

He took the strawberry from her fingers. "Allow me."

He stole a bite of the fruit himself, then offered it to her, and his pupils darkened as she parted her lips and took a bite.

"I've dreamed about this wicked mouth of yours." He leaned in and kissed the strawberry juice from her lips. "Please tell me your collection of naughty prints includes a picture of a woman pleasuring a man with her mouth."

Tess's heart began to pound, but she didn't feign ignorance. She'd glimpsed just such a thing in Case's collection, and it had piqued her curiosity to an unholy degree.

Daisy claimed that whatever felt good to Tess would be equally pleasurable to her partner, and considering how much she enjoyed Justin kissing her, down there, it seemed logical that he might like the same.

Tess gave him a little push, taking the initiative, and he rolled onto his back without the slightest bit of resistance. She followed him down, continuing their kiss, and he groaned when she moved on top of him, her chest pressed to his.

He tasted of champagne.

Delighted that he was letting her take the lead, she kissed her way down his jaw to his chin, sliding her hands over the swells of his chest and abdomen until she reached his falls. She cupped him through the fabric, thrilled that he was so hard, so ready for her.

He let out a labored breath, almost a laugh. "Perfect, naughty duchess."

With trembling fingers, she unbuttoned his falls and he sighed as she clasped his bare skin. "God, yes."

Tess bit back a smile. She'd held him in her hand like this at Careby's, in the dark, but now she was at full leisure to explore. He threaded his fingers through her hair as she slid down his body and settled herself between his thighs.

When she lowered her lips and kissed him, he hissed out a breath and rocked his hips. Hesitant at first, she pressed kisses along his warm flesh, loving the dichotomy of soft skin and hard muscle. She gave the tip a tentative lick.

"Bloody Hell. That's good."

Blood was pounding in her temples and her whole body felt warm, as if his pleasure was somehow transferring itself to her. A heady sense of victory, of power made her dizzy. *He loved what she was doing!*

Buoyed by his reaction, she opened her lips and took him inside her mouth and he clutched her head with a smothered sound of pleasure. Tess closed her eyes, remembering how he'd teased her with the maple syrup, and swirled her tongue.

She lifted her head. "Say my name."

His groan of frustration echoed through the trees. "Tease!"

Tess smiled up at him, wicked and wanton. "Can't you remember?" She gave him another taunting lick, loving the salty taste of him. He thrust into her hand. "I'll give you a clue: it's not Scarlet."

In a lightning move, he rolled them both over onto the grass, and she let out a startled shriek at his unexpected ambush. There was no escape; his hands rucked up her skirts and she wriggled—but only to assist him, as desperate for him as he was for her.

He didn't remove her drawers. He simply found the slit in the fabric and pressed into her in one smooth slide that made both of them catch their breath.

For an instant he stilled, savoring the moment, and then he caught her thigh, urging her leg up and around his hips. The perfection of the fit, the way his body matched hers in every curve and hollow, made her bite her lip in wonder.

He raised himself up on his forearms, still pressed deep within her, and smoothed his thumb over her lips.

His gray eyes stared into hers. "Tess."

Happiness filled her. Her name on his lips felt like a vindication, an acknowledgment of something profound. As if he was seeing her, *truly* seeing her, for the first time.

She pulled him down for a kiss just as he rocked his hips, sending a shimmer of pleasure through her body.

He didn't try to make it last. He took her hard and fast, almost roughly, and Tess reveled in it, loving the way she frayed the edges of his control. She wrapped her legs around him, digging her heels into the back of his thighs.

Her climax claimed her in a breathless rush, but just before he reached his own peak, he withdrew. She sent him a confused, questioning look, afraid that she'd somehow displeased him, but he merely guided her hand back between his legs.

"Don't want to leave you with a mess to clean up," he panted. "Not out here."

His thoughtfulness was something she hadn't expected; she'd been so lost in their lovemaking that the aftermath hadn't even crossed her mind.

Satisfied that it wasn't lack of desire that had caused him to pause, she set about pleasuring him, loving the way his big body arched and shuddered at her touch. It still amazed her that such power could be mastered by such gentle pressure, the way a bull could be steered by a ring through its nose.

He groaned her name again when he climaxed, and Tess smiled in delight. If he could recall it when he was half delirious with passion, that was excellent progress.

He used one of the linen napkins to clean himself, but instead of righting his clothing, he tugged his shirt over his head and deftly removed his boots and stockings.

"Time for a swim."

"You aren't going to remove your breeches?"

He shook his head. "The shrinking effects of cold water are well documented. I refuse to provide you with anything but happy memories of my cock."

Tess laughed, even as the bittersweet implication of his words gave her heart a pang. He still imagined them going their separate ways.

He sent her a questioning look, his brows raised in challenge. "Are you coming in?"

She laughed again, refusing to be dismayed. "Not for a hundred pounds. But you go ahead. I'll sit here and watch. You might need rescuing."

Chapter Thirty

Tess watched Justin test the strength of the rope swing with obvious mistrust. Apparently satisfied that it would hold his weight, he let out a bellowing shout and flung himself out over the water. He released it at the perfect time and plummeted into the pool below with a splash that reached her on the bank.

He surfaced with another shout, and this time Tess didn't hide her laughter at his indignant expression.

"Bloody Hell, it's as chill as the rivers in Canada!"

"I warned you!" she shouted back. "Daisy always said it was colder than a belt buckle at the Frost Fair, whatever that means. It's certainly bracing."

He set off across the pond in a brisk crawl and she watched in silent appreciation as his muscled arms and rounded shoulders cleaved through the water. When he reached the far bank he stood, giving her a delicious view of his broad back tapering to a narrow waist and hips. His buff breeches clung like a second skin, and she gave him a spontaneous round of applause.

"Bravo!"

He turned, pushing his wet hair from his face. He really was the most extraordinarily handsome man.

"Sure you won't join me?"

Tess shook her head. "I'm enjoying the view."

He waded over to a partly submerged tree trunk that jutted out into the water and climbed up onto it with an agility that belied his size. He extended his arms to the sides.

"In Canada, they transport timber this way. They cut down the trees, and float them down the rivers until they reach the sawmills. The log drivers, men called *draveurs*, balance on the logs like this and jump between them, making sure they don't get jammed."

"That sounds incredibly dangerous."

"It is. Which is why I rejected it as a vocation. Shipping has far better odds of survival."

A ray of sunlight slanted through the tree branches, gilding the water droplets on his high cheekbones and making him glitter like some unearthly fairy prince.

He smiled at her—a genuine smile of uninhibited enjoyment—and her heart gave a little stutter. An answering smile tugged her own lips. His happiness was infectious.

"You should smile more. You're very handsome when you smile."

She said it softly, but he heard. His brows rose, and the sardonic curl returned to his mouth.

"I thought all ladies liked brooding, surly heroes?"

She shrugged. "Dark and brooding is all very well in principle, but on a day-to-day basis I can see it becoming very tedious. No woman wants to be glowered at. We want someone who can find the humor in the darkest of situations. For someone who can make us laugh, not make us cry."

"Duly noted." He jumped down from the log with a splash and waded forward until he was forced to swim.

He'd just reached the middle of the pool when a frantic barking and the thrashing of undergrowth sounded behind him. He turned in time to see a fat squirrel bound out of the ferns, leap onto one of the overhanging trees, and scamper up the branch and out of sight.

The puppy, Oliver, burst out of the greenery like a tiny cannonball, clearly in hot pursuit. Unfortunately, he hadn't anticipated the stream, nor the abrupt end to the solid ground.

Propelled by his forward momentum, he hurtled over the edge of the bank, scrabbling and skidding on all four paws in a vain attempt to stop, then tumbled into the water with an enormous splash.

Tess let out a shout of alarm, but the puppy's head bobbed back up a moment later, and she could have sworn its little face held the exact expression of indignation and shock as Thornton's had done earlier.

The pup let out a shrill yelp, and splashed around, apparently astonished at finding itself able to swim.

He set out toward the far bank, paddling frantically, but Justin was there. He caught the pup by the scruff of the neck and scooped it up into his arms, ignoring the sharp little claws that scratched at his bare chest.

Realizing it was saved, the puppy quieted in his hold, and he waded through the shallows and up the bank toward Tess just as she grabbed the picnic blanket from the ground.

"Oh, you poor thing!" she exclaimed, half laughing. "That naughty squirrel played a mean trick, didn't he?"

She took the squirming puppy from Justin's arms, wrapping it tightly in the blanket and trying to rub it dry as best she could.

Oliver gave a pitiful yowl. His once-fluffy fur now lay flat; he looked like a drowned rat. She clutched the tiny body to her breast as shivers wracked his tiny frame.

Justin used his shirt to dry his chest, then pulled it on, followed by his jacket and greatcoat. "Give him here. I'll warm him up."

He took the dejected little scrap and placed him inside his shirt, against his skin, then wrapped his jacket around them both. The puppy's forlorn little face peeked out from between his lapels, and Tess felt herself melting.

She turned quickly away, bustling about to pack the remnants of the picnic in the hamper while Justin cuddled the dog.

He crooned to the animal like a lover as they hastened back to the gig, and she tried to ignore the dangerous softening in the region of her heart.

She took the reins as he clambered up into the seat, the puppy nestled against his throat.

"Mr. Collins lives just over there." She pointed down the track. "Oliver must have escaped from the garden. Let's take him home."

They heard Collins and his wife, Anne, calling for the dog as they neared the end of the lane. Collins shook his head in dismay when he saw the creature bundled in Justin's clothes, but Justin brushed away his profuse apologies, and offers of a new shirt, with a good-natured laugh.

"No need for that, Mr. Collins. Oliver here just decided to keep me company while I swam."

He handed the bedraggled pup over to Mrs. Collins, who blushed at the sight of his wet shirt and exposed chest. Tess hid a smile. Even a practical mother of six wasn't immune to his charms.

"You be off home now, Your Grace," she scolded

gently, as if he was one of her own boys. "You'll catch an ague. Take a good, hot bath, and ask Mrs. Ward for a nice hot toddy, with brandy and lemon."

Justin nodded dutifully, and Tess ushered him back into the gig.

It was late in the afternoon, and the air was beginning to cool. She had no doubt that Justin would be feeling uncomfortable, so she set the horses to a brisk trot.

They were less than a mile from the house when they hit a rut in the road and a hideous crack sounded from the right-side wheel. Before Tess could do more than give a shout of warning, the entire wheel gave way with a sickening, bone-jarring jolt, and the seat tilted sideways at an alarming angle.

The horse reared at the sudden change. Tess pulled hard on the reins, even as she started to topple sideways off the seat.

"Tess!" Justin grabbed her skirts, barely stopping her from falling out of the dangerously listing cab. He grasped the reins with his other hand, adding his strength to hers, and together they managed to drag it to a juddering, bouncing halt.

Justin leapt down and went to the horse's head to quieten him. Tess climbed to the ground and bent over, panting and shaking in delayed reaction.

Dear God, that had been close! Either one of them could have fallen and broken a leg. Or worse.

Justin unhitched the horse, stroking its neck to soothe it. He tied it to a tree, then returned to inspect the wheel.

"That was bloody close," he frowned. "What happened?"

Tess stared at the splintered wood. "I've never had three spokes give way at the same time. Jones, the cartwright, must have used a defective piece of timber."

Justin ran his hands over the wheel, and his expression clouded with anger. "We were incredibly lucky. It wasn't even a big rut. If we'd been going faster, or if the horse had bolted, you could have been thrown and killed."

The thought made Tess feel nauseous. "Or you," she said.

Since the gig was clearly unusable, they left it where it was and led the horse toward the house. Tess's feet were aching by the time they finally reached the stables, and she was sure Justin felt equally miserable; his breeches were still damp and he must be getting chilled.

He handed the horse over to the stablemaster and explained what had happened, then sent two of the stable boys to retrieve the gig. That done, he escorted Tess inside.

She touched his arm. "You need to get warm. I'll have a hot bath sent up for you right away."

He nodded, clearly distracted, and she tried not to feel snubbed by his curt, "Yes. Thank you," before he strode away.

Chapter Thirty-One

Justin's anger simmered as he waited for Simms to attend him in his rooms.

His blood was pounding, his nerves on edge, as he re-played the carriage incident in his mind.

Bloody Hell. It had been a miracle that neither one of them had been seriously injured or killed. Tess had seemed genuinely surprised and bewildered by what she saw as a freak accident, but it wasn't in his nature to be so trusting. The odds of three spokes giving way natu-rally were extraordinarily long. The odds on them having been tampered with were far shorter.

He stripped off his damp clothes and threw them onto the bed.

If he was correct, and someone had meant for the wheel to fail, then who had been the intended target? Tess? Or himself?

It seemed unlikely to be Tess. He'd seen the respect and affection she garnered. Everyone from the baker's boy to the prince regent was in love with her.

He, on the other hand, could well have been the in-tended recipient of a nasty fall. But was it because of his business dealings, or because of his position as the new duke?

Simms's knock halted his aimless pacing.

"You called, Your Grace?"

"I did. I was wondering if you'd had any luck in finding out who might have shot at us in the woods yesterday afternoon?"

Simms shook his head. "Sadly not, sir. The truffle hunter, Collins, was undoubtedly in the vicinity, but he was seen showing the truffle you found to the landlord of the Dog and Duck in the village not ten minutes after you say the shots were fired. He did not appear out of breath, as if he'd recently been running through the trees."

Justin nodded. He hadn't really imagined the kindly old man to be the culprit. Besides, those dogs of his would have made a noise at hearing a shotgun, had they been close by.

"Remind me, how did the previous heirs to the duchy die?"

If Simms was surprised by the topic, or by Justin's state of complete undress, he didn't show it.

"The eighth duke's brother drowned in a canal in Venice. The next heir fell from his horse after a drunken attempt to jump a fence. Another one died after very unwisely attempting to dress himself without a valet." Simms shook his head at such patent foolishness. "He put both feet in the same trouser leg, lost his balance, and hit his head on the grate. He never regained consciousness."

"Go on."

"Your grandfather died in his mistress's bed in Paris, your uncle George was shot in a duel, and your father, God rest his soul, died of a fever on his last expedition."

"Could any of them have been . . . not accidental?"

Simms raised his brows. "Deliberate, but made to look like an accident, you mean?"

Justin nodded.

The majordomo pursed his lips. "Well, yes. A few of them, I suppose. But not all. The death in Venice could easily have been murder, but the drunken fall from the horse would have been harder to orchestrate, although not impossible. The head injury *might* have been inflicted by someone other than the deceased. There were no witnesses to that one, after all."

He continued. "Your uncle might well have been goaded into accusing someone of cheating at cards, but I don't recall the particulars. He was always hotheaded. The other deaths, however, I don't think could have been planned. Certainly not your father's. You and I were both with him when the doctor said there was no more that could be done."

Justin hissed out a breath at the unhappy memory. "That's true. And half the crew died of the same fever. There was no foul play there."

"Indeed. Might I ask why the sudden interest in your predecessors?"

"Because I'm starting to think that someone's trying to kill me," Justin said. "Or possibly Tess. But that's less likely."

"Why do you say that?"

"Do you remember a few weeks ago, in London? I was almost knocked down by that brewer's cart in Charing Cross. At the time I dismissed it as a freak accident, but now I'm not so sure. When you add it to the fact that someone took a shot at us in the woods yesterday, and that both of us narrowly avoided serious injury from a suspiciously unsafe cartwheel today, it all adds up to too many near-misses for my liking."

Simms nodded, and Justin ran his hand over his face, struggling with a niggling suspicion that refused to be ignored—that all his near-misses had started at the same time he'd become involved with Tess.

Was it possible that his beautiful, brilliant wife might not be as naive—nor as innocent—as she appeared?

In his experience, anything that seemed too good to be true, generally *was* too good to be true. There was always a catch, some reason to be wary. He'd seen it a million times in his business dealings: spices at a price so low they had to have been adulterated with lesser-quality ingredients; a ship whose freshly painted boards attempted to hide myriad structural failings.

Such deals might fool the greedy, the unwary, but life had given him a healthy suspicion of all that glittered.

Was Tess herself too good to be true? Was he being blinded by lust and infatuation, guilty of ignoring the very logic for which he prided himself? When viewed unemotionally, the facts seemed to paint a very incriminating picture.

She'd definitely lied to him. He didn't truly believe that saucy print was the sole reason she'd been at Case's house. And she wasn't above using subterfuge, either—she'd been happy to dally with him incognito at Careby's. How many other times had she done such a thing?

He shook his head, annoyed at himself for being so disloyal, so untrusting, but unable to stop.

Tess could have been seriously hurt herself this afternoon. She could have been thrown from the cart, or crushed if it toppled, or trampled by the horse.

The thought of her in any kind of pain made him feel queasy, even as a cynical little voice in his head reminded him that it could have been a calculated risk to appear innocent and allay suspicion.

Bloody Hell.

He resumed his naked pacing. He had to think clearly. To push emotion aside.

What would Tess gain from disposing of him? She'd keep her title whether he was alive or dead, so it couldn't be that. And while she'd get her widow's portion if he died, just as they'd agreed in writing, she'd lose the allowance he'd promised her while he lived. Financially, she'd be worse off with him dead. That couldn't be a motive.

Could there be an emotional reason, though? Had she lied to him about having a lover? If not Case, then someone else? Did she regret their bargain, and long for another man's embrace?

He'd glimpsed a letter addressed to a "Charles King" yesterday when he'd added his own correspondence to the outward pile. At the time he'd assumed it was some business matter, but now he wasn't so sure.

His chest tightened with what he assured himself was anger at being deceived, and not jealousy. Jealousy would require the presence of other, more complicated emotions, the likes of which he was unwilling to entertain in relation to Tess. He'd instituted his three-month rule to avoid precisely this kind of painful situation.

Belatedly realizing that Simms was still watching him as one might a caged tiger, Justin pulled himself up short. Unwilling to voice his suspicions of Tess, even to his most loyal employee, he merely frowned.

"I want you to look into it, Simms. Talk to the coachman and see if there's any proof that the gig wheel was tampered with. See if you can find any suspicious circumstances regarding the previous heirs. And find out what you can about a man named Charles King, of Lincoln's Inn Fields."

Simms, the soul of discretion, merely bowed. "Of course, sir."

The hot water for Justin's bath arrived at that moment, and he dismissed Simms and sank into the steaming tub with a sigh.

He'd bloody known inheriting a dukedom would be nothing but trouble.

As the heat from the bath sank into his bones, he told himself he was being overly sensitive. He closed his eyes, and Tess's beautiful face swam in his mind. She'd seemed so passionate, so loving, this afternoon. And the way she felt in his arms, the ardency of her kisses—surely that wasn't feigned? It was ridiculous to think that she could be plotting against him. He was a cynical, jaded fool.

If she was pining for a lover, well, he'd simply have to make her forget the man even existed. He'd love her so thoroughly that she'd never want to let him go.

Of course, the reverse side of that coin was that Justin might never want to let *her* go, but he dismissed that possibility as absurd. She might be the most fascinating, most beguiling woman he'd ever met, but he was in no danger of falling in love with her. The organ that had pounded so loudly when she'd been in danger hadn't been his heart. He didn't have one to lose.

Chapter Thirty-Two

Tess dismissed Hannah and eyed her bath with a sigh of pleasure. The expensive copper tub had been a luxury purchase she'd never regret, and the water, when she tested it with her hand, was the perfect temperature: a degree below uncomfortably hot.

The rising steam formed little beads on her hairline as she added a few dops of rose-scented oil to the water, looking forward to feeling the aches and pains of the near-miss with the gig melt away.

The click of the adjoining door made her jump, and her heart stuttered at the sight of Justin in the doorway. He'd already bathed; his hair was damp, and he'd donned a clean white shirt and breeches.

He was not wearing stockings, and she found herself intrigued by his lean, bare feet as he came toward her.

She cleared her throat. "I was just about to have a bath."

"So I see." He stopped in front of her and she sucked in a breath as he untied the sash of her dressing robe with slow deliberation. She was naked underneath, and a muscle ticked in his jaw as the fabric parted down the middle.

Without a word, he slid the robe off her shoulders and

then caught her hand, helping her step into the tub as if she was royalty.

Slightly confused—she'd expected him to kiss her— Tess sat in the deliciously warm water. Her skin turned pink almost immediately, adding to her self-conscious flush at being so exposed. Before, she'd been shielded by clothes, or bedcovers.

She sank down until only her knees and her head were above the water, and glanced up at Justin, unsure of his intentions.

He seemed to have a plan. With brisk movements he turned back the cuffs of his shirt and rolled his sleeves up to his elbows.

Tess bit back a groan. The sight of his forearms, corded with muscle and a smattering of dark hair, made her a bit lightheaded. And when she thought of those wonderful hands of his—

Still silent, he picked up the bar of rose-scented soap from her dresser and knelt behind her, on the floor.

She'd piled her hair haphazardly on top of her head, and she shivered in excitement as his warm breath teased the tendrils that curled at her nape. He dipped the soap in the water and made a froth of bubbles in his hands, then slid the foam over her shoulder and along her clavicle.

Tess closed her eyes, savoring the wicked slide of his hands. The soap reduced the friction, but she could still feel the slight calluses on his hands. When she dropped her head forward, he kissed the slope of her shoulder, and she arched, silently willing him to move lower, to her breasts.

But the perverse creature pulled back instead, and she watched in a daze as he rose and crossed back to her dressing table. He dried his hands on his breeches, and opened the case that held her jewelry.

Tess frowned as he selected the necklace he'd given her. He detached the diamond bow and pendant and placed it on the table, then returned to her with the pearl strands cupped in his hands.

Tess sat up a little higher in the bath. *Did he mean to put the necklace on her? In the bath? How decadent!*

She bent her head again, expecting him to fasten the clip at her nape, but he merely pressed another kiss there instead.

"When I ordered this necklace, I wanted, *so badly*, to see them against your skin." His voice was low, gravelly with desire.

Tess shivered as he draped the heavy strands over her shoulder. The cool pearls heated to match her body almost instantly, but the end dangled dangerously close to the water.

"You'll get them wet!" she scolded, a little breathless.

His low laugh made her belly somersault. "They've spent most of their existence under water. I doubt a dip in your bath is going to do them any harm."

Tess exhaled. "Oh, I didn't think of that. But surely the stringing shouldn't—"

"I'll have them restrung. A hundred times, if necessary."

Whatever she was about to say next was lost in a gasp as he rolled the pearls down over her breast. Her nipples peaked, despite the heat, and she bit back a groan at the incredible sensation of the tiny smooth globes teasing her skin.

He was toying with her, playing. Leaning over her from behind, he made a bubbly lather on her left breast with the soap while gently massaging her right with the pearls, polishing in lazy circles that made her whole body tingle.

Tess tilted her head back against his shoulder and he moved lower, dropping his hand below the waterline. She could barely think. The world had contracted to this room, this man, this moment.

Her stomach muscles tensed as the pearls rolled lower still, to the curly hair at the juncture of her thighs.

She was panting now, her body aflame.

"Do you like this, Tess?" His rough voice at her ear only added to her excitement.

She swallowed; her mouth was dry. "Yes."

"Shall I continue?"

"Yes."

The sight of his forearm stretching down her body made her weak. The contrast between his tanned skin and her paler flesh seemed outrageously erotic. She tried to imprint the image on her brain for future recall.

He reached down, completely disregarding his shirt-sleeves, and she let out a shocked moan as he pressed the pearls directly between her legs.

"Justin!" She grasped the edge of the tub for support. "Oh!"

"Nice?" He moved his hand, and the multiple rows of pearls rolled against her most sensitive skin, back and forth, an amazing combination of hard ridges and slippery smoothness.

She shuddered. Every sensation centered between her legs, an aching, throbbing heat that felt almost like a sickness.

He didn't stop. He massaged in circles, rolling and polishing them against her until she was squirming against his hand, her feet pressed to the end of the tub. She was wanton, unashamed of her desire. A sensual creature of his creation.

He knew exactly what she wanted, the devil. But he

taunted her with the pearls, and as her frustration grew, she almost hated him.

He'd created this ache; he could bloody well finish it.

She reached back, her arm dripping water, and grabbed his hair. She arched her back, offering herself, wordlessly trying to force him to release her from the torment.

He let out a harsh exhale, as if the sight of her was unbearably arousing. He pressed the pearls to her opening, not quite pushing inside, then drew them upward, bump by bump, a wicked, maddening friction that almost made her scream.

"Please!"

He took pity on her. He reached forward and slid his finger inside her, and she arched up into his hand, lifting her hips to find the perfect angle.

"Is this what you want, Duchess?"

"Please!" she panted. "Yes!"

Her reward was a second finger. A sweet stretch and slide, in and out, slow stabs that made her writhe as the tension ratcheted higher.

It still wasn't enough. She wanted *him* inside her. To be filled so completely there was no knowing where she ended and he began.

She pushed him off and stood abruptly, water streaming down her body. He rose, too, and she threw her arms around him, heedless of his clothing or the absurdly expensive rug. She mashed her lips to his, and he gave a low groan of surprise and delight.

In one smooth move he picked her up, out of the bath, urging her legs around his hips so she clung to him, his hands cupping her bare bottom, a blur of wet limbs and soaked clothing.

He practically threw her onto the bed. She landed with a bounce, a shock of cold sheets as they absorbed the water from her skin. He pulled his shirt up over his head with gratifying haste, tore at the buttons of his falls, and kicked them off. And then he was on her, his whole body pressing her down, skin against skin, warming her, his hair-roughened legs sliding between hers with delicious friction.

He captured her jaw and kissed her, almost roughly, devouring her like a starving man, and she reveled in his need, in his lack of restraint.

His passion matched her own.

His hand slid back between her legs, but only to guide his cock to her entrance. She was so ready for him there was no resistance. He entered her in a single thrust, like a knife through warm butter. Sweet, slick perfection.

"Tess." The groan came from deep within his chest.

And then he threaded his fingers through hers and drew their joined hands over her head. He pressed her down and started to move, and she'd never felt so loved. So smothered, yet so cherished. So crushed and yet so free.

She bit his shoulder lightly, the muscle that joined his neck, and he gave another delicious thrust; a punishment that was all pleasure.

She angled her hips and met his every stroke and he tightened his fingers on hers.

"Keep doing that. God, please, exactly that." She was babbling, but she didn't care. She needed to reach that peak.

"This?" His teasing voice was rough against her temple.

"Yes!" Tess scrunched her eyes closed. Held her breath. Higher, closer. She was almost there.

He kissed her, hard, his tongue plunging deep, and she dug her nails into his shoulders, holding on for dear life, kissing him back, eyes closed. The breathless darkness grew, swelling into a glorious golden wave that crested and broke in a shower of pulsing sparks.

Her inner contractions triggered his own. She held him close, loving his lack of control, the way his big body shuddered in total abandonment.

Chapter Thirty-Three

Neither of them made it downstairs to dinner. At Justin's suggestion, they ate cheese on toast at the small drop-leaf table in the shared drawing room that linked their rooms.

Hannah, who served them, took one look at Tess's still-damp hair and pink cheeks and started humming something cheerful under her breath. She sent Tess a conspiratorial smile as she deposited the tea tray and backed out of the room.

Tess bit back a good-natured groan. No doubt the staff were making bets on the probable arrival date and gender of the next Thornton.

There was certainly a possibility that she might become pregnant. She and Justin had made love several times now without taking any precautions, and she realized that she truly wouldn't mind if she ended up with a "honeymoon baby" if Fate decided to deal her that hand.

The meal was the most intimate she'd ever shared, but there was no awkwardness. Justin seemed determined to draw her into conversation, and before she knew it, she was telling him all about the estate, and the vagaries of truffles, and the grossly unfair dog tax that had been imposed some twenty years ago by William Pitt on any "sporting dog"—which included truffle-hunting hounds like Nell and Oliver—a charge of five shillings per dog.

He, in turn, told her about his adventures in Canada, and his warehouses in Bristol, and his plans to invest in the new technology of gas lighting that had recently been introduced to the capital.

Tess was so much in charity with him that she almost told him about King & Co., but natural caution held her back. Part of her felt guilty for not revealing such a large part of her life, but she was still unable to predict how he'd react.

As a member of the merchant classes himself, he might understand the need to fill her days with something more satisfying than mere social calls, but as her husband, he might dislike the thought of her putting herself into potentially dangerous situations.

The last thing she wanted was for him to forbid her to continue—because she'd refuse to comply. The work she did at King & Co. was too important to abandon. Each case they solved might only count for a single drop in the vast ocean of crimes against women, but Tess was still proud of the fact that they were changing lives for the better.

Besides, she'd become too accustomed to her own independence to lose it now. She would keep her secrets until she knew Justin better.

For a brief moment, she wondered how Daisy and Ellie were handling the princess's case in her absence, then scolded herself. She would know soon enough if there was any news. The girls would tease her mercilessly for dwelling on work when there was a far more enjoyable subject before her: namely, her handsome husband.

Tess hadn't wanted the evening to end, but when she yawned for the second time, Justin sent her an amused smile and rose to his feet.

"The excitement of the day is clearly catching up with you. Time for bed."

She hoped he'd invite her to share his bed, or suggest they go to hers, but he merely made his way to his own doorway. "I'll see you in the morning."

౭

The morning brought a letter from Ellie, written in her usual cryptic style, designed to frustrate any unintended reader.

> S—has provided a letter, which Mrs. King has con-
> firmed to be genuine. He wishes to meet the Lady
> in Red at Vauxhall Pleasure Gardens this Saturday.

Tess let out a sigh. She'd hoped to spend a little longer at Wansford with Justin, but duty called.

Things were bound to change once they returned to London. He'd agreed to live at Wansford House, at least for a while, to maintain the fiction of a love match, but would he spend any time with her, or would he disappear to his offices and only visit her bedchamber whenever he wanted physical release?

True, Tess herself planned to be at King & Co. most days, but the thought of the two of them leading completely separate lives was rather depressing.

Why couldn't she resign herself to settling with what they had? Wishing for more was only asking for heartache.

And yet foolish hope persisted.

She refolded the letter just as Justin entered the breakfast room, looking his usual handsome self.

"I need to return to London," she said without preamble.

He glanced at the paper in her hand with a frown. "Nothing bad, I hope?"

"Oh no, just a small business matter."

"Is it anything I can help you with?"

A hot flash of guilt swept over her at his seemingly genuine offer. She disliked having to conceal the true reason from him.

"Thank you, but no. It's not connected with the duchy, just an appointment I must attend."

He nodded and she let out a tiny huff of relief that he wasn't questioning her further.

"Very well. I could do with getting back to business myself. If you don't want to ride with me, I'll have the carriage readied for you. We can leave after lunch."

"Have you had your belongings transferred to Wansford House?"

"I sent Simms back to town yesterday evening to see to it."

She smiled at him. "In that case, I look forward to giving you a tour."

∽

Justin stared at Tess across the breakfast room. Was he a fool for wanting to believe her? Did she truly have business in town, or was that letter in her hand a summons from a lover?

He willed her to leave it on the table so that he might lower himself to some shameful snooping, but she tucked it into the pocket of her skirts.

He was glad she'd suggested leaving Wansford Hall. He'd been about to suggest it himself.

His pulse pounded at the sight of her, sitting there, looking so beautiful it made his chest hurt. She appeared so guileless, so content.

Perhaps it was his imagination, but she seemed to have become even more lovely since they'd arrived. There was something different about her, a satisfaction he couldn't quite pinpoint. She seemed more sensual, more alluring than ever. A poet might even have said that she'd *bloomed*.

Not that he'd ever subscribe to such flowery nonsense.

Perhaps *he* was the one who had changed? Had he, like so many others before him, fallen dangerously under her spell?

No. She was a distraction. He needed to go back to London and throw himself into his work, to rid himself of this terrible desire to be with her. Not just to make love with her, but at other times, too. To make her laugh, or to listen to that husky voice of hers. She could make even the most prosaic description of drainage ditches sound seductive.

Justin ran his hands through his hair. For the first time in his life, the thought of going back to work was . . . unappealing. The need to prove himself, to succeed, had paled. In fact, the only reason he could think of to earn money now was to spend it on Tess. To clothe her in the most beautiful dresses. To shower her with jewels.

What was wrong with him? He had everything he'd set out to achieve. With Tess at his side, as his hostess, he should have been looking forward to conquering yet another section of society, to widening his connections, increasing his profits. And yet it all felt hollow.

Perhaps by the time they got back to London Simms

would have discovered something that either condemned or exonerated her when it came to the "accidents."

Could she really be so duplicitous as to wish him harm while melting so passionately in his arms? He hated to consider it, but experience had shown that people were quite capable of looking him in the eye while planning to rob him blind.

He prayed to God that Tess wasn't one of them.

Chapter Thirty-Four

"Daisy, Ellie, I think I'm in trouble."

Tess sank into one of the armchairs at King & Co. with a ruffle of skirts.

Daisy waggled her eyebrows. "Well, you can't be pregnant already. I'm sure it wasn't for lack of trying, but a week really is too early to tell."

Tess smiled, despite her worry. "No. Definitely not that. My monthly courses arrived this morning."

Ellie sent her a sympathetic grimace.

"So, what seems to be the problem?" Daisy asked. "Don't tell me the duke didn't provide satisfaction, because I shan't believe it. You're practically glowing."

Tess put her hands to her cheeks. She'd thought the same thing when she'd looked in the mirror that morning.

"Oh, the duke kept his part of the bargain extremely well," she said, with a blush. "But that's not it. Or, at least, that's only part of the problem. The truth is, I think I've made the very grave mistake of falling in love with him."

"Oh, Hell," Daisy muttered.

"What did he do?" Ellie demanded. "He didn't turn out to be nice, did he?"

"Did he steal our 'rehabilitation home for puppies, veterans, and fallen women' idea?" Daisy asked.

"Worse. He listened to me ramble on about agriculture. And truffles. And taxes." Tess sighed. "He fed me liquid sugar. Some ambrosia of the gods called 'maple syrup.'"

"The swine!" Daisy gasped, only half joking.

"And that's not all." Tess recounted the incident with Oliver, plus the near-misses with the poacher and the broken carriage wheel.

Ellie shook her head. "You say he scooped up the wet poodle—the same one that had previously ruined an expensive pair of boots—hugged it to his chest—with no thought of ruining his shirt in the process—and then buttoned his coat around the puppy?"

She sounded like she was cross-examining a witness in court, trying to get the facts right for the jury.

"Yes. Exactly."

Daisy scowled. "That's a dirty trick. *Of course* you fell in love with him. What woman wouldn't? 'Wet puppy in the coat' is right up near the top of the list of things we can't resist."

"There's a list?"

"Of course there's a list. It's one of those unwritten laws. Like the fact that the week before you get your monthly courses, you have to force yourself not to stab everyone with a letter opener because they're being so irritating."

"We do all have 'stabby week,'" Tess agreed. "But go on. What are the things we can't resist?"

Daisy stood and started to pace. "May I present for the prosecution: item one. Rescuing wildlife. Especially adorably small, helpless wildlife."

"She's not wrong," Ellie said. "I once saw a very

ordinary-looking man save a hedgehog from a drain, and I almost kissed him on the spot."

"Item two," Daisy continued. "Wet shirt. Preferably transparent. Plastered to the chest."

"Also true. As long as the chest in question is reasonably muscular," Ellie clarified.

Daisy nodded, accepting the amendment. "Item three: Rescuing a woman not once, but twice, from mortal peril."

"I'm not sure you could count a broken cartwheel as *mortal* peril *per se*," Tess said.

"Fine. A 'reasonably dangerous situation,' then," Daisy conceded. "It still fits the 'damsel in distress' rule."

"He didn't even hug me for comfort on either occasion."

"Doesn't matter. He probably *wanted* to. There's a lot to be said for restraint, too."

"I think he's guilty of at least one other item on the list," Tess said.

"Did he kiss you in the rain? Threaten to beat another man to a pulp because they'd insulted you?"

"He kissed me in the *bath*," Tess said.

"Close enough."

"And that was after he rolled up his sleeves and flaunted his forearms at me."

Ellie sucked in a disapproving breath. "Oh, now that's just not playing fair!"

"We should add wrists to the list, too," Daisy said. "As well as forearms. Have you noticed how men have these protruding bones, in their wrists? It makes me a little lightheaded just thinking about it."

"And shoulders," Ellie breathed. "They have marvelous shoulders."

"Eleanor Law, you're blushing!" Tess laughed. "Whose shoulders are you thinking of?"

"None in particular." Ellie smiled. "It was more a general observation from that time we visited that boxing match in Holborn. Those gentlemen were prime anatomical specimens."

"I have something else to add," Tess said. "He treated me as his intellectual equal, instead of a feebleminded simpleton. He deferred to my greater knowledge of running the estate without once trying to tell me I was wrong, or suggesting I do something differently."

"A rare man indeed," Daisy muttered.

"And the way he says my name." An involuntary sigh escaped Tess. "As if it's his dying breath, and it's the last thing he wants on his lips before he leaves this world. Nobody else says it like that."

"Bloody Hell," Daisy said. "You *are* in love with him."

"But is he in love with you?" Ellie asked.

Tess shook her head. "He is not. At least, I don't think so." She put her hands to her forehead and squeezed her temples. "God, I'm such a fool. He calls me Tess now, instead of Scarlet, which is a definite improvement. And I want to believe we could be friends. But he still seems perfectly able to ignore me. I've hardly seen him since we got back to Wansford House yesterday."

"Well, he did say he'd leave you alone during your monthly courses. Perhaps he's just being considerate."

"Maybe. But I feel like he's avoiding me."

Ellie nibbled the end of her pencil. "He's probably halfway in love with you already, but refusing to admit it. He's burying himself in work just to avoid temptation."

"I wish I had your confidence," Tess said. "But enough about me. What's the latest news about Stockdale?"

Daisy slid behind her desk. "He wants to meet you, in your red dress, at Vauxhall Gardens on Saturday. You're to wait by the fireworks tower, at the east end of the grounds, at ten o'clock."

"Another good choice," Ellie grumbled. "It's far away from the entrance and most of the amusements. And it's almost completely surrounded by trees."

"He's agreed to bring the remaining letters written by the princess, but he's changed his mind about how he wants to be paid."

Tess raised her brows.

"Before, he was asking for five hundred pounds, but in his last note he demanded payment in jewels."

"Why?"

Daisy shrugged. "They're small, easy to dispose of, and almost untraceable. If he were given a necklace, for example, he could break it up and sell the pieces separately. Five hundred pounds in small-denomination bank notes is quite an unwieldy bundle to conceal. And he could theoretically be traced by the serial numbers on each one."

"The queen has agreed to lend us a necklace," Ellie added. "It's real, not paste, in case he can tell the difference. Daisy and I will hide nearby, so as soon as you get the letters, we'll emerge from the trees and force him to return it at pistol point."

"The queen isn't sending any of her own guards to help capture him?"

Ellie shook her head. "We advised against it. Stockdale will be wary of being double-crossed. He might call it off if he sees a bunch of burly-looking men lurking about in the bushes. If he sees Daisy and I, he'll probably just think we're tarts, waiting for an assignation. Or lovers."

Tess nodded. "Shall we meet at Vauxhall? Or do you want to travel together?"

"You won't be asking Thornton to escort you?"

"As much as I'd like his company, I don't see how I'd be able to slip away from him to meet Stockdale without arousing suspicion. I don't want him thinking I'm breaking our agreement and meeting another man. It would be better if he wasn't there."

A stab of guilt flashed through her at the thought of excluding Justin, but it had to be done. She would make it up to him some other time.

"In that case, we'll share a carriage. Unless you prefer to take a boat down the Thames from Whitehall?"

Tess shook her head. "No. It's always so windy on the river, even though it's faster. I'll call for you both at eight on Saturday."

Chapter Thirty-Five

Tess descended the stairs for breakfast on Saturday morning eager to encounter Justin. True to his word, he hadn't visited her chamber while she was "indisposed," and she'd barely seen him over the past few days. He'd spent a great deal of time at his offices, and at his club, presumably dealing with business matters and the myriad other things requiring a new duke's attention.

Her cheeks heated as she recalled the one time his cool, polite façade had cracked. It had happened last night. Unable to sleep, seized by a sudden craving for the syrup Justin had gifted her, Tess had tiptoed down the stairs, heading for the pantry. It had been too late to rouse the servants, so she'd decided to make an impromptu visit to the kitchens herself.

She'd just replaced the stopper when Justin entered through the back door from the stables. He turned in surprise, presumably thinking she was a servant, or an intruder, but stilled when he saw it was her.

"Tess!"

Tess tried to still her pounding heart. His hair was

slightly damp, thanks to the late-night drizzle, and droplets of water glimmered on the shoulders of his coat in the light from her solitary candle. His cheeks were dark with a faint shadow of stubble, and her fingers itched to touch him.

"I was . . . err . . . just getting a little snack." She gestured guiltily toward the stoneware flagon of syrup.

His gaze barely flicked to the bottle before it returned to her, and her stomach tightened as she realized what she was wearing. Knowing he wouldn't be visiting her rooms, she'd donned her plainest cotton chemise, but from the look on his face she might as well have been wearing one of the beautiful silk nightgowns she'd bought from Madame Lefèvre.

His gray gaze roamed hungrily over her, lingering on the shadowed V of her breasts, then back up to her mouth.

Her heart started to pound. Self-conscious, she licked her lower lip, and a muscle ticked in his jaw.

"Tess," he said again, more a groan this time. His throat bobbed as he swallowed.

Tess cast around for something sensible to say. She gestured at the maple syrup.

"It's really quite addictive, you know . . . the sweetness."

Ugh, she was a stammering wreck.

He started toward her, a silent prowl. She backed up until her bottom bumped the huge wooden table in the center of the room. A copper jelly mold rattled as he stepped in close, caging her with his body, and her pulse skittered at the waft of cool night air and cedar-scented man he brought with him.

"Addictive," he growled. "Sweet." He sounded almost accusing.

He leaned closer.

Tess gripped the edge of the table, determined to resist the temptation to slip her hands inside his coat.

And then he was kissing her. His big hand caught the back of her head, cradling her skull, and desire leapt between them. He took her mouth hungrily, as though starved for her taste, and Tess answered in kind, loving his roughness, his urgency.

But just as she raised her hand to cup his cheek, he pulled back with an anguished groan.

"I'm sorry . . . I know it's your time of the month . . . I promised to leave you alone . . ." His voice was low, gravelly. "But . . . I . . . You . . ." He made a helpless gesture between them, as if that explained everything. "I forgot myself."

They were both breathing hard. Tess pressed her fingers to her throbbing lips, desperate to tell him to keep on kissing her anyway, but instead he took a decisive step back.

"I'll bid you good night."

And then he was gone. Tess heard him taking the stairs two at a time, almost as if he couldn't wait to get away from her, but a small, feminine smile curved her mouth. He wanted her. Even in her most unattractive nightgown, he could barely keep his hands from her.

She considered following him, imagined knocking on his door with an offer to ease him with her hands or her mouth. But what she *really* wanted was for him to hold her in his arms while they slept, as he'd done that first night they'd been together.

To love her, not just make love to her.

And that was something he'd told her he'd never do.

"Do you have plans for this evening?"

Tess froze in the doorway to the breakfast room as

Justin's seemingly casual question jolted her from her reverie.

"I'm afraid I do, actually. Daisy, Ellie, and I are going to Vauxhall to see the balloon ascent and Madame Saqui's rope dancing."

"Would you like me to accompany you?"

Tess gave an airy wave and tried to keep her tone light. "No, it's all right. I'm sure you'll just be bored."

His gray eyes rested on hers and she felt a guilty heat rise on her skin, along with the sensual frisson his gaze always produced.

"I could never be bored in your company. But if you wish to go alone, I wouldn't dream of stopping you. Be careful, though. There are always hidden dangers at places like that."

"You mean pickpockets and drunkards? Yes, I know."

He tilted his head. "Among other things."

His cryptic comment made her feel even more uneasy. Was he annoyed that she'd refused his company? What other dangers did he envisage?

"I'll make sure to stay alert," she said lightly. "The rack punch there is notoriously strong."

Would he go to a different party without her? Would he flirt with other women because she wasn't there? The thought made her irrationally cross. She'd much rather be meeting Justin in the shrubbery for an illicit assignation than a blackmailing printmaker, but the princess's letters had to take precedent.

Business before pleasure.

⁓

Justin kept his expression bland as he watched Tess. He'd felt guilty for asking Simms to retrieve the letter she'd received at Wansford Hall from her writing desk, but his guilt had been replaced by anger when he'd read the contents.

He had no idea what the references to a letter, or to a Mrs. King meant, but it was clear that Tess was the "Lady in Red" who was to meet the mysterious *S* at Vauxhall.

Was she reprising her role of Scarlet to meet a lover in the pleasure gardens?

Jealousy gnawed at his gut. Had he failed to satisfy her physically? What was she seeking from another man that he himself had not provided?

He'd deliberately kept his distance from her for the past few days, throwing himself into work, and he'd hated it. He'd found himself drifting off in the middle of meetings, thinking of her laughing on the banks of the stream, her eyes sparkling, her hair a beautiful windblown mess. He'd mistakenly confused his banker with his solicitor, simply because he'd been dreaming of her lips.

This had never happened with any other lover. It was if she'd bewitched him, infected his brain so that it constantly turned to her. What she might be doing. When he could see her next.

The power she held over him was disturbing. Last night, when he'd surprised her in the kitchen, it had taken all of his willpower not to keep on kissing her until they were both out of their minds. It had been on the tip of his tongue to invite her to his bed anyway. Not to make love, but just to hold her in his arms.

Which was stupid and irrational. He still couldn't trust her. Years of negotiating had taught him how to spot when people were being evasive, and she'd had all the classic tells: avoiding his eyes and fidgeting with her hands when she'd spoken of her plans.

Justin ground his teeth. In one way, her meeting a lover would be better than the alternative: that *S* was the person she'd hired to engineer the spate of "accidents" that had been plaguing him. Was she meeting a potential assassin to arrange the next misfortune?

Neither option was good, but whichever it was, he had to know.

~

Justin had just come into the hall and was laying down his gloves when Tess appeared at the top of the stairs in her red dress that evening.

His heart missed a beat, and it took more strength than he knew he possessed not to bound up the steps, catch her in his arms, and kiss her until she abandoned all thought of leaving him.

He swallowed instead, and sent her what he hoped was an easy smile.

"Scarlet. You look magnificent."

She stilled, just for a moment, at his use of that name, then continued her graceful descent. "Thank you."

Could one kidnap one's own wife? Could he carry her aboard one of his ships and simply set sail? Keep her in his cabin and make love to her, *love her*, until they were oceans away from dukedoms and intrigues and lovers and accidents? Until they were simply Tess and Justin. Nothing more, nothing less.

He dismissed the foolish thought and picked up her cloak. She allowed him to drape it over her shoulders, and he almost begged her not to go. To stay with him. To choose him.

When she turned and smoothed her hands down the front of his shirt his body reacted predictably, growing hot and hard in her presence. The guileless, slightly shy smile she gave him made his chest ache.

"I'd much rather stay here with you," she murmured. "But Ellie and Daisy are waiting."

The cynical part of him had to admit that she was good. So utterly believable. He succumbed to the need to stroke his thumb along her jaw, and she tilted her face up, angling for a kiss.

He forced himself to step back. "Have fun."

A flash of disappointment crossed her face, and he regretted not taking the kiss that was offered, but she turned and swept out the door before he could grab her back.

Justin strode into the study and pulled the bell rope for Simms.

Chapter Thirty-Six

Tess heard Vauxhall before she saw it. The distant sound of an orchestra and the occasional shout floated over the rooftops, and the golden glow of lights twinkled through the trees as the carriage rocked to a stop.

They paid the fee of one shilling and made their way along the dark, narrow passageway that was the entrance to the pleasure grounds. In a deliberate *coup de theatre*, the tunnel opened up onto a dazzling vista, a brightly lit dreamworld that had delighted Londoners for over a century.

Thousands of oil lamps with colored-glass shades provided illumination, lit to the sound of a whistle at nine o'clock sharp every evening. Gravel crunched beneath their feet as they made their way past the rotunda, a circular building used as a concert venue in inclement weather, and entered the open area known as the Grove.

A marble statue of the composer Handel was positioned in a break in the vaulted colonnade that curved around three sides of the piazza, housing countless open-fronted supper boxes, like theater boxes, for those who wished to dine partly *alfresco*. Each box was large enough to seat six or eight guests, and they were identified not only by a number, but also by the unique painting that hung on the back walls.

Waiters in red coats served the notorious rack punch, along with cold ham, lobster salad, and all manner of other culinary delights. An orchestra played in an octagonal bandstand in the center, and a series of paths led off into the gardens beyond.

"It's a good thing we arranged a specific spot to meet Stockdale," Ellie murmured. "This place covers almost twelve acres. We'd never be able to find him otherwise."

"It's the perfect place for getting lost," Daisy agreed with a sly smile. "Whether intentionally, or not."

Tess had no doubt that it would look sad and neglected in the harsh light of day, but at night it was a magical place, the perfect setting for a thousand small dramas to unfold—intrigues and flirtations, love affairs and brawls. A palpable excitement filled the air, music and laughter, and people determined to enjoy themselves.

The Grand Walk, a wide boulevard with trees planted on either side, stretched before them, but Ellie steered them to the right, toward the Druid's Walk and Lover's Walk.

"Have you ever had your fortune told by the Hermit?" Daisy asked idly.

The Hermit—a wizened gentleman with a beard so long Tess had always assumed it to be fake—could be found within a rudimentary grotto, made from wood, pasteboard, and canvas, complete with views of a fantastical landscape and a bizarre interior ravine, into which the Hermit disappeared, only to reemerge with one's fortune written on a cream parchment scroll.

"I have," Ellie said. "Last year. It said I'd marry a mysterious stranger."

"And mine said I'd meet my true match on a dark highway," Daisy chuckled. "Perhaps I should take up highway robbery, to hurry things along?"

"I'm sure he writes them ahead of time and only personalizes them with your name once you've paid your sixpence," Ellie said.

"Of course he does," Tess agreed. "Mine said I'd receive undying fidelity from my husband."

Daisy snorted. "That was definitely true of your *first* husband. But only because he didn't have time to be unfaithful. Whether it's true for your second remains to be seen."

Tess's heart gave a foolish little flutter. To have a man like Justin be hers forever sounded like an impossible dream. She should be happy with the few months they'd agreed. And yet a tiny spark of optimism persisted. Perhaps he would come to realize how good they could be together.

The crowds thinned as they ventured deeper into the grounds. A rush of people raced in the opposite direction to witness the balloon ascent, and by the time they reached their destination they hadn't seen anyone for several minutes.

The Dark Walk was aptly named. Unlike the straight main thoroughfares, it consisted of a series of twisting, serpentine paths through the trees at the farthest edge of the gardens. It was a favorite place for furtive assignations.

The firework tower was accessible from several directions, ringed by a circle of trees. It was, in truth, less a tower and more a series of wooden battlements surrounding a small stage, like an empty open-air theater, a place from where the fireworks were launched.

The cheerful lanterns did not extend this far into the park. In the moonlight it seemed forlorn, almost eerie.

The pyrotechnic display was already over; the fire-works had provided an accompaniment for Madame Saqui, the famous tightrope artist, who'd run down an inclined rope suspended above one of the main walks. The distinctive scent of spent gunpowder still hung on the cool night air.

Tess stopped at the periphery of the clearing, within the cover of the trees, and waited to see if anyone was lingering near the wooden scenery. She could see no movement, but that didn't mean that Stockdale wasn't lurking in the shadows, waiting for her to make an appearance.

"You need the necklace from the queen."

Daisy reached into her reticule and Tess groaned in dismay as she saw what Queen Charlotte had provided for the exchange.

Justin's words echoed in her head.

Scarlet would wear rubies. Something huge, and wonderfully vulgar.

The necklace was precisely the kind of thing Scarlet would wear: a brash, glittering statement of wealth and excess. Tess immediately wished for her pearls, and her body heated as memories of her interlude with Justin flooded her.

Not the time to get distracted.

She'd left her neck deliberately unadorned, and she shivered as she fastened the necklace at her throat. In the semidarkness the rubies glittered like dark drops of blood.

"Pretend you can't undo the clasp," Daisy reminded her softly. "Stockdale will need to use both hands, which means he won't be able to hold a gun. That's when Daisy and I will reveal ourselves."

Tess nodded. They'd been over the plan several times.

Ellie gave her a brief hug. "It's almost ten. Good luck. We'll be here, even if you can't see us."

The two of them melted into the shadows, and Tess pressed herself against the trunk of a tree, peering out toward the meeting place. The rough bark beneath her palms reminded her of kissing Justin against the tree at Wansford, before they'd been so rudely interrupted by that poacher.

She forced herself to concentrate on the task at hand.

With a deep breath she pulled herself up tall and strolled toward the wooden structure. Her heart beat against her ribs and her skin pricked in awareness of being watched. Whether it was Daisy and Ellie's regard she could sense, or Stockdale's, she couldn't say.

She waited in the shadows beneath the wooden struts of one of the towers for what seemed like an eternity, listening for the sound of approaching footsteps. Her heart leapt when a feminine giggle echoed through the trees, followed by a deeper masculine reply, but the amorous couple quickly disappeared into the woods.

She was about to start pacing when a tall, male figure appeared at the edge of the stage. He sent her a mocking bow.

"Well met, my scarlet lady. Are you enjoying the night air?"

Tess was in no mood for pleasantries. She was chilled and ill at ease, irritated by the seemingly inexhaustible schemes men could devise for their own enrichment. She had no sympathy for this blackmailing vermin.

"I'll enjoy it a great deal better when our business is done," she said coldly.

She pushed back her hood, untied the drawstring that secured her cloak, and draped the heavy material over her arm, providing Stockdale with a clear view of the necklace that glittered against her throat.

She had a knife in her pocket, accessible via a slit in the pleats of her skirts, and she used the cloak as cover to retrieve it. The handle felt reassuringly solid against her palm.

"Do you have the letters?"

Stockdale drew closer. "I do." His eyes lingered greedily on the necklace at her throat. "And I see you have my payment. I'm so glad your employer decided to be sensible. Discretion is such a valuable trait. Young ladies can't be too careful with their reputation."

His sly tone made Tess grind her teeth. What an ass.

She held out her hand, palm up. "Hand them over."

Her fingers tightened on the handle of her knife as he reached into his coat. She half expected him to draw a pistol, but she relaxed a fraction when he merely withdrew three folded sheets of paper.

Tess had studied the one genuine letter he'd already returned. The princess's script was childishly distinctive, sloping heavily to the right, with large flourishes for the capital letters. As Stockdale watched, she unfolded one of the letters and scanned it in the dim light to confirm he wasn't trying to dupe them.

"This appears to be genuine," she conceded curtly.

Stockdale sent her a cheeky smile. "'Course it is. Wouldn't double-cross you, now would I? Bad for business."

She almost rolled her eyes. There was no honor among thieves, despite what he claimed. He just wanted the convenience of a single, guaranteed payment, instead of having to expend the effort of publishing and distributing this damaging gossip himself.

She slipped the letters into her cloak, then reached up

to the nape of her neck. She'd arranged her hair in an up-swept style, and with her cloak still draped over one arm she fiddled with the necklace's clasp.

"Oh, blast. I can't seem to get it undone."

Stockdale's brows rose at her feigned exasperation and an oily smile curved his mouth. "Allow me."

Tess quashed an instinctive shudder as he stepped closer, turning her back to him so he could more easily access her nape. His legs brushed the back of her skirts and she tamped down a wave of revulsion as his warm breath skimmed over her neck. He smelled of onions and beer.

His cold fingers fumbled with the clasp and she found herself holding her breath, praying that Daisy and Ellie would make their move.

"It's been a pleasure doing business with you, Your Grace," he murmured softly, and she flinched as his palm caressed the slope of her neck in a totally gratuitous touch.

"Did you see the amusing little sketch I drew of you and that brooding new husband of yours?" He was still fumbling with the clasp.

"I did," Tess said stiffly.

"He's a lucky man. But if you ever get bored, you know where you can find me."

Tess was about to tell him she'd leap into the filthy Thames before she'd consider him as a partner, but a movement in her peripheral vision caught her eye. A wave of relief swamped her and she turned, expecting to see Daisy and Ellie with pistols drawn, but her relief turned to horror as she recognized the dark-coated figure emerging from the trees.

Her husband, looking as coolly murderous as one of the Four Horsemen of the Apocalypse.

"What the Bloody Hell is this?" Justin growled.

Chapter Thirty-Seven

Both Tess and Stockdale froze, and she could only imagine the damning tableau they made. From Justin's vantage point it must look as if Stockdale was placing the necklace around her throat, instead of removing it.

Shit. Bloody. Buggering Hell. What in God's name was he doing here?

Stockdale was the first to recover his wits. He made a chiding little sound, as if Tess had disappointed him.

"Your Grace. What a pleasant surprise. Your wife and I were just concluding a little business."

Justin's hand closed into a fist at his side. "So I see."

His tone was glacial, and the look he shot Tess made her heart pound. The clasp of the necklace finally gave way, and the heavy gems slithered over her chest and caught in the front of her low bodice. She clutched at it as Stockdale slid his hand over her breast and snatched it, his fingers tangling with hers.

A muscle ticked in Justin's jaw. "Get your hands off my wife."

Stockdale tugged the necklace from her grip and

slipped it into his coat pocket. "Oh, I don't think she minded, did you, love?"

Her blood boiled at the malicious amusement in his voice.

Justin's gaze bored into hers. "It appears I'm interrupting a lovers' tryst."

Tess found her voice. "Not at all." She took a step away from Stockdale. "This is not what it looks like, my lord."

Justin's lip gave a scornful curl. "Oh really? Because it *looks like* your lover, here, is giving you a very gaudy present."

The fury in his face made her quail, but Stockdale gave a low chuckle.

"Oh, no. The boot's on the other foot. Your charming wife's giving *me* the gift. For services rendered."

Tess almost groaned at the way he deliberately made it sound as if she'd used him as some kind of male whore.

Justin advanced. "Who are you? Charles King?"

"Not me, mate. He must be another of your wife's *friends*." Stockdale's insinuating tone was an insult.

Tess's frustration was mounting. Where had Justin heard the name Charles King? And why would he think she and King were lovers? Or she and Stockdale, for that matter? Either way, his unwelcome interference couldn't be allowed to jeopardize this case. It was too important. She had to make him leave; she could explain later.

"Go away, Justin," she said coldly. "I have some important business with Mr. Stockdale, here, and you are decidedly *de trop*."

He glared at her. "Are you paying him to have me killed?"

Her mouth dropped open in shock. "What on earth are you talking about?"

"Are you trying to get me out of the way so you can be with your lover?" He gestured at Stockdale. "Is he the one responsible for the 'accident' to our carriage wheel? Is he the 'poacher' who can't shoot straight? The cart driver who almost ran me down?"

Behind her, Stockdale sucked in a breath. He stepped to her side, both hands raised in an attitude of innocent surrender.

"You've got this all wrong, Yer Grace. I've never set out to harm you in my life." He took another step sideways, edging toward the trees. "I deal in scandal, not murder. My business was with the duchess, and it's done. If you want to play the jealous husband, that's none of my affair. I'm off."

"You stay right where you are," Justin growled.

Tess shook her head in exasperation. "Let him leave, Justin!"

Ellie and Daisy would be watching this farce from the trees, waiting to accost Stockdale in the shadows. If Justin would just allow him to leave, they could grab him and retrieve the necklace before he left the grounds.

But Justin wasn't having any of it. As Stockdale kept moving, he leapt forward and tackled him.

"Bastard!"

Tess gave a shriek as the two men sprawled on the ground, rolling over and over in the mud and the leaves. Stockdale tried to push Justin off him, then punched him in the ribs. Justin gave a furious grunt and slammed his elbow hard into Stockdale's belly, then landed a blow to his jaw that made the other man's head snap back.

"Stop it, you idiots!" Tess scolded. They were like two dogs, blinded by rage. If only she had a bucket of water to throw over the pair of them.

She'd seen a boxing match in Holborn, once, as part

of an investigation. There, the fighters had been methodical, almost scientific in their ducking and delivering of blows.

This was nothing like that. It was savage and lawless, like a tavern brawl, with both men kicking and punching at any body part they could find. Gentlemanly it was not.

Justin kneed Stockdale in the groin, and the other man curled into a ball with a howl of pain. As Justin staggered to his feet, Stockdale recovered enough to kick out and land a horrible blow to his knee.

Justin hissed in fury, and as Stockdale rolled and got to his feet, he curved his arm around the printseller's neck in a brutal choke hold. Stockdale squirmed and bucked, trying to free his head, and a glittering lump fell from his pocket and into the mud.

Neither man noticed, in their distraction, and Tess darted forward and scooped up the necklace when the scuffle spun away.

"Justin!" she commanded. "Let him go. I can explain."

He glanced up at her, his face flushed. He still had Stockdale bent over in a headlock, but he stilled. A red mark that would undoubtedly become a bruise was already darkening his right cheekbone, and his lip was split and oozing blood.

Stockdale grasped his forearm and gasped an unsteady breath. "Mercy! Let me go, you madman!"

With a disgusted sound Justin released him and Stockdale staggered back, clutching his throat and gasping for air. He eyed Justin as if he were an inmate straight from Bedlam.

Justin sent him a dismissive glare. "I never want to see your face again, do you hear me? Now go."

Stockdale didn't need telling twice. With a furious, accusing look at Tess—as if this debacle was somehow *her* fault—he turned and staggered off into the trees as fast as his shaking legs could carry him.

Justin's chest was heaving with exertion. He wiped the blood from his lip with a disdainful swipe of his cuff, then turned his attention back to Tess.

His eyes glimmered in the faint light and her heart couldn't seem to find a steady beat.

"Care to explain, Scarlet?"

∾

Justin was furious, not just with Tess, for whatever perfidy this was, but also with himself, for losing control. Where had his icy calm gone? His ability to reason? He'd seen another man's hands on her and reacted like some hotheaded Casanova in a Drury Lane melodrama.

He was a stranger to himself. And it was *her* fault. She made him insane.

When she didn't answer immediately, he took a step forward and tilted his chin at the necklace in her hand. The man she called Stockdale must have dropped it during their fight.

"*I* gave you jewels," he panted. "Were they not to your liking?" He took a deep breath, filling his lungs with the cool night air. "I made love to you, too. Was that not good enough, either? What do you *want*, woman?"

She shook her head, and he couldn't tell if she was furious, disgusted, or simply disappointed.

"You're mad," she breathed, sounding as if she truly believed it. "You're acting like a jealous fool. Which is impossible, because you've told me on numerous occasions that what's between us is only business and physical pleasure."

Her scathing tone made him flinch, and her eyes narrowed in a fury that matched his own.

"Which means," she continued, "that you're just guarding something you see as your possession. You don't want any other man touching what you see as your own."

That there was a grain of truth in her accusation made him even more irritated. And defensive.

"You didn't interrupt a lovers' meeting," she said hotly. "You interrupted a private investigator—*me*—foiling a plot to blackmail the queen." She reached into her cloak and drew out a sheaf of folded papers. "The man you just tried to beat to a pulp was a printmaker from Covent Garden who was threatening to publish Princess Charlotte's love letters." She brandished the bundle in front of his face. "These."

Justin tried to conceal his surprise. Tess was some kind of female Bow Street Runner? Bloody Hell. If that was true, then he'd misjudged her—and the situation—quite horrifically.

"Sounds like he deserved a good beating, then," he drawled.

She scowled at his flippant attempt at levity.

"This necklace," she said, lifting it in her other hand, "was his payment. It's not a lover's gift, nor is it blood money for some imaginary assassination attempt."

Justin winced at the hurt and anger in her tone. "Why didn't you tell me you were working for the queen? That you're some kind of—what? Secret spy?"

"I had no reason to trust you! I didn't even know you a month ago. You were a stranger." Her eyes glittered. "You *still are* a stranger, in fact. And you don't know me at all if you think I could have ordered someone to hurt you."

She shook her head, and her voice sounded choked.

"Do you honestly believe that I could do something so awful? That I've been trying to *kill* you?"

Justin took a step toward her, but she moved back, keeping the distance between them and putting her hands up to ward him off.

"I admit, it does seem far-fetched," he admitted. "But not impossible. Your past actions led me to believe that you would do anything to secure your position. Both socially and financially."

She gasped in offense, but he forged on, determined to make her see that he'd had valid reasons for his mistrust.

"You can't deny that becoming the Duchess of Wansford greatly improved your situation. Your father was in dire financial straits. You didn't even bring a dowry to the marriage—I read the settlement your father agreed with the old duke."

Her eyes widened, but she said nothing.

"And as luck would have it, you barely had to endure the old man's company for long. One night only, in fact. As his widow you were well provided for, and since no subsequent heirs lived long enough to come and claim the title, you were left to enjoy your life without unwelcome interference for almost two years."

He ran his fingers through his disordered hair. "You seemed to be enjoying your widowhood. You'd found a solution to satisfy your physical needs that didn't risk losing your income from the duchy: cavorting with men like *me* at Careby's. We were intimate, without even knowing each other's names."

She pressed her lips together in a tight line, unable to refute that particular truth.

"And then I came along, the new duke, and you jumped at the chance to improve your lot yet again. The only downside was that you had to endure my company for a few months before we separated."

Tess shook her head. "You think I married both you, and the first duke, for money and position?" Two red spots flamed on her cheeks. "If that were true, then why would I be trying to kill you? Financially, I'm better off with you alive."

She sent him a scathing look, and he cursed the fact that he found her attractive, even now.

"Perhaps," she continued, her tone practically dripping scorn, "I couldn't stomach sleeping with you, even for a few weeks. Perhaps I missed my endless procession of lovers and my life as a merry widow?"

Her bosom swelled in outrage. Justin opened his mouth to make a counterargument, but she spoke before he could get a word out.

"Do you think I faked my attraction to you?" she demanded. "That I only pretended to enjoy your kisses, your lovemaking?" Her angry words echoed through the clearing. "The only thing I faked was my experience!"

Chapter Thirty-Eight

Tess stilled, appalled by what she'd just admitted. But indignation was heating her blood, boiling her from the inside out.

Justin was staring at her as if he didn't understand the bombshell she'd just delivered, but she was too furious at his accusations to backtrack now. She would spare him nothing.

She took a step forward, advancing on him until they were barely a foot apart.

"I married the last duke because my father *forced* me to."

She enunciated every word so there was no chance he could miss her meaning. "I tried to escape, but he locked me in my room until the wedding. Even after I'd said my vows, I still had no intention of submitting to the duke. I took a pistol to my chamber to protect myself from his advances, but he died of natural causes before I had to use it."

She shook her head, reckless, yet oddly liberated. "I was a virgin on my first wedding night. And I was a virgin on my second one, too. With *you*."

She glared at him, meeting his eyes with a defiant kind of pride.

Justin's gaze narrowed in disbelief, but as she watched, his expression changed as he obviously began to think back over their previous interactions, reassessing everything.

"Oh, Bloody Hell," he breathed.

"Yes!" she snapped. "I pretended to know what I was doing. And you only saw what you expected to see: a woman with vast experience. You'd been so quick to think the worst of me, it never occurred to you to think anything else."

She took another step closer until her skirts brushed his legs.

"You've *consistently* thought the worst of me, ever since we met. You are cynical, and suspicious, and you only married me to improve your standing in society and to benefit your business."

Justin shook his head in denial, but she wasn't finished.

"Well, I married you to protect *my* business, too." She let out a hollow laugh. "Of course, I stupidly hoped we might become friends, despite what you said, but you've made it abundantly clear that's not possible. I'm just a temporary body to sate your physical needs."

Justin shook his head, more emphatically this time. "No! Tess, that's not true."

"Ha! It is!"

He sucked in a breath that made his chest rise and fall. "It might have been true at first," he conceded slowly. "But not anymore. I *feel* things for you. Things I've never felt for anyone else."

"You specifically told me you'd never have any deeper feelings for me. That you didn't have a heart to give."

His gaze held hers and she felt herself captured, held against her will.

"I admire you, Tess. More than you can imagine. Your cleverness, your loyalty, your wit. The fact that you're working as an investigator only makes me admire you more. You are so much more than your physical beauty. Although I'm damned if I'll deny that I desire you, because I do, more than any woman I've ever met."

His brows lowered in a frown, as if a new thought had occurred to him.

"God, Tess, I *love* you."

He sounded quite aggravated at the revelation.

Her heart stuttered in her chest, but she shook her head.

"You don't love me. If you did, you'd never have thought I could plot your demise. You'd have given me the benefit of the doubt—however compelling the evidence against me might have been. You should have had faith in me, trusted me."

Even as she said it, she realized she was being unfair, to demand his trust when she hadn't given it herself, but he just nodded.

"That's true, and I'm sorry. How can I make it up to you?"

He reached for her hand, but she pulled it away, out of reach. She didn't want to touch him. If she did, she might crumble.

"You can't. Actions speak louder than words, and all *your* actions have proved you're incapable of overriding your natural cynicism. You're not in love with me, Justin. You won't allow yourself to be. You're confusing desire and convenience with real intimacy, real emotion."

She stepped back, putting cool, rational distance between them.

"I know what I said when we made our agreement," he said tersely. "But I didn't *want* to love. Not you. Not anyone. All I could see were the negatives." Insistence made his voice rough. "You've shown me the positives. That there's passion beyond the physical—passion of the soul. It's longing for someone when you're apart. Missing their smile, their presence, their humor. It's wanting to share more than a bed with them. It's wanting to *stay*."

Tess took another step away from him. She was in no mood to be persuaded, and his nearness made her want to throw herself into his arms, despite everything.

She drew herself up and pulled her cloak around her shoulders. "I want you to move your things out of Wansford House. You can stay at your Curzon Street house tonight. I want to end our agreement."

"Tess, no."

"Yes."

"Even if you're angry with me, at least let me stay to protect you."

"Protect me? From what?"

"That broken wheel on the gig wasn't an accident. I spoke to the cartwright, and he told me someone had tampered with it. The spokes had been sawn through to make them fail."

She frowned, but he continued.

"And what if those shots fired at us weren't an innocent mistake by a poacher? What if they'd meant to hit one of us?"

"Considering the size and scope of your business dealings, I'd say you're far more likely to be the target, not me," Tess said irritably. "In which case, your proximity is likely to put me in *more* danger than if you left me alone."

"I can't do that."

"You can," she said sternly. "You should set whoever you asked to investigate *my* affairs to turn his attention to your business rivals instead. It will be a better use of his time and your money."

Her heart was breaking, but she sent him one last look in the darkness. "Goodbye, Justin."

And then she walked away. Her head was high, but her eyes were blinded by tears.

Chapter Thirty-Nine

Princess Charlotte Augusta, only daughter of the prince regent and his wife, Caroline of Brunswick, beamed at Tess from her seat beside her grandmother in the front office at King & Co.

"I cannot thank you enough for retrieving those foolish letters." Charlotte shook her head and her pale blond ringlets bounced. "Now that I see them again, I'm mortified by my youthful indiscretion. Two years ago, I was convinced I was in love with Charles, but now I think it was more that I was flattered by the attention. I loved the idea of being in love, the excitement, the thrill of a secret correspondence."

Daisy sent her a smile. "There's nothing wrong with that. I think everyone deserves at least one youthful indiscretion. What *nobody* deserves is having that indiscretion printed in a public gossip rag so they're mocked and pilloried."

"Quite so, Lady Dorothea," the queen said.

"What I feel for Leopold is so very different from what I felt for Charles that I can't believe I ever mistook it for love," Charlotte said. The way she spoke was oddly direct, not at all the soft, modulated tones expected of a princess, but she was charming along with it. "I can't wait until we're wed."

"We all wish you the greatest happiness, Your Highness." Tess smiled. "Have you chosen a wedding dress yet? I hear silver is all the rage."

The queen gave a knowing smile. "From what I hear, it's *red* dresses that have caused quite a stir in recent weeks. But that's certainly not a color for a wedding. Perhaps silver would be best."

Tess nodded, and tried not to look so disheartened by the princess's obvious aura of happiness whenever she spoke of her betrothed.

Had she looked so glowing and besotted with Justin? Had her infatuation with him been so obvious?

Memories of the last time she'd seen him, bruised and yet unbowed at Vauxhall, crowded her brain but she shoved them away. She couldn't think about him. It made her throat tight and her nose sting.

The ruby-and-diamond necklace lay on the desk before her, taunting her.

Queen Charlotte nodded at it. "You ladies may keep that necklace as payment. It was never a favorite of mine. And I do not wish to be reminded of this unpleasant business every time I put it on. You shall also receive the hundred pounds we agreed upon, of course, for successfully retrieving the letters."

"Thank you, ma'am."

"I have decided not to pursue any further action against the blackmailer. Since he ended up with neither the letters nor the necklace, I hope he will be sufficiently chastened."

"He received a good beating, too," Daisy said, then snapped her mouth shut as she realized her error. They hadn't told the queen the particulars of the evening at Vauxhall.

The queen's brows rose in interest. "From yourself?"

"Sadly not," Daisy said. "Although it would have been a pleasure. Our man had an altercation with the Duke of Wansford, just after we'd made the exchange."

Amusement lit the queen's face. "How delightful! As a rule, I generally advise against violence, but in this case, I can only say I hope the duke gave him a sound thrashing."

Tess managed a faint smile. "He did indeed, ma'am."

The queen nodded and rose, and the princess did the same. "In that case, justice seems to have been served. Come, Charlotte."

Tess, Daisy, and Ellie all rose, too, and as the queen bustled into the hallway, Charlotte glanced at the needlepoint sampler that hung on the wall above Daisy's desk.

"A badly stuffed sausage?" Her eyes sparkled with mischief. "I *do* hope that's not the case with Leopold!"

Sheltered she might have been, but it was clear the princess possessed a bawdy sense of humor.

Tess laughed. "We wish you all the best, Your Highness."

The queen turned to Tess as she reached the front door. "Oh, I almost forgot! I have instructed my secretaries to look for proof of that loan your father made to the king. I shall let you know if they meet with any success."

Tess bobbed a curtsey. "Thank you, ma'am."

When the two women had left, Tess returned to the study and eyed the ruby necklace with dislike.

"I've always been of the opinion that rubies bring bad luck."

Ellie nodded. "Me, too. I can't imagine any of us ever wearing it."

"We should have it remade. Let's ask Rundell and Bridge to sell the rubies, and turn the diamonds into earrings for us all."

"Excellent idea," Daisy said. She brushed her hands together. "Well, that's another happy customer. But you don't look too pleased, Tess."

Tess forced a smile. In truth, she was feeling rather deflated, despite the success of the case. She hadn't seen Justin for almost a week, and she missed him. Regret at the way she'd dismissed him so curtly had been gnawing at her for days.

Ellie and Daisy had been too far away to hear what had passed between herself, Stockdale, and Justin at Vauxhall, but they'd been outraged and incredulous on her behalf when she'd told them of Justin's unfair accusations.

Daisy, however, had seen a ray of hope. "I know his behavior was appalling, but it really does sound as if he was following his heart and not his head. Which is extremely out of character. Perhaps he really *has* fallen in love with you? Love does make perfectly rational people do the most irrational things."

Tess let out a sigh. "I know. But where does this leave us? He sent me a note saying he would call at Wansford House tomorrow to discuss ending our agreement. If he really loved me, he wouldn't be so eager to let me go."

Ellie sent her a sympathetic look. "If he really loved you, and thought you wanted to end the contract, then he'd do anything to make you happy. Even at his own expense."

Tess put her head in her hands. "Lord, what a mess."

Chapter Forty

"Before you say anything, I would like to apologize. Again."

Tess sank back into her chair behind the desk as Justin strode into the study, and her heart galloped in precisely the same way it had done when she'd seen him standing there the first time.

He took the vacant seat opposite her and ran his fingers through his hair, and she drank in the sight of him. The bruise on his cheek had faded in the week they'd been apart, and his lip had healed.

She'd kissed those lips.

She tore her eyes away from the temptation.

"Apologize for what?"

"For accusing you of wishing me harm. Simms and I have been investigating all week, and we've found the culprit. A competitor of mine named Connor MacKenzie. I'd met him in Montreal, but he came to see me in Bristol a few weeks ago wanting to go into partnership. I said no, because I disliked the bullying way he did business, but it seems he didn't like that answer and decided that if I wouldn't join him, then he would eliminate me as a rival."

"How did you discover it was him?"

"I recalled seeing him across the street just before I was almost run down by that cart. When I gave his description to the staff at Wansford Hall, and to the villagers, I found that a man matching his features had called at the Hall asking for work the day before we arrived. Withers had turned him away, but the landlord at the Dog and Duck also remembered him loitering around the day we were shot at in the woods."

Tess pressed her lips together, determined not to lower herself to saying something as childish as *I told you so*.

"Simms and I discovered the address of a warehouse he rents here in the docklands, and we paid him a visit."

She tightened her hands in her lap. "That could have been extremely dangerous."

"Oh, it wasn't just the two of us." A faint smile ghosted his lips. "I took Edward and eight of my burliest deckhands from *The Tempest*, in case he decided to give us a violent welcome."

"And did he?"

Justin tilted his head. "We had a small altercation. But in the end, he admitted to being the one behind the attacks. Since his confession was witnessed by Edward Hussey—a noted barrister—it was agreed that Mr. MacKenzie would henceforth conduct his business from the other side of the Atlantic, on pain of being immediately arrested and tried for the attempted murder of a peer should he ever set foot in this country again."

"Goodness," Tess said faintly. The phrase *small altercation* was clearly an understatement, but she was glad to see that Justin didn't appear to have sustained any additional injuries.

He leaned back in his chair and his gray eyes lingered on hers. "You were right. It was nothing to do with you, and I was an idiot to suspect you for a moment."

"Yes. You were."

He reached into his coat and withdrew a sheaf of papers.

"I was also an idiot to draw up our agreement. I release you from it with immediate effect." He tore the paper neatly in two, and in two again, and placed the scraps on the desk before her.

"You will, of course, continue to receive all the benefits from the duchy that we agreed. I'll have Turnbull make it official. We are still married, and will remain so, but that is all. You never have to see me again if you don't want to."

Tess's heart felt heavy in her chest. A bizarre combination of relief and disappointment warred within her. Was that it? Wasn't he going to try to persuade her to reconcile? Were they to be no better than strangers from this moment on?

She cleared her throat. "I have some news, too. The queen's secretaries found details of the loan my father made to the king. It did exist. There's an agreement in the king's own hand that confirms it."

"How much was it for?"

"A thousand pounds. With interest at a rate of five percent per annum for the past ten years, it's over two thousand pounds now."

A muscle twitched in his jaw as he pressed his lips together. "I am happy for you. It's the least you deserve." He let out a long exhale. "You're wealthy in your own right now. You can do whatever you please from this day forth."

Tess didn't know what to say. This was the goal of self-sufficiency she'd dreamed of for so long, but now that it was here, she felt oddly hollow.

Despite Justin's words, she wasn't truly free. She might not be dependent on the duchy financially, but she was still caught in an emotional entanglement with *him*.

To be married to him, but forever estranged, seemed the worst kind of torture. A lifelong punishment, like that of King Midas: having him so close, yet being unable to touch him.

Could she really let things end this way? Yes, he'd been an untrusting fool to suspect her, but he'd admitted his mistake. And he'd said he loved her, which was something she'd never thought to hear from his lips, considering his views on romance.

It's the antithesis of reason and logic.

It's imbecilic.

Love ruins everything.

A bittersweet ache tightened her chest as she recalled his words. Maybe he *was* in love with her. His recent actions certainly fitted those definitions.

As did hers, for wanting to throw herself into his arms now and forgive him. To ask him to move his things back into the house and live with her as her husband in every sense of the word.

To have and to hold, for better, for worse, for richer, for poorer, in sickness and in health.

She hadn't told him she was in love with him. He probably thought he was releasing her from an unwanted attachment.

Her silence seemed to unnerve him. He stood, and his face held nothing but regret and stern affection as he looked down at her.

"I'm sorry things have ended this way. Please know that I wish nothing but the best for you. You are an extraordinary woman, Tess."

Tess opened her mouth, still unsure what she was

about to say, but he shook his head and drew himself up tall.

"Now, if you'll excuse me, I plan to get exceedingly drunk."

Tess gaped at him. "It's ten o'clock in the morning!"

He glanced at the clock on the mantel and gave a careless, despairing shrug. "So it is. Good day."

Chapter Forty-One

"It's a disaster. The worst. I *love* her, Eddie. What am I going to do?"

Justin finished the brandy in his glass and immediately poured another. It wasn't even noon, and White's was almost entirely devoid of guests, which was probably a good thing, considering their advanced state of inebriation.

Edward grabbed the bottle he set down before it could topple off the table.

"Well, for one thing, we should probably shtop drinking," he said, his voice a little slurred. "And you've told me you love her a dozen times now. It's old news."

Justin grunted. "I told *her*, too, but she doesn't believe me. Not that I blame her. I told her time and again that I wouldn't love her. Couldn't love her. But I have. And I do. Bloody Hell."

Edward shrugged. "It's not an ideal situation, certainly."

"It's a bloody awful situation. But I can't let her go. I know I *should*. But I can't."

"In legal terms, one could argue that this is a case of *par delictum*. When both parties are equally at fault."

"How so?"

"Well, you lied to her about not being able to fall in love. But she lied to you about being a woman with extensive experience in the boudoir."

Justin snorted. "Not the same. Her crime was only one of omission. I stated my opinion several times, quite vehemently."

"Ah, but you said it in good faith—*bona fides*—because you didn't think you had a heart to give. *Nemo dat quod non habet*."

Justin groaned. "Speak English, Eddie. For God's sake."

"It means, 'Nobody can give what he has not.'"

"Well, I was wrong about the heart," Justin said morosely. "I did have one. But now it's hers and I can never get it back."

"There must be something you can do to prove you love her. Some ridiculous grand gesture. Harry Chesterfield hired a hot-air balloon to hover above Hyde Park with a banner declaring his undying love for Veronica Smurthwaite last season."

"That is truly nauseating." Justin shuddered and took another fortifying gulp of his drink. "I'm willing to grovel, but does it really have to be so public?"

"I think it does," Edward said sadly.

"Bloody Hell. Fine. I'll get one of those caricaturists in Covent Garden to draw me as her lap dog on a leash. Or as a carpet, crushed beneath her feet." He took another gulp of brandy. "Or tied to a stake and pierced with arrows like that Saint whatsisname—"

"Sebastian," Edward supplied.

"That's the one. Like Sebastian, shot through the heart. And Tess, as Aphrodite, with a bow and arrow. They can title it 'Her Grace makes a conquest of her husband, or: Oh, how the mighty have fallen!' I'll have five thousand printed and take out an advertisement in *The Times*."

Edward shook his head. "That's good. But when a prisoner's looking to be paroled, he has to prove to the judge that he's changed. That he's a different man now, who will never make the same mistake again."

"I have to do that?"

"I think so. What's something you would never normally do?"

"Make a bad investment," Justin said immediately. "Put money into a venture that's guaranteed to fail."

"Well, there you have it. That's what you have to do."

"I have to *lose* money to *win back* my wife? That's ridiculous."

Edward shrugged. "It makes a funny sort of sense. If love makes fools of us all, then you have to prove that you're a fool for her. You have to do something humiliating and foolish that shows the world that nothing matters as much as her. That you would gladly lose your fortune, your reason, and your wits, if only you can have her."

"Bloody Hell. You've been reading those opium-soaked poets again, haven't you?" Justin accused. "Shelley and Byron and Keats. It's addled your brain."

Edward shrugged. "I'm not the one sitting here in a drunken despair because he's married to the woman he loves."

"Fair point." Justin frowned. "Wait. Did you say fool for love? Ha! Edward, you're a genius!"

"I am?"

"You are. I know the perfect way to prove to Tess that I love her."

"How?"

"I'm going to buy her a horse."

"A horse."

Justin nodded, suddenly animated. "A racehorse. Called Fool For Love. The prince regent's been trying to sell it for months, and I've never seen a more miserable creature in my entire life."

"I'm not sure you've really grasped the concept of—"

"It's perfect. It hasn't won a race for the last two seasons and it's hideously overpriced. If she enters it into a race it is guaranteed to lose."

"How is this going to prove your love, exactly?"

"In several ways. Firstly, it will physically pain me to pay such an exorbitant sum for such a flea-ridden nag. People who hear about it will think I've gone mad. They'll think I only bought it because of the name. Because I'm besotted with my wife."

"They might. Or they might think you're just saddling her with a flea-ridden nag as a present. She might think you're mocking her with a literal gift horse, like that one the Greeks gave the Trojans."

"There's more," Justin said. "I'll tell Tess to enter it into a race. Somewhere like Newmarket or Stamford. The odds against it winning will be astronomical. I'll place an enormous bet on the thing to win, and when it doesn't, she'll see I care for her more than I care about money or winning or my reputation as an infallible businessman."

"Humph," Edward said, clearly unconvinced.

"I will lose. Deliberately. Publicly. For her. She'll understand the significance of it. If that's not a big enough declaration of love, I don't know what is."

Justin poured another finger of brandy into his glass and took a triumphant swallow. It felt good to have a plan, a way forward. For the first time since he'd returned from Wansford Hall, he felt optimistic about the future.

Against all the odds, against his own wishes, he was in love with his wife.

Now he just had to make her believe it.

Chapter Forty-Two

Tess put a hand to her bonnet to stop it from blowing away in the wind.

The racecourse near Stamford was set on a hill a little way to the south of the town, between the villages of Collyweston and Easton-on-the-Hill, and while it commanded a beautiful view of the surrounding countryside, it was a little breezy.

Hundreds of spectators milled around. A two-level grandstand had been erected some years before, with the top level reserved for the gentry and aristocracy. Rows of carriages had been lined up behind the fence that delineated the oval track, for those who didn't wish to pay the five shillings for a seat in the grandstand.

A series of gaily striped tents lined the periphery of the course, with vendors selling everything from spiced cider to honeyed almonds. There were games of pitch-and-toss and a woman telling fortunes, and even a raffle where the owner of the winning ticket could win a handsome four-wheeled post chaise. The air was abuzz with a sense of jollity and excitement.

"Fool For Love has been entered into the Noble-men and Gentlemen's sweepstakes at three o'clock," Ellie said, studying the race timetable. "The prize is a gold cup worth one hundred guineas."

Tess snorted. "There's no chance of winning that. What on earth was Justin thinking to insist the poor thing be raced?"

She slanted a look across to the opposite side of the racecourse, where an area had been set aside for the competitors and their grooms. The horse Justin had apparently bought for her was tied to the back of a cart, being brushed by a small stable lad in a cap.

"He looks healthier than I'd expected," Ellie said, with her usual boundless optimism. "I mean, his coat is shiny and he's more than just skin and bone. He's a handsome-looking horse."

"But hardly winning material," Tess said with a frown. "He hasn't won a race for the past two seasons. Is Justin trying to humiliate me? I don't understand."

"I don't think that's his aim," Daisy said slowly. "After all, he claims to be in love with you. Embarrassing you in public is hardly likely to convince you he's telling the truth."

Tess shook her head. Last week, when she'd seen Justin's distinctive scrawl on the letter informing her that he'd purchased Fool For Love, she hadn't known what to think. She'd been missing him so much that even receiving a note from him made her heart beat in a dangerously irregular rhythm.

When she'd put the sheet to her nose, she could have sworn she could smell an echo of his distinctive scent, and her stomach had clenched in misery.

But a flutter of hope had stirred in her, too. He hadn't abandoned London for Bristol, or boarded one of his ships and sailed halfway across the world to avoid her. Any indication that she was still in his thoughts was a positive sign. Even if she didn't understand his intentions.

He'd requested her presence at the weekend's races at Stamford, and Tess had eagerly complied. The chance to see him again had kept her awake for most of the night, and now she was here she was almost quivering with nerves.

She'd never spent so long worrying about her appearance, and it had taken three different changes before she finally settled on the summer dress of white cotton with a floral design picked out in silver thread.

"Who owns the other horses in the race?" Ellie asked.

Tess studied the race sheet. "There's Ghost, owned by Lord Burlington, Twist owned by Lord Fitzwilliam, and Kestrel owned by the Marquis of Exeter. There's also Arbiter, owned by Lord Grosvenor, and a horse called Sweet Lips, owned by a Mr. Watson."

"That's definitely named for a lady," Daisy chuckled. "I wonder if Sweet Lips is his wife, or his mistress."

"Ghost, the gray, is by far the favorite," Ellie said. "I've been listening to the bookmakers taking the bets. He's won three of the last four races he's entered."

"And Fool For Love has the longest odds of all." Tess shook her head.

At that moment an audible buzz began to ripple around the crowd and she glanced over toward the betting stands run by the bookmakers known as blacklegs, due to the high top-boots they always wore.

Her heart stilled as the crowd parted and she glimpsed Justin, shaking hands with another gentleman and surrounded by a group of several others. His smile made her ache, and she couldn't tear her eyes from his tall, lean figure.

He was dressed in an exquisitely cut coat of blue superfine, with buff breeches and a white cravat, and a pair of boots so well polished they couldn't possibly have been the same ones the puppy Oliver had abused.

Tess drank in the sight of him, and it was only Daisy's hushed whisper that brought her out of her reverie.

"Your husband has placed the most outrageous bet."

Tess tore her gaze away. "What?"

"It's all anyone can talk about. He just placed a bet of two hundred pounds with each of those five blacklegs for Fool For Love to win the three o'clock race."

Tess's mouth fell open in shock. "Are you sure? Surely he bet on him to *lose*."

Daisy shook her head with a grin. "I'm sure. A thousand pounds total, to win. And that's not all. I just saw your cousin Edward, Ellie, and he told me that Justin's also put a bet in the book at White's. If Fool For Love loses, he'll pay every single member of White's ten pounds."

Tess gasped. "He's going to lose a fortune. How many members of White's are there?"

"Edward says at least two hundred and eighty. It's usually around three hundred."

"Dear God. The man's lost his mind. Fool For Love is bound to come in last, which means he'll lose not just the thousand pounds he's bet here today, but also another *three thousand* to the members of his club. What is he *thinking*?"

Daisy couldn't seem to stop smiling. She looked almost gleeful with excitement. "I don't think he's thinking at all. At least, not with his head. And not with his cock, either. I think for the first time ever he's letting his *heart* make the decisions."

Chapter Forty-Three

Around them, Justin's extraordinary bets were the main topic of conversation. Speculation was rife. Some racegoers rushed to place similar bets, convinced that he must have some inside knowledge, or swayed by his reputation as a successful businessman.

"Shall we head up to the stand?" Ellie asked. "The race is about to start."

Tess could only nod dumbly. Part of her wanted to go over and demand an explanation from Justin, but the other half wanted to go somewhere quiet to hide.

The three of them climbed the stairs to the upper level of the grandstand, and Tess's gaze immediately found Justin, now in the owner's enclosure opposite them, talking to a short, slim man in a red shirt she assumed was the jockey.

In no time at all, the horses were led to the starting line.

"Only five horses are starting," Daisy said. "Look, Kestrel has been pulled."

Sure enough, a disappointed grumble rippled through the crowd as those who'd bet on Kestrel discovered he'd been withdrawn from the race.

"Must be sick. Or injured."

A few of the horses pranced, picking up the nervous excitement from the crowd, and the jockeys tugged on the reins to control them. But not Fool For Love. The chestnut stood calmly at the starting tape, flicking his ears and looking entirely disinterested in the proceedings.

"That Fool For Love looks like he's asleep!"

Tess almost groaned at the amused comment from a gentleman to her left. Disaster was about to unfold right before her eyes. She could hardly bear to watch.

A pistol shot heralded the start of the race and four of the horses leapt forward. Fool For Love's rider had to give him a few good kicks with his heels to get him to move. The other horses were already ahead by the time he decided to bestir himself, earning him a raucous, derisive cheer from the crowd.

"Hoi! I've seen donkeys with more go!" the man next to Tess snorted.

"It's two laps of the track," Daisy said excitedly. "Come on, Fool For Love!"

Flecks of turf flicked from the horse's hooves as they thundered past on their first lap.

To Tess's right an announcer used a cone-shaped speaking trumpet to amplify his commentary in an effort to be heard above the baying crowd.

"It's Ghost in the lead, closely followed by Arbiter and Twist."

Tess gripped the wooden railing in front of her. Fool For Love was clear last, several lengths behind Sweet Lips.

"Oh no, look!" Ellie's excited voice broke her concentration. "Arbiter and Twist have bumped together."

A roar went up from the crowd as the horses in second and third place collided as they rounded the second bend.

"Tom Fennell on Arbiter's lost his stirrup!" The announcer shouted.

Arbiter stumbled, but didn't go down, and the crowd gasped in unison. But the contact unsettled Twist. He veered off sharply to the right, galloping across the track, and began to buck. His rider, in blue silks, made a valiant effort to keep his seat, but he was thrown clear of the saddle and landed on the ground.

The crowd groaned in sympathy, but the valiant jockey rose to his feet and hobbled away to duck under the fence. The horse gave a delighted snort and cantered off along the rail, neatly avoiding the reaching hands of the crowd trying to catch his reins.

"And there's Sweet Lips, gaining ground on Arbiter, who still hasn't regained his stirrups!" the announcer roared.

Ghost was still in the lead, but Sweet Lips overtook the struggling Arbiter to go into second place.

Twist, delighted to have lost the burden of his rider, galloped back to the inside rail to rejoin the race, and the crowd gasped as he veered straight in front of Sweet Lips and Arbiter.

Both jockeys were forced to pull up sharply on the reins to avoid a collision. Sweet Lips's rider reached over and grabbed Twist's dangling reins and pulled him to a bouncing stop.

"That's both Arbiter and Sweet Lips out of the running," the announcer called. "But just look at Fool For Love!"

Tess swung her gaze to the last horse in the pack. Justin's jockey was wearing a scarlet coat and a matching cap. Was it a nod to her?

As she watched, Fool For Love seemed to shake off his ennui and come out of his sleepy trance. It was as if he suddenly remembered what he was supposed to be doing. His nostrils flared, his ears flicked forward, and he bounded ahead with an easy stride that ate up the distance.

"Look at that!" Daisy whispered in awe.

Sweet Lips, Arbiter, and Twist were still partly blocking the course, but Fool For Love went wide and galloped around them.

"Fool For Love is in second place!" Ellie squealed.

"Only because there's only two horses left," Tess croaked. "He'll never beat Ghost."

Her heart was in her mouth. She searched the crowd for Justin, but couldn't see him anywhere.

"There's one lap to go, but it . . . looks like Ghost is tiring." The announcer sounded as if he couldn't believe his own words. "He's been raced hard this season, and his win at Newmarket last week may have exhausted him."

"The ground's too wet to favor him," a punter in a striped shirt next to Ellie said sagely. "It rained last night, and he doesn't favor soggy ground."

The crowd, always appreciative of an underdog, and sensing the possibility of an upset of epic proportions, suddenly seemed to switch their allegiance to Fool For Love. As he thundered past, clearly gaining on Ghost, an enormous cheer went up.

Tess could hardly catch a breath as the horse put on an extraordinary burst of speed that put him within a length of Ghost.

Ghost's rider turned to see who was approaching, and his look of astonishment at seeing Fool For Love was visible to half the grandstand.

Guffaws of laughter rang out around the ground.

Ghost's rider kicked his heels to the horse's flanks, and

gave him a quick flick on the hindquarters with his whip, but it was clear that the gray was indeed tiring.

The two horses rounded the final corner. Ghost's gait was labored, but Fool For Love was flying.

"Fool For Love has drawn level with Ghost!" The commentator's voice had risen an octave in excitement. "Ladies and gentlemen, are we about to see a miracle unfold before us on the turf?"

The two horses were thundering down the final straight toward the finishing post, which was directly in front of the grandstand.

"They're neck and neck!" Daisy screamed, bouncing up and down. "Run, Fool, run!"

The entire crowd was screaming now, a deafening cacophony of noise that swelled like a wave to envelop them. Tess found herself holding her breath, unable to believe what she was witnessing.

As the two horses neared the finishing line Fool For Love just edged ahead, and the crowd exploded in ecstatic jubilation.

"And Fool For Love WINS by a nose!" the commentator screamed. "By God, what a race! Phenomenal!"

"The Duke of Wansford must be the luckiest bastard in Christendom!" the fellow next to Tess bellowed.

"I have to find Justin," Tess breathed.

Chapter Forty-Four

Tess elbowed her way through the crowd and raced down the stairs, desperate to find her husband.

She pushed through the crush of people and headed in the general direction of the owner's encampment. She was almost there when she rounded a carriage and came face-to-face with Justin, who seemed to have been heading the opposite way, toward her.

She stopped short, breathless at the sight of him.

"Justin!"

"Tess!"

His hair was mussed, and his cravat was askew. She reminded herself to be cool, calm. Rational.

"Congratulations," she said stiffly. "On winning. Everything you touch turns to gold."

He shook his head, and his expression was tortured, desperate. It was not at all the face of a man who'd just won a small fortune.

"He wasn't supposed to win!" There was an urgency, a desperation in his voice she'd never heard before. "You have to believe me. That wasn't the plan *at all*."

"What do you mean?"

"Fool For Love was supposed to lose. *I* was supposed to lose. All that money? It was my grand gesture. I was trying to prove how little it all means without you." His eyes bored into hers as he took a step closer. "You, Tess. I did it all for you."

The ground was suddenly unsteady beneath her feet. The buzz of the crowd receded until it felt like they were the only two people in the world.

Justin took another step, slowly, as if she were a skittish horse who might bolt at any moment.

"I love you," he said simply. "And I know you can live without me, but I honestly don't think I can live without you."

He took another step and she could feel herself swaying toward him.

"Please stay with me. Be my duchess. Not because of some stupid agreement, but because you want to. Because you want *me*. Completely. As I want you."

Tess couldn't seem to find words. Happiness was bubbling up inside her, but she was still afraid to hope.

A faint smile curled the corner of his mouth, and her breath caught at the familiar sight. She'd missed such secret things. Missed being in the same room as him, missed the laughing glances that made her skin heat and her toes curl in her slippers.

"You wore a silvery dress like that the first time I ever saw you." His voice was low, almost reverent.

Tess frowned. "No, I was wearing that scandalous red dress. At Careby's."

He shook his head and gave her his heartbreaking smile. "That was the first time you saw me. But I saw you long before that. Almost two years before, in fact."

"What? When?"

"You know that rumor I started? The one about how I'd dreamed of you for years?"

Tess nodded.

"It was true. I saw you in a silver-white gown at some party or other, before I even left for Canada, and I thought you were the most beautiful woman I'd ever seen."

Tess's lips parted in astonishment. "I had no idea. Why on earth didn't you introduce yourself?"

"To save myself from heartache," he said wryly. "I had a premonition, a conviction that if I spoke to you, got to know even a tiny part of you, that I would fall completely and horribly in love. And I was a realist. What chance would I have had against your legions of suitors? Your father would never have let you throw yourself away on a lowly merchant."

"No, probably not," Tess acknowledged sadly. "But perhaps we could have eloped?"

He gave a despairing sound, half laugh, half resignation. "Perhaps. But maybe it's best that we didn't. Trying to become someone worthy of you drove me from that moment on. Even if I didn't fully admit it to myself."

"If we'd met back then," Tess said severely, "you'd never have made enemies who tried to kill you."

"That's true. I'm so sorry about that."

Tess clenched her fists in her skirts. Her heart was pounding, but she was determined that there would be no more misunderstandings between them.

"Charles King doesn't exist. King & Co. is run by Ellie, Daisy, and myself. We investigate crimes that Bow Street's too busy to handle. Mainly ones that involve women. I didn't tell you, because I was afraid you'd try to stop me from doing what I love."

"I would never do that." He let out an odd half laugh.

"Because I love you. I didn't *want* to. In fact, I did everything in my power to prevent it."

He ducked his head, then met her eyes again. "When my mother died, and I saw my father's pain, I vowed to save myself that, in any way I could. I thought that if I never allowed myself to get too attached to anything—to anyone—then I couldn't get hurt. I insisted on a stupid three-month rule for my relationships, for my own protection."

He shook his head, as if amazed at his own foolishness. "What I failed to take into account was that love doesn't need three months. Sometimes it doesn't even need three *minutes*."

His lips curved in a rueful smile. "It didn't with you. I can't tell you the precise moment I fell in love with you, but I can tell you the precise moment I finally admitted it to myself. It was at Vauxhall, when I thought I was losing you. It *hurt* to let you go."

Tess sucked in a shaky breath, but he wasn't finished.

"My father was right: grief is the price we pay for love, but it's worth it. He wouldn't have exchanged one minute with my mother for any lessening of his pain, and I don't want to waste any more time denying my feelings for you. I love you. And I want to keep on loving you for the rest of my days. I can't say I'm thrilled at the thought of you putting yourself in danger, but I hope you'll let me do everything in my power to keep you as safe as possible while you do it."

He was so close his boots brushed her skirts, but he still made no move to touch her.

"You are beautiful, but that's only a tiny part of what makes you so lovely. You're clever, and brave, and kind. I don't know why I was surprised that you'd run an investigative agency. You're always trying to help people, to find solutions for their problems. Witness how you badgered me to appeal against the tax for working dogs, and how you combined the crops at Wansford to improve the yield."

He shook his head, even as he smiled at her. "You *amaze* me, Tess. Even if you don't return my feelings, I want you to know that. You have my heart. Now and forever."

Tess finally closed the distance between them.

"I do."

"Do what?"

"Return your feelings." She gave a sudden, incredulous laugh. "I love *you*, Justin Trevelyan Thornton, and I refuse to let you leave me. You're going to have to stay with me and love me until you die of extreme old age."

For a moment he looked stunned, as if he couldn't believe his good fortune. And then he caught her in his arms and enfolded her in a hug that crushed the breath from her body.

Tess closed her eyes in delight as she breathed in his familiar scent and her body molded to his as if they were two halves of the same whole, perfectly aligned.

He released her only enough to clasp her face between his palms. "I am the luckiest man in England," he breathed.

Tess smiled. "You certainly are. I can't believe you won even *more* money, while specifically trying not to. There is no justice in this world."

He pressed his forehead against hers with a laugh. "That's true. If there was, an undeserving bastard like myself would never have married a nice girl like you."

"Daisy would suggest there's a nun somewhere about to be hit by lightning."

"Sounds fair. Perhaps you can think of a worthy cause to benefit from my undeserved winnings?"

"What about a rehabilitation home for puppies, harlots, and veterans?"

His amused exhale huffed against her nose. "All in one place? That sounds like a recipe for disaster. But I'll agree to whatever you say, my love."

Tess tilted her face upward. "In that case, I say you should kiss me."

"With the greatest pleasure on earth."

The world slipped away as his lips found hers. Tess threw her arms around his neck and returned the favor, matching his passion with her own. It was only the insistent shouting of one of the grooms that forced them reluctantly apart.

"'Ere, Yer Grace, you've got to go up an' accept yer winner's cup!"

Justin groaned at the interruption, but he smiled down into her eyes.

"I don't need a golden cup to know that I've won. I have everything I need right here."

Tess sent him a mock scowl. "Come on, Your Grace. I'll accept on your behalf. And then we can take poor Fool For Love back to Wansford Hall and set him out to pasture. He's more than earned his happiness."

Justin gave her bottom a playful pinch. "As have we."

Epilogue

King & Co., Lincoln's Inn Fields.

Tess lifted her face for a kiss as Justin bent over her shoulder.

"Good evening, my lady."

She smiled against his lips. "Good evening, yourself."

He straightened and gestured at the pile of correspondence in front of her. "Are you almost finished? Simms promised to have dinner ready for us at seven."

Tess dipped her nib into the inkpot and signed *Charles King, Esquire* in elegant script at the bottom of an invoice requesting payment from a countess. In the months since their success on behalf of the princess, business had almost doubled.

"Now, I'm done." She glanced outside, at the softly falling snowflakes fluttering past the window, then back at her husband, who had rounded her desk and was now leaning negligently against the doorframe.

He really was obnoxiously handsome. She could hardly believe he was hers.

"So much for your 'three months, no feelings' rule," she teased softly. "You were supposed to be back in Bristol by now, if I remember rightly. And yet here we are, in snowy December, still happily married."

Justin sent her a rueful grin. "What can I say? The best laid plans of mice and men go oft awry, and all that. To misquote poor Robbie Burns."

"I ruined your plans?"

"You did. But they were terrible plans." He sent her a hot, suggestive look across the room. "I have *much* better ones to show you."

Tess chucked. Her husband was a wonderfully wicked man.

In truth, she suspected she'd already guessed one surprise he had planned for her. The faint sound of barking had been coming from the stables that morning, and when she'd peered out the window, she'd glimpsed a familiar figure climbing furtively into a cart. Justin, she was sure, had bought her one of Mr. Collins's latest litter of puppies, and she couldn't wait to meet the adorable little creature—nor to show her husband just how much she appreciated such a sweet gift.

As she stood to leave, she picked up the hastily scrawled note that had been delivered by courier earlier. "It sounds as if Ellie may have found us another interesting case."

"Concerning what?"

Tess tilted her head. "I'm not entirely sure."

Ellie's note had been unusually cryptic, even for her. She'd simply written, *New job. Urgent. P.S. Just kissed Charles King.*

Justin frowned, confused, when she read it aloud.

"I thought *you* were Charles King? The three of you. You, Ellie, and Daisy."

"We are. So I don't know what Ellie means. But I'm sure we'll find out tomorrow. She and Daisy are coming for dinner, remember?"

"As if I could forget." Justin wrapped her cloak around her shoulders and stole the opportunity to press a kiss against her neck. "All the more reason to enjoy our time together now," he murmured. "In fact, maybe I can show you one of my better plans in the carriage."

Tess gasped in mock outrage. "The carriage? How very scandalous, Your Grace."

He grinned and tugged her hand. "Only if we're caught. Come on."